## BRIDAL NIGHT

It was very dark. . . . Moving with caution I sat up in bed. The room was warm as if a fire blazed. . . . But in my body there was a spreading cold. All of a sudden it was very necessary to see—to see not only the room, the bed, but most of all what lay upon that bed and slept so soundly. . . .

I thrust at the shutters, sending them flying open. Moonlight—it was very clear and brighter than I had ever seen it before. . . .

"Ahh—" Voice—or snarl?

I turned to look to the bed I had left. What lifted heavy head and looked at me green-eyed? Fur, sleek and shining fur, the fanged mask of awakening fury— . . . The lips wrinkled, showing even more the fangs meant to tear, to devour—It was horror beyond any horror I had ever dreamed upon.

*This—this you have chosen!—*

**The WITCH WORLD**
**of**
**ANDRE NORTON**

WITCH WORLD
WEB OF THE WITCH WORLD
THREE AGAINST THE WITCH WORLD
WARLOCK OF THE WITCH WORLD
SORCERESS OF THE WITCH WORLD
and
TREY OF SWORDS
YEAR OF THE UNICORN
ZARSTHOR'S BANE (Illustrated)

**from**
**ACE SCIENCE FICTION**

**SF**

# YEAR OF THE UNICORN

SF
ace books

A Division of Charter Communications Inc.
A GROSSET & DUNLAP COMPANY
360 Park Avenue South
New York, New York 10010

An ACE Book

First Ace printing: October 1965
Second Ace printing: July 1969
Third Ace printing: May 1974
Fourth Ace printing: January 1976
Fifth Ace printing: March 1979

Printed in U.S.A.

# CONTENTS

# I  NEWS OF FAR FARING AT NORSTEAD

How DOES ONE KNOW coming good from coming ill? There are those times in life when one welcomes any change, believing that nothing can be such ashes in the mouth, such dryness of days as the never altering flood of time in a small community where the outside world lies ever beyond gates locked and barred against all change. From the bell tower of Abbey Norstead—and how many years had sped since a bell had pealed from there?—one could see the unending rippling of the Dales, on and on to the blue-gray of Fast Ridge. On bright days, when the sun drove away the mist curtain, the darkened fringe of the forest cloaking Falthingdale broke the moss-carpet to the west, and the harsh, sky-clutching claws of Falcon-Fist made a sharp point to draw the eyes eastward. But otherwise there were just the Dales with their age-old shutting out of man and his affairs. They had lain so before his coming; they would remain so at his going. But as yet he had his part in them, and here in Norsdale it would seem that quiet land had conquered the natural restlessness of the breed of mankind, slowing all life force to the pace of those everlasting hills.

Yet this was a land lately embattled, wherein war flashed like a drawn sword, thrust as a cruel spear, sung in the flight of arrows, or lay panting of breath behind a half-riven shield. War . . . uneasy peace for a hand-finger count of years

. . . then war again. In the first days open field battle, with one army at the throat of another. And then, as men fell, as time gnawed, small raiding bands flashing out of a wilderness to use wolf-fangs. Then—with the invaders from overseas driven back to their first handhold on the coast—a final destruction and peace which those, who had been nurtured from their cradles under the flapping hawk banners, who had heard naught but sword talk for the span of their lives, met awkwardly and ill at ease.

This we of Norsdale knew, yet the war tongues had never licked inland so far as to sear our valley. And only those who had survived terror and worse and fled to us for refuge bore battle tidings within the gates of the Abbey. We had never seen the Hounds of Alizon at their harrying, and for that, the Dames of Norstead gave thanks on their knees night and morning in the Chapel.

Abbey Norstead held me because of that war tide, and there were times when I thought that its stifling peace would choke me. For it is very hard to live among those who are no kin to you, not only in blood but in spirit and desire and mind. Who was I? Any one walking those precise paths in the garden below could have given me name and past, and would have told you at the asking:

"That one? Ah, that is Gillan, who works with Dame Alousan in the herbarium. She came here eight years ago with the Lady Freeza, being a handmaiden of her household. She has some small knowledge of herbs, a liking for her own company, no beauty, no great kindred—naught to give her any importance in the world. She comes to the chapel services morn and night, she bows her head, but she takes no vows. She sits with the maids at times and plies her needle as is fit, but she has not asked to serve the Abbey. She speaks little—"

Aye, she speaks little, my Dames, and maids, and those laides who have taken refuge here. But she thinks much, and she tries to remember. Though that is another thing which times denies, or perhaps the unchanging pattern of this land and life denies.

For Gillan is not of the blood of High Hallack. There was a ship. Always can I remember so much, of the tossing of a ship on a sea where waves ran high, avid to feed upon the work of men's hands. A ship of Alizon, that much also I remember. But that I am of Alizon—no. There was a purpose in my being on that ship, and, small and young a girl child as I then was, I feared that purpose. But he who brought me there was under a mast which the wind and wave brought down upon the deck. And then no other of his company knew why I was among them.

That was during the time of raids when the lords of High Hallack, fighting to free their homeland from the Hounds of Alizon, swept down and struck a lightning blow at the port through which came the invaders' lifeblood of supplies and men. And so was I also swept up with those supplies and taken to one of the mountain holds.

The Lord Furlo, I believe, had some private knowledge or suspicion of my past. For he sent me under guard to his lady wife, with the command that I be well cared for. Thus I was a fosterling in that household for a space. But that also did not last, for Alizon arose in might and the Lords were driven back and back. In the depths of harsh and heavy winter we fled across the barren land and into the upper dales. At last we came to Norstead, but the Lady Freeza came only to die. And her lord lay with an arrow in his throat back in the passes—whatever he had suspected concerning me unsaid. So that I was again adrift in strange, if placid, waters.

I need only to look into any mirror within these walls to know that I was not of the breed of Hallack. Whereas their womenkind were fair of skin, but with a fine color to their faces, their hair as yellow as the small flowers bordering the garden walks in the spring, or brown as the wings of the sweet singing birds in the stream gullies, I was of a flesh which browned under the sun, but held no color in cheek. And the hair I learned to plait tightly about my head, was of a black as deep as a starless night. Also . . . I thought odd thoughts. But even before I came to Norstead, while still I played the part of fosterling, I had learned to keep such thoughts to myself, for they alarmed and dismayed those about me.

There is a loneliness of spirit which is worse than loneliness of body. And in all Norstead during those years, I had found only two to whom I might turn for company of a kind. The Dame Alousan was past the span of middle life when I came. She, too, was apart from her companions of the Order. Her life was in the gardens, and in the rooms wherein she worked with herbs, distilling, combining, making those powders and salves, those flasks of liquids, which soothed, healed, pleasured mankind. Noted she was, so that fighting bands in the high hills would send men trained for swift traveling to beg her for those products of her knowledge and hands which would aid in the healing of sore wounds, or the fevers and rheums which came of living in the open no matter what the season or weather.

And when I was set adrift in Abbey Norstead, she looked upon me, keenly, as usually she looked only on some herb new come to her (for she was sent packets of strange things from time to time, by her ordering gifts). Then she took me into her service and I found that at first all I needed, for it was learning of a demanding kind, and my mind was thirsty for occupation. For some years thereafter I was content.

I was working in the garden, weeding beds, when I first knew that other one who was to trouble my balance of learning and labor. There was always a humming of bees, since bees and gardens needs must lie close together, each serving the other. But now there came another thread of sound, entering my ears, and then my mind. And I sat back on my heels to listen, because my memory stirred, yet I could not summon aught clearly to the surface of my mind.

As if that humming were a cord to draw me. I arose and went through an arch into the inner garden which was for pleasure only, a place with a fountain and a pool, and flowers according to the season. A chair had been placed there, half in sun, half in shade. And in it, well cushioned, draped about with shawls though the day was warm, was one of the very ancient Dames, those who seldom ventured from their cells, who were almost legend among the younger members of the community.

Beneath her hood and coif, her face was very small and white, yet the wrinkles of age were tight only in the corners of her eyes and about her lips. They were wrinkles, too, such as come from smiling, and looking upon the world with a blithe spirit. Her hands were much crooked with the painful twisting of one of the blights of aging, and they lay in her lap unmoving. But on one of her fingers perched a jeweled lizard, its small head raised, its sparks of eyes fixed upon her as if they two communed happily together.

She looked still at the lizard, but the humming stopped and she said quietly, "Welcome, my daughter. This is a fair day."

So short a speech, and words such as you might hear from any lips, yet they drew me into a warmth of spirit, and I came and knelt by her chair eagerly. Thus did I meet with Past-Abbess Malwinna and from her, too, I learned. But hers was not the lore of plants and growing things, but of those winged, and fourfooted, and wriggling lives which share our world, and yet so often are made servants or foes of man.

But the Abbess was in the far twilight of her life, and she was to be my friend for only a short, so short, a time. In all of Norstead she knew my secret. I do not know just how I betrayed myself to her, but she showed no uneasiness when she learned that sometimes I could see the thing behind the thing that was. On the last meeting between us—she was abed then and could not move the body which imprisoned her free rang-ing spirit—she asked me questions, as she never had done before. How much could I remember . . . aught at all behind the ship from Alizon? And when had I learned that I was not like those about me? And to those questions I made the fullest answers.

"You are wise for one so young, my daughter," she said then, her voice the thinnest thread of speech. "It is our nature to mistrust that which we do not understand. I have heard tales of a country overseas where some women have powers beyond the common. And also that Alizon stands enemy to those people, just as her hounds now tear at us. It may well be that you are of that other race, prisoner for some reason."

"Please, Mother Abbess"—I took fire from her words—"where lies this country? How might I—"

"Find your way thither, my daughter? There is no hope of that. Accept that fact. And if you venture to where Alizon may again lay hands upon you—that may be courting greater pain than any sword thrust which ends life cleanly. Do not shadow your years with vain longings. Naught moves save by some purpose of Those Who Have Set The Flames. You will find that which is meant for you to do in the proper time." Then her eyes smiled, though her lips could not. "Ill hearing for the young this promise of a better future. But accept it as the last gift I have to give you, my daughter. I say it by the Flames, there will come that which will fill your emptiness."

But that had been said three winter seasons past. Now there was a stirring within Norstead with the war's end. Lords would come riding to claim wives, sisters, daughters. There would be a marrying season and there was a fluttering in the narrow rooms below my tower perch.

A marrying—which made me think of that other tale which had come to us through many lips—the Great Bargain. Now would come the settling of the Great Bargain.

It was during the days of the first spring flood in the Year of the Gryphon that the Lords of High Hallack had made their covenant with the Were Riders of the waste. They had been sore driven by Alizon, knowing the fading hope of very desperate men, and the fear that they faced the final shadow of all. Thus hate and fear drove them to set up a call banner in the salt dunes and treat with the Riders.

Those who came to speak with the harried lords wore the bodies of men, but they were not humankind. They were dour fighters . . . men—or creatures—of power who ranged the northeastern wilderness and who were greatly feared, though they did not trouble any who touched not upon the territory of their holding. How many of them there were no man knew, but that they had a force beyond human knowledge was certain.

Shape-changers, warlocks, sorcerers . . . rumor had it they were all that and more. But also when they spoke upon oath they held to that oath-taking and were loyal. Thus they would fight, under their own leaders and by their own strange ways, yet for the right of High Hallack.

The war continued through the Year of the Fire Drake, and that of the Hornet, until Alizon was utterly broken and downcast. From overseas came no more ships to supply her men. And now that last port was taken. Her forts on the high places were stinking rubble, and she was erased from the coast she had invaded.

Now approached the new Year of the Unicorn, and the Great Bargain must be kept with the Riders as they had kept theirs with High Hallack. The promises of the Riders had been two: that they would come to the support of the Lords; and then, they would ride out of the wastelands, withdrawing from the land they had helped to cleanse, leaving it to the humankind alone.

And the other side of that bargain—the payment the Lords of High Hallack had sworn dire and binding oaths to render? That was to be in their own blood, for the Riders demanded wives to carry with them into the unknown.

As far as the Dales knew, the Riders had always been. Yet among them no female had ever been sighted, or talked of. Whether they were the same, with a life span far beyond that of humankind, was not known. But it was true that no child had ever been sighted among them— though Lords from time to time had sent envoys into their camps, even before the Bargain.

Twelve and one maids they asked for—maids, not widows, or those who had chosen to live beyond custom's bonds. And they must not be younger than eighteen years of age, nor beyond twenty. They were also to be of gentle blood, and well of body. Twelve and one to be found and delivered on the first day of the Year of the Unicorn at the borders of the waste, thereafter to ride with their strange lords into a future from which there would be no return.

How would they feel, these twelve and one? Fearful? Yes, fear would be a part of it. For, as

Abbess Malwinna had said, fear is our first reaction to that which is alien to us. Yet to some of them it would be an escape. For the girl who had no dowry, nor face bright enough to excuse that lack, no kinfolk who would shield and care for her, or who might perhaps have kin who wished her ill—for such this choice might be the better of two evils.

Norstead now sheltered five maids who answered all the requirements. Two of those, however, were already betrothed, waiting impatiently for marriage in the spring. The Lady Tolfana was the daughter of a lord so highly born that surely a great alliance would be arranged for her, in spite of her plain face and sharp tongue. And Marimme, with her flower face, her winning softness—no, her uncle would have her out of this Abbey and off to the first Fold Gather where he could pick and choose wisely among her suitors for good addition to his standing. Sussia—

Sussia—what did anyone know about Sussia? She was older, she kept her own council, though she talked readily about the small concerns of Norstead in company. Perhaps few realized how little she ever spoke of herself. She was of gentle blood, yes, and had, I thought, a good and even quick mind. Her home was in the lowlands of the sea coast, and so she had been exiled from her birth. She had kin with the host, but how close they were . . . Yes, Sussia was a possibility. And how would she welcome news that such a choice had fallen upon her? Would that outward amicability crack and let us see what lay beneath it?

"Gillan!"

I looked down over the parapet of the tower. There was the sheen of rime, the covering of snow across the gardens. I had a doubled shawl about me against the bite of the wind, yet the sun made a diamond glitter on the cloak of winter and a small, sharp wind tugged at Dame Alousan's coif veil.

To be summoned by my mistress in this fashion was a thing out of daily pattern. And in me stirred a feeling which I had half forgotten since I had so well schooled myself against that which was trouble. The dust of time was being blown upon— Dared I hope for a wind of change?

Though I had learned to walk calmly, with unhurried step according to Abbey custom, yet now I ran down the stairs, round and round the wall of the bell tower, setting a curb on my haste only when I came into the open.

"Dame?" I sketched the curtsy of greeting and she gestured in return.

"There has been a message, and a full convocation is ordered." She was frowning. "Go you and tend the small still. This is not a time when my work should be so interrupted."

She pulled at the flapping ends of her veil and went past me with a firm step as one who would speedily answer some hail that she might the more quickly return to her task.

A message? But no one had ridden through the Dale, past the village. The flapping of wings past the tower when I had first ascended? A bird? Perhaps one of the trained, winged messengers used by the host. Abbess Malwinna had lessoned many of them in her active days. The war—had our belief in peace been only rumor? Did the Hounds now bay on the borders of Norstead?

But these were only thoughts, and come war or lasting peace, if I did not give thought to Dame Alousan's distilling there would be real trouble for me in due time.

The still room was odorous as always, though most of those smells were sweet and clean. And now there was a fragrance, arising from the vessel by the still which was so entrancing that I feasted my nostrils as I obeyed the orders laid upon me. That task was done, the liquid safely bottled, the apparatus washed thrice as was the custom, and yet Dame Alousan returned not. Outside afternoon became early winter evening. I blew out the lamps, latched the door, and crossed to the main hall of the Abbey.

There was the twittering of voices, growing the shriller by the moment as women's voices do when there are no lower masculine notes to hold them in scale. Two lay sisters were setting out the meal for guests on the table, but none of the Dames were present. By the fireplace gathered all those who had taken refuge, some for years, within these walls.

I hung my shawl on the proper hook by the door and went to the fire. In that gathering I was neither bird nor cat. I do not think that some ever knew just how to accept me: whether as a fostering of a noble house once on a time and of the rank, say, of a Captain of company's daughter; or whether I was to be counted one of the community though I did not wear the veil and coif. Now, as I joined them they took no note of me at all, and the chitter-chatter was deafening. I saw that some, usually sparing of word, were now striving to outtalk their companions. Truly a stoat had been introduced into our house of hens!

"Gillan, what think you!" The Lady Marimme was all rounded lips and wide, astonished eyes. "They are coming here—they may reach here by the Hour of the Fifth Flame?"

Kinsmen home from the wars, I thought. Truly something to set the Abbey a flutter. But—why the convocation lasting to this hour? The Dames would not be moved by any such guesting, not even that of a full company of horse. They would merely draw into their apportioned section of the Abbey until the men of the world had departed beyond their gates once again.

"Who comes?" I then named her nearest kin. "Lord Imgry?"

"He and others—the brides, Gillan, the promised brides! They march to the waste border by the north road and they will guest here this night! Gillan, it is a fearsome thing they do— Poor, poor ones! We should offer prayers in their names—"

"Whyfor?" The Lady Sussia came up in her usual unhurried way. She had not the soft beauty of Marimme. But, I thought, she will be regal all her life, and eyes will follow her after other beauty fades with the years.

"Whyfor?" repeated Marimme, "Whyfor? Because they ride into black evil, Sussia, and they will not come forth again!" She was indignant.

It was then Sussia repeated aloud what had been something of my own thinking on the subject. "Also they may ride from evil, birdling. All of us have not soft nests nor sheltering wings about us." She must be speaking for herself. Did she indeed have some foreknowledge that the train which would guest with us this night would take her with it in the morning?

"I would rather wed steel, in truth," cried Marimme, "than ride on such a marriage journey!"

"You need not fear," I said then, for I guessed she spoke the truth, if somewhat wildly. Her fear was like a sickness, stretching out its shadow from her mind and heart.

But over Marimme's shoulder I saw Sussia look at me oddly. Again it was as if she had foreknowledge. And in me a second time that warning of my own stirred. I could breathe in trouble as I could the aromatic smell of the leaves burned with the firelogs to freshen the hall.

"Marimme, Marimme—"

I think she was glad to turn from us to answer that call, to join the maids who were betrothed and so safe from alarms, as if their safety could cloak her also. But Sussia still faced me, her face locked as ever against any revealing of herself.

"Watch her, as shall I this night," she said under cover of their chatter.

"Why?"

"Because—she goes!"

I stared at her, for the moment struck dumb with amazement. Still I knew she spoke the truth.

"How—why—?" I did not finish either question for she was speaking swiftly, her hand on my arm drawing me a little away, her voice low and for my ear alone.

"How do I know? I had a private message this seven night. Oh, yes, I thought that I might be chosen, there was much to warrant it. But my kinsmen have had other plans for a year, and when the suggestion was made that I might be

included in the Bargain, they made sword troth
for me at once. While war raged I was landless.
Now that the Hounds are hurled back into the sea
from whence they came, I am mistress of more
than one manor, being the last of my immediate
line." She smiled thinly. "Thus am I a treasure
for my kin. I go to a wedding indeed this spring,
but one in the Dales. As to why Marimme—
beauty draws men, even when there is no dowry
to fill the purse or line manor with manor. But a
man who wants power can try for it in different
ways. Lord Imgry has the granting of her hand.
He is a man who hoards power as a captain
hoards his men—until the attack trumpet. Then
he will risk much to get what he wants. He has
offered Marimme in return for certain favors.
And the others believe that such a flower offered
the Riders will sweeten the dish, since all the
brides are not so choice."

"She will not go—"

"She will go—they shall see to that. But she
will die—such a draught is not for her drinking."

I glanced across to Marimme. Her face was
flushed, she made quick graceful gestures with
her hands. There was a feverish gaity about her I
did not like. Though what was all this to me,
who was an outsider and none of their blood or
company?

"She will die," again that statement delivered
with emphasis.

I turned to Sussia. "If the Lord Imgry is set on
this and the others agree, then she can not
escape—"

"No? Oftentimes have men agreed upon a
thing and women changed their thinking."

"But even if another were offered in her place,

would they agree to the choice, seeing as how it is her beauty which made her it in the first place?"

"Just so." Sussia continued to watch me with that strange, knowing look, almost as if she sensed in me something so closely kindred that we thought with one thought and had no need for words between us. And I was thinking of Norstead, of the dust of changeless years, of my own place and part in this my world. And as many thoughts, some less than half formed, sped thus through my mind, the Lady Sussia retired a little, dropped her hand from my arm. Once again there was a curtain between us and matters were as they had always been.

I knew a spark of anger then, thinking—"she has used me!" But that lasted only for the space of an eye-wink. For it did not matter what tool of That Which Abides is used to open the future. To let some small resentment cloud one's mind is the action of a fool. Twelve brides would guest here tonight, twelve and one would ride out in the morning. Twelve and—one!

As to planning, I knew much about the Abbey and its inhabitants. Much I could learn through eyes and ears in the hours to come. And proudly I set my wit and will against any of High Hallack, be they Dame, lady, or lords of the host!

## II  BRIDES—TWELVE AND ONE

THE HALLS OF the Abbey were dim with the winter twilight. Here and there a wall lamp gave off faint light, which did not draw back the arras of shadows. To leave the fireside and the company in the great hall was to step into another world, but it was one I knew well. I passed the chamber of convocation. No light showed beneath its ponderous but time warped door. The Dames must all have returned to their cells in the wing forbidden to their guests.

Their guests—as I sped along that dark and chilly corridor I thought of those guests. Not those who had been so long housed at Norstead that they had become a part of its life, but rather the party which had ridden in before the last close down of night, who had shared our board and fare about the long table.

Lord Imgry, very much in charge of that company—his brown beard cut short to the jaw line for the better wearing of battle helm, its wiry strength shot here and there with silver, which showed again above his ears. His was a strong face, but with determination and will in every line of it, deep graven. This was man to yield not to any plaint, save when it pleased his own plan to do so, when that yielding meant advantage.

With him two others, lesser men, and ones who had little liking for their present task. Soldiers used to the ordering of their coming and going, never looking beyond those orders to what prompted their giving—now ill at ease and more centered upon that unease than upon the surroundings which gave it cause. As for the troop of men-at-arms—they had retired to quarters in the village.

Last of all—the brides. Yes—the brides! My acquaintance with weddings had been limited to those of village maids, when I had accompanied the Dame delegated to represent the Abbey at such festivities. Then there had been smiles, and if tears, happy ones, and singing—a festival, in truth.

Tonight I had faced across the board a new kind of bride. They wore the formal travel garb, robes well padded against winter blasts, skirts divided for the saddle, and, under their cloaks the short tabards, each embroidered with the arms of their houses, that they might proclaim their high birth to the world. But there were no loose locks and flower crowns.

There is a saying that all brides are fair of face on their wedding days. Two or three of these, now glittering of eyes, feverishly flushed, too talkative, were notably pretty. But there were heavy, reddened eyelids, too palid cheeks, and other signs of misery among them.

And in my ear had sounded the too-carrying whisper of the Lady Tolfana sharing her knowledge of the gathering with her seat mate.

"Fair? Ah, yes, too fair as her sister-by-blood, the Lady Gralya would tell you. Lord Jerret, her bedmate, is a notable lifter of skirts. It seems that lately he fingers, or would finger, robes closer to home. Thus you see Kildas in this party. Once wedded to a Rider she will not trouble that household again."

Kildas? She was one of the feverishly alive brides. Her brown hair was touched with red gold in the lamp light, and she had the round chin, the full lower lip of one fashioned for the eyes of men. Even behind the stiff tabard there were hints of a well rounded body, enough to inflame the lecher her sister's lord was reputed to be. A reason good enough to include Kildas in this company.

Her seat mate was a thin shadow to her ruddy substance. The 'broidery of her tabard was carefully and intricately wrought. Much care and choice had gone into that stichery, as if it were indeed a labor of love. Yet the robe beneath it was well worn and showed traces of being cut from another garment. The girl sat with her lids tear puffed, downcast and scarce ate, though she drank thirstily from her goblet.

I searched memory for her name—Alianna? No, that was the small girl at the far end. Solfinna—that was it. While Kildas had been sent forth in fine trappings, mayhap salving in some small way the consciences of those who had so dispatched her, Solfinna wore the thread-bareness of poverty long borne. Daughter of an old but impoverished house no doubt, with no dowry, and perhaps with younger sisters to be provided for. By becoming a bride she put the lords under obligation to serve her family.

In spite of Sussia's suggestion, none of the girls were ugly. By the covenant they could not be diseased nor ill formed. And several, such as Kildas, were fair enough to marry well. For the rest, youth granted them some pleasantness or prettiness—thought their unhappiness might cloud that now. I began to consider that the

Lords of High Hallack were fullfilling their part of the bargain with honor—save that the brides were unwilling. But then, in High Hallack, weddings did not come of mutual liking and regard, not among the old houses, but rather were arranged alliances. And perhaps these girls were not facing anything worse than they would have faced in the natural course of events.

It was easy to believe that until I looked upon Marimme. She did not display the strained vivacity she had shown in the hall, but now sat still, as a bird when a serpent eyes it coldly. And she ever watched Lord Imgry's face, though she made no attempt to attract his eye, rather turned her gaze from him quickly when it would seem he was about to return it. Had he broken the news to her yet? I thought not. Marimme, who had never been able to retain her composure when faced by small difficulties of the day, would have been in hysterics long since. But it was also plain she suspected something.

And when it did come . . . Plans made on the spur of the moment may go awry, but also may those which have been most carefully wrought over days and years. I was shield-backed now by my own sense that this was one of those times when Fortune not only smiled but put out her hand to aid, and that I needed only keep my wits about me to have matters go as I willed.

So now that the feast was past—mock feast and shadowed as it had been—I sought my own answer for what must happen soon. The shawl over my arm I whipped about my shoulders. To have sought my own would have perhaps marked my going, so I had one found on the back of a chair—dull green instead of gray, but no color in the night.

The way I took was a private one long known to me by my labors in the still room, and it was to that chamber I went, crossing the winter blasted garden at a run. There were snow flakes, large and feathery, falling. A storm such as this was another stroke of good luck. Within the still room the chill was not yet complete, and the good scents hung in the air. What I had come to do must be done swiftly and yet with care.

There were bags on a side shelf, each quilted into pockets of different sizes and shapes. One of these in my hands—and then, moving with care, for I dared not show a light, I made my way about the cupboards and tables, from shelves to chests, thankful that long familiarity made my fingers grow eyes for this task. Phials, boxes, small vials, each to its proper pocket in the bag, until at last I slung over my shoulder such a bag of simples and healing aids as Dame Alousan had supplied to the war bands. Last, not least but foremost, I groped my way to a far cupboard. It was locked by a dial lock, but that was no bar to me who had been entrusted with its secret years ago. I counted along a row of bottles within, making that numbering twice, then working loose a stopper to sniff.

Faint indeed was the odor—sharp, rather like the vinegar from the orchard apples. But it told me I was right. The bottle was large and difficult to carry. However, to try to decant what I needed for my purpose was impossible here and now. I gripped it tight between crooked arm and breast as I relocked the cupboard.

There was always the chance that Dame Alousan might find it in mind to check her storehouse, even at this hour and season. Until I reached my own room I was in danger of discovery. Yet in me the exultation grew with the belief that all was moving as I wished.

My small chamber was in a turn of the hall, a meeting place between the corridor of the Dames' cells and the portion given to visitors and boarders. Lights shone dully about the frames of some of the latter doors, but only the night lamp was alive at the far end of the cell hallway. My quick breath slowed as I closed my door behind me, though I had as yet taken only the first and far lesser steps on the path I had chosen to walk this night.

I set spark to my own lamp on the small table and set down thereon the flask I had brought out of the still room. A tray—so—then the small horn cup always used for medicinal doses, a spoon—all laid out. Last of all—the dose! I poured with care—filling the smaller bottle from my cupboard with the colorless liquid out of the flask. This much, no more—then—into it drops—five, six—from another phial. I counted under my breath, watching the mixture and its changing color, until it was a clear and refreshing green.

Now—to wait— And deep inside me grew a wonder as to how I could be so sure that this would be the way of it. My long suppression of my "power," if that was the word one might apply to my strange bits of knowledge and feeling which warred against controls I kept on them, might that not now have led to deception, a self-confidence which could defeat me? I could not sit still, but stood by the narrow window looking out into the night and the snow. There were lights in the village, marking the inn where Lord Imgry's escort now took their ease. Beyond that only the dull dark of the dale. North—the brides were riding north to the waste border— down Norsdale, and on past the Arm of Sparn, into Dimdale, and Casterbrook, and the Gorge of Ravenswell, off the map of our knowing—

Yet all the time my eyes watched the outer world my ears listened for sounds of the inner one, for I had carefully left my door ajar to better that hearing. And in me excitement bubbled and boiled.

The swish of a robe, the quick beat of slipper heels on uncarpeted stone— All that was in me wanted to rush to the door, throw it open to greet who came. But I kept control and at the scratch of nails on the wood, I moved with deliberation.

It was no surprise to front the Lady Sussia. Nor was she in turn amazed, I was sure, to find me still dressed as if I awaited a summons.

"Marimme—you are needed to tend her with your healcraft, Gillan." Her eyes swept past me to the table where waited the tray and its burden, and there was the faintest curve of smile to her lips as she then glanced back to me. Again there were no words between us, but understanding. She nodded as if agreeing to some comment unheard by me.

"I wish you good fortune for what you do," she said softly. But it was not of heal-craft that she spoke, and we both knew it.

I went down the hall, bearing the tray. As I came to the door of Marimme's room I saw that it also stood ajar and there were voices to be heard.

One was low, a murmur which seldom arose to intelligible speech. The sound of it stopped me, struck against the confidence which had been heady wine for my drinking all evening.

Abbess Yulianna! To govern any Abbey-stead was a task demanding wit and force of character which made any Abbess a formidable adversary. And Yulianna was not the least of those who had ruled here. To play my game before her required far more skill than any I thought would be demanded of me. Still I had long passed the point where withdrawal from battle-to-be was allowed.

"—maidish vapourings! Yes, Lady Abbess, this I will make allowance for. But time marches along the hills. We ride with the morn to keep our covenant. And she goes to the marriage made for her! Also she goes without wailing. I have heard you are skilled in heal-craft. Put down her some potion to end these mad humors she has treated us to this past hour. I would not take her gagged or tied in the saddle—but if that must be—so it will! We keep our bargain with those we have hand-sealed to the treaty."

Not choleric was Lord Imgry—no—cold and as one stating facts which not even the winds and tempests of the heavens could nay-say. He was one who would be as unyielding as the earth and the stone bones of the Dales.

"Those who use heal-craft for ill are not among us, my lord." As unyielding in turn was the Abbess. "It remains, do you wish to reach your trysting place with a girl out of her wits with fear? For this is what well may happen should you force this matter—"

"You enlarge upon this past all reason, Lady

Abbess! She is startled, yes, and she had heard too many wild tales. Makes she any marriage she will do it to order and not to silly liking. We tryst within three days, so we ride in the dawn. By honor are we bound to give twelve and one brides into their lords' care. Twelve and one we have under this roof tonight. We do not take fewer with us—"

I steadied the tray upon my right hand and scratched upon the door with my left during the small interval of silence which followed his cool statement, one which he certainly did not intend to be challenged.

There was an exclamation and the door was opened. Lord Imgry looked out and I dipped knee in curtsy, but as would an equal in blood.

"What's to do?"

"The Lady Sussia says that heal-craft is needed," I schooled my voice. I waited an answer, not from him, but from her who stood by the bed on which lay Marimme. Her veil was pushed a little back so that her face was in the light. On it, however, I could read no expression as Lord Imgry stepped back to allow me entrance.

"Come in then. Come in and be about your work—"

I think he paused then because he did not know just how to name me. Though my under-robe was drab of color, I wore neither coif nor veil. Instead I had on a feasting tabard bright with stitchery. No crest for a nameless, landless one, of course, yet the fabric was richly stiff with an intricate design of my own wandering fancy.

But for now the Lord Imgry was not my concern. I continued to watch her who looked over his shoulder. And toward the Abbess Yulianna I launched the full force of what power of will I could summon, even as an archer on a field of grave doubt would loose the last of his shafts at the captain of the enemy. Though in this time and wise I did not wish to compel foe but one who might stand my friend.

"This is not your healer," Imgry said sharply.

I waited then for the Abbess to nay-say me in agreement. But rather did she move a step or two aside and wave me to the bed.

"This is Gillan who is help-hand to our healer and lessoned in all such matters. You forget, my lord, it is past the Hour of Last Light. Those of the community must soon be in the Chapel for night prayer. Unless the need approaches great danger, the healer can not be summoned from such a service."

He gave a bitten-off exclamation, but even his confidence could not prevail against the custom and usage under this roof. Now the Abbess spoke again:

"You had best withdraw now, my lord. Should Marimme awake from her swoon to find you here—then perhaps needs must we again have the wailing and crying which you so dislike—"

But he did not move. There was no scowl on his face . . . only the lines of determination which I had marked at the table grew a fraction deeper. For a moment there was silence and then the Abbess spoke, and now her tone was that which I had heard now and again, infinitely remote and daunting.

"You are her guardian-by-rule-and-blood, my lord. We know well the law and will not move against your will, no matter how ill we think your decision. She shall not be spirited away in the night—how could she be? Nor is it necessary for us to give oath on such a point under this roof!"

He did then look a little ashamed, for it was plain she had read aright his thoughts. Yet at the same time her voice carried the conviction of one taking that oath she had denied the need for.

"My daughter," again her eyes sought mine and held them. I could not read her thoughts. If she read mine, or guessed my intention, she did not reveal the fact. "You will heal as you can, and watch through the night, should that be needful."

I made no direct answer, only bent knee in curtsy, and that more deeply than I had to my lord. He was at the door, still hesitating there. But as the Abbess advanced upon that portal he went, and she, following, closed it with a click of falling latch.

Marimme stirred and moaned. Her face was flushed as one in a fever, and she breathed in uneven gasps. I set the tray on the table and measured by spoon a portion of the liquid into the horn cup. I held it for a moment in my hand. This was the last parting between present and future. From this point there was no back-turning—only complete success, or discovery and ill will of the kind I could never hope to escape. But I did not hesitate long. My arm behind her shoulder raised Marimme. Her eyes were half open, she muttered incoherently. The horn cup to her lips . . . then she swallowed with soft urging from me.

"Well done."

I looked around. Sussia stood by the door, but it was safely closed behind her. Now she came forward a step or two.

"You will need an ally—"

That was true. But why—?

Again it was as if we were mind to mind, one thought shared.

"Why, Lady Gillan? Because of many things. First, I have more than a little liking for this soft creature." She came to the end of the bed and stood looking down at Marimme. "She is a harmless, clinging one of the kind who find the world harsh enough without bending and breaking under blows never meant for their shoulders. No—you—and I—we are of a different breed—"

I settled Marimme back on her pillows and stood up, putting down the horn cup with a hand I was pleased to see was steady.

"And second, I know you, perhaps better than you think, Gillan. This Norstead has become a prison to you. And what other future could you look to but endless years of like living—"

"The dusty years—" I had not realized I spoke aloud until I heard her small chuckle of amusement.

"I could not have said it better!"

"But why should my fate be a matter of concern to you, my lady?"

She was frowning a little. "To me that is also a puzzle, Gillan. We are not cup-fellows, nor sister-friends. I can not tell why I wish to see you forth from here—only that I am moved to aid you so. And I think this is truly a venture for you. It is one which I would have chosen, had I been allowed a choice."

"Willingly?"

She smiled. "Does that surprise you?"

Oddly it did not. I believe that Sussia would have ridden on such a bride trek with tearless eyes, looking forward with curiosity and desire for adventure.

"I say it now again, we are of one breed, Gillan. Therefore this abbey is not for you, and since there is naught else within High Hallack for you—"

"I should go forth with a high heart to wed with a shape-changer and sorcerer?"

"Just so." Still she smiled. "Think what a challenge and adventure that presents, my Gillan. Greatly do I envy you."

She was right, very right!

"Now," she spoke more briskly. "What dose have you given her? And what do you plan?"

"I have given her sleep, and shall give it again. She will wake refreshed a day, perhaps more, from now. And also she will awake with soothed mind and nerves."

"If she sleeps here—" Sussia put finger tip to lips and chewed upon it.

"I do not intend that she shall. In her sleep she will be open to suggestion. As soon as the Hour of Great Silence begins I shall take her to my chamber."

Sussia nodded. "Well planned. You are taller than she, but in the morning dark that will not be marked. I will bring you riding robe—and with her tabard, and the cloaks— You can be allowed some weeping behind a wind veil. I do not think Lord Imgry will question if you walk with face hidden to your horse. But there is the leave taking with the Abbess, she is to bless the brides at the chapel door—"

"It will be very early, and if it snows— Well, there are some things one can only leave to chance."

"A great deal in this ploy must be left to chance," she countered. "But what I can do, that I will!"

Thus together we pushed onward my plan. Marimme lay at last in my bed and beside it I did don the underclothing for a long winter ride, setting over it the divided robe Sussia brought me. It was a finer stuff than I had worn for years, though plain of color, being a silver gray to match the cloak she also gave me. Over it the tabard was a bright splash of color, the striking hippogriff of Marimme's crest picked out in bright scarlet with touches of gold, prancing over a curve of blue-green representing the sea.

I braided and pinned very tight my dark hair and then coiled a travel veil and hood over that, leaving veil ends loose to be drawn mask-fashion over my face. When I was done, Sussia surveyed me critically.

"To one who knows Marimme well, this would be no true counterfeit, I fear me. But the Lord Imgry has seen her little, and those you will ride with on the morn do not know her at all. You must use all wits to keep the play going until they are past the place from which they might return. The time for the meeting with the Riders comes very close, ill weather in the highlands could mean more delay, so Lord Imgry would not dare return. After all, he needs but twelve and one brides, and those he shall have. That will be your safeguard against his wrath when discovery is made."

And that was the only safeguard I would have.

A little shiver ran through me, but that I would not let Sussia guess. My confidence must be my armor.

"Good fortune to you, Gillan."

"I shall doubtless need all such wishes and more, too," I replied shortly as I picked up the bag of herbs and simples I had earlier packed. Yet at that moment had I been given a chance to retrace all I had done that night and be free of the action I had embarked upon, I would have scornfully refused it.

Back in Marimme's chamber I rested for the rest of the night, having fortified myself with another cordial from my store, so that while I did not sleep much, I was vigorous and eager when there was a morning scratching at my door.

I had my veil about my head, my cloak over my arm. For a moment I did not move to open and then I heard a whisper:

"Ready?"

Sussia again. When I came forth she put her arm quickly about my shoulders as one who supported a friend in distress. Thus I adapted my action to her suggestion, and walked in a feeble, wavering fashion down to the hall. There was food waiting: cakes of journey bread and hot drink. And of this I managed to eat more than appeared with Sussia sitting as a cup-companion, urging me on in a solicitous fashion. She told me in whispers that she had warned off Marimme's other friends, saying that I was so distraught that their sympathy might prove disastrous. And after Marimme's hysterical fit of the night before when the news was broken to her, they believed this readily.

Thus it went as we had hoped. When Lord

Imgry, who had avoided me heretofore, came to lead me forth, I went bent and weeping, so I hoped, in a piteous fashion. The last test came as we knelt for the Abbess's blessing. She gave each the kiss of peace and for that I needs must throw back my veil for a moment. I waited tensely to be denounced. But there was not a flicker of change on the Abbess's face as she leaned forward to press her lips to my forehead.

"Go in peace, my daughter—" She spoke the ritual words, but I knew they were truly meant for me and not Marimme. Thus heartened, I was aided by Lord Imgry into the saddle and so rode out of Norstead forever, after some ten years of life within its never-changing walls.

# III THE THROAT OF THE HAWK

IT WAS COLD, and the falling snow thickened as the road wound out of Norsdale, across the uplands, where the fringe forests made black scars against the white. In the spring, in the summer, in autumn, the dale lands were green with richly rooted grass and tree, bush and briar, but in winter they held aloof, alien to those who dwelt in village or upland farm.

Into Harrowdale the road narrowed. Before the long war of the invasion, men had spread out and out to north and west, putting under tillage land uncut by plow before. And then there had been travel on these roads, pack merchants, hill lords and their men, families with their worldly possessions on carts, driving their stock, moving out to fresh new lands. But since the war years communication across the Dales had dwindled, and what had been roads became mountain tracks—narrowed and blurred by the growth of vegetation.

There was little or no talk among our party as we rode, not mounted on such horses as the host kept for raiding and battle, but rather on shaggy coated, short legged beasts, ambling of pace, yet with vast powers of endurance and deep lungs to take the rough up and down going of the back country with uncomplaining and steady gait.

At first we rode three and four abreast, one or two of the escort with each pair of women. Then we strung out farther as the brush encroached and the road became a lane. I was content to keep silence behind veil and hood. For a space I had ridden stiff of back, tense, lest some call from the Abbey . . . a rider sent after . . . would reveal me for what I was. Still did it puzzle me that the Abbess Yulianna had not unmasked me in that farewell moment. Did she have such tenderness for Marimme that she was willing to let the deception stand to save a favorite? Or did she consider me a disturbing factor in her placid community, of whom she would be well rid?

Every hour we traveled lessened the chance of any return. And Imgry forced the pace where he could, conferring with the taciturn guide who led our party at least twice during the morning. How far away was our rendezvous? I only knew that it lay upon the edge of the waste at some point of landscape which was so noteworthy as not to be mistaken.

Harrowdale with its isolated farms was gone, and yet the road climbed with us. Save for our own party we might have passed through a deserted countryside. No animal, no bird—and certainly no man—came into sight. When winter wrapped the farms their people kept much indoors, the women busy at their looms, the men at such tasks as they wished.

Now followed the sharper descent into Hockerdale and the murmur of water, for the swift flowing stream there was not yet completely ice roofed. We passed a guard post at the head of that dale, and men turned out to salute our leader and exchange words with him and the guide. It was at that pause another pony edged close to mine and she who rode it leaned a little forward in her saddle.

"Do they mean to never give us any ease?" she

asked, perhaps of me, perhaps only of the air, that her words might carry to Lord Imgry.

"It would seem not so," I made my answer low-voiced, for I did not want to be heard abroad.

She pulled impatiently at her veil and her hood fell back a little. This was that Kildas whom Tolfana had pricked with her spite at the table. There were dark shadows under her green-blue eyes in this wan light, a pinching about her full lipped mouth, as if both harsh dayshine and the cold had aged and withered her for the nonce.

"You are his choice," she nodded to Lord Imgry. "But you ride mum this morning. What whip of fear did he use to bind you to his purpose? Last eve you swore you would not come—" There was not any sympathy in her, just curiosity, as if her own discomfort might be eased a little by seeing the sores of another sufferer exposed.

"I had the night for reflection," I made the best reply I could.

She laughed shortly. "Mighty must have been those reflections to produce so collected a mind this day! Your screams had the halls ringing bravely when they took you forth. Do you now fancy a sorcerer bridegroom?"

"Do you?" I countered. The thought that Marimme had made such a show of her fear and revulsion was a small worry now. I was not Marimme and I could not counterfeit her well. Lord Imgry had been engrossed all morning in his urge for speed. But what would happen when he found he had been befooled? He needed me to make up the tale of the Bargain, and that should protect me from the full force of any wrath that he would feel upon learning of the substitution.

"Do I?" Kildas drew me out of my thoughts. "As all of us, I have no choice. But—should these Weremen share much with those of our own kind, then I do not fear." She tossed her head, strengthened by her confidence in herself and those weapons chance and nature had given her. "No, I do not fear that I shall be ill received by him who waits my coming!"

"What are they like? Have you ever seen a Rider?" I set myself to explore what she might know. Until this time I had been far more intent upon escape and what lay behind me, than what waited at this ride's end.

"Seen them?" she answered my last question first. "No. They have not come into the Dales, save on raids against Alizon. And they are said then to travel by night, not day. As to what they are like—they wore man forms when they treated with us, and they have strange powers—" Kildas' confidence ebbed and again her fingers pulled at the veil about her throat as if she found it hard to breathe and some cord pressed there against her flesh. "If more is known—that has not been told us."

I heard a catch of breath, not far removed from sob, to my left. Another had come level with us. Her travel worn robe—she was Solfinna who had shared Kildas' plate the night before—her poverty put farther to shame by the other's display.

"Weep out your eyes if you wish, Solfinna," snapped Kildas. "A pool of tears as deep as the sea will not change the future."

Solfinna started, as if that voice, whip-sharp, was indeed a thong laid about her hunched shoulders. And I think that Kildas then took shame, for she said in a softer voice:

"Think you—this was a free choice for you. Thus are you the greater than the rest of us. And since you believe in prayer, do you not also believe that right and good come to just rewards, even if there must be a time of waiting?"

"You chose to come?" I asked.

"It—it was a way to help." Solfinna paused and then spoke more firmly, "You are right, Kildas. To do a thing because it is right, and then to bewail the doing because one fears, throws away all that one must believe in. Yet I would give much to see my lady mother, and my sisters and Wasscot Keep once again. And never shall I."

"Would that not also be so in regular marriage?" Kildas asked with a gentleness she had not shown before. "If you had been betrothed to lord or Captain of the south Dales, there would have been no returning."

"So do I remember. To that thought I hold," Solfinna said quickly. "We are betrothed, in truth. We go to our weddings. It is as it has been for womenkind for untold years. And for my going so, those left behind gain much. Yet the Riders—"

"Look upon this thought, also. Test it in your mind," I said. "These Riders so wanted wives that they set up a war bargain to gain them. And when a man so much wants a thing that he will gamble his life to its gaining, then I think once it is in his hands he will cherish and hold it in no little esteem."

Solfinna turned to look at me more closely. Her red-rimmed eyes blinked as if she would focus them upon me for keener sight. And I

heard a little exclamation from Kildas, who
urged her mount even closer.

"Who are you?" she demanded with a force
which disputed any denial. "You are not that
wailing maid they carried from the hall last
night!"

Need I try to play the counterfeit with my
fellows in the train? There was no great reason
for that. Perhaps we were already past the point
where Lord Imgry could make adequate protest.

"You are right. I am not Marimme—"

"Then who?" Kildas continued to press, while
Solfinna watched me now with eyes rounded by
astonishment.

"I am Gillan, one who dwelt at the Abbey for
some years. I have no kin and this is my free
choice."

"If you have no kin to compell you, nor to
profit from your free choice," that was Solfinna
her amazement now in her voice, "why do you
come?"

"Because, perhaps there are worse things then
riding into an unknown future."

"Worse things?" prompted Kildas.

"Facing a future too well known."

Solfinna drew back a little. "You have done
that which—"

"Which makes this the lesser choice of ill
fate?" I laughed. "No, I leave no crimes behind
me. But neither do I have any chance of life
outside the Abbey-stead, and I am not of a nature
to take veil and coif and be content with such a
round, one day so like unto another, so that during the years they become just one endless series
of hours none differing from its fore or following
companion."

Kildas nodded. "Yes, I think that could be so. But what will chance when he," she nodded towards Lord Imgry, "discovers the truth? He was set upon Marimme because of some project of his own. And he is not a man to be lightly balked."

"That I know. But there is this drive he has shown, a fear of passing time. He will not be able to return to Norstead and he is honorbound to furnish the full toll of brides."

Again Kildas laughed. "You have a good way of thinking to a purpose, Gillan. I believe that both your weapons against him will serve."

"You—you do not fear the—the wild men? You chose for yourself alone?" Solfinna asked.

"I do not know about future fears. It is best not to see shadows on mountain crests while you still ride the valleys at their feet," I replied. Yet I thought that I could not claim unusual courage in this. Perhaps I had turned my back on a lesser trouble to embrace a greater. Still I would not admit that now, even to myself.

"A good philosophy," Kildas commented, but there was more a note of raillery than approval in that. "May it continue to guide and preserve you, sister-bride. Ah, it appears that we shall be granted a rest within after all—"

For at word from Lord Imgry the men of the escort came forward to help us dismount and lead us into the post. In the guardroom we crowded to the fire, holding out our hands, moving about to drive the stiffness from our legs and backs. As always I kept as far from our leader as I might. Perhaps he would believe that my avoidance of him was only natural, that Marimme's fear and hatred would keep her from the man solely responsible for her being here. If he believed so, he meant to leave well enough alone, for he did not approach me where I stood with Kildas and Solfinna, sipping now at the mugs of hot stew-soup dipped out of a common kettle.

We were not yet finished with this meal, if meal it might be named, when Lord Imgry spoke out, addressing us as a company.

"The snow has stopped in the heights. Though it is uncomfortable, yet we must press on to the Croffkeep before night. Time grows short and we must be at the Throat of the Hawk in another day's time."

There was some under-the-breath complaining at his words, but none of them spoke out loud. He was not a man to be fronted on a matter of comfort alone. Throat of the Hawk—the name meant nothing to me. Perhaps it was our ordained meeting place.

My luck still held. When we reached the Croffkeep, a mountain fort now only a quarter manned, we were given a long room to ourselves, with pallets laid on its floor, reducing us to the "comforts" of those who had fought from this rocky perch in years past.

Fatigue pushed me into sleep, deep and dreamless. But I awoke from that suddenly, alert of mind, as if I had been summoned. Almost I could hear the echo of some well known voice—Dame Alousan's?—calling me to a necessary task. And so strong was that feeling that I blinked at the dim lamp at the far end of the room, found it hard for the moment to recognize the sounds of heavy breathing from the pallets around mine and realize where I lay and for what purpose.

My weariness was gone. Instead I was filled with a restlessness, the kind of anticipatory unease which haunts one before some momentous and life changing event. And also my old talent, which had been stirring in me since I first thought of this, was as awake as I.

There was that reaching out in me which I did not exactly fear, which some inner part below the level of my daymind knew and welcomed, as one drinking a cordial for the first time might know the refreshment of a herb the body craved but which hitherto had been denied it. It was a brave excitement and it worked in me so that I found it impossible to lie still.

With what stealth I could summon, I put on my outer clothing. The divided skirt of my riding robe was still damp and the chill unpleasant but that did not matter to the thing forcing me into the night and the open, as if I must have freedom in which to breathe.

Kildas stirred in her sleep as I rounded the end of her pallet, next to mine, and murmured—a name perhaps. But she did not wake, and then I laid hand on the door latch. I could hear the tread of a sentry in the corridor. Yet my need for the open drove me on.

When I edged open the door he was back towards me at the end of his beat. I had taken but a step or two without when he began to turn. And in that moment I was possessed by that which I had known only dimly—a will which was as much of the body as it was of the mind. I looked upon that man who in a moment would see me, and I willed, fiercely and with all the force in me, that he would not do so—not for the seconds which would see me gone.

And he did not! Though, as I reached the side corridor, I leaned limply against the cold stone of the wall, spent with the effort of that willing. And the excitement in me was augmented by another emotion—that of wonder and triumph mixed. For a period out of real time I stood so, savoring what I believed I had done—but one cool portion of me doubted, acted as a brake. Then I went up the stairs facing me and out onto a terrace or lookout walk. The snow gave a certain lightness, but the bulk of the dark heights were only slightly silvered by the moon veiled by drifting clouds.

There was a wind, fresh, as it blew from yet higher peaks—free lands where the dust of the Dales could never linger. Only, now that I had reached this place, that urge which had brought me here was fast dying, and I could find no reason for it. In spite of my cloak I shivered in the wind, drew back to the doorway for protection.

"What do you here?"

There was no mistaking that voice. Why or how Lord Imgry shared my need for deep night wandering, I did not know. But our meeting I could not escape.

"I wished the fresh air—" My reply was stupid, meaningless. But to seek delays was useless.

As I turned I held my hand to my eyes for he swept me with the dazzling light of a hand lamp. He must first have read the device on Marimme's borrowed tabard, for his hand flashed out and gripped my shoulder with punishing force, dragging me closer to him.

"Fool! Little fool!" Passion stirred under that adamant tone, not one soft-turned to Marimme,

but rather one concerned with his good or ill.
And somehow that thought armored me and I
dropped my masking hand to meet him eye to
eye.

"You are not Marimme." He kept grip on my
shoulder, swung the lamp still closer to me.
"Nor are you any other rightfully of this company. Who are you?" And his fingers were five
sword points in my flesh, so that I could have
cried out under their torment but did not.

"I am of this company, my lord. I am Gillan,
out of Norstead—"

"So! They would dare, those mouse-squeak
women, to do this—"

"Not so." I did not strive to throw off his hold,
since I knew that I could not, but I stood
straight-shouldered under it. And I think my
denial of his accusation broke the surface of his
anger and made him listen. "This was of my own
planning—"

"You? And what have you to do with deci-
sions beyond your making? You shall rue
this—"

Passion curbed, but perhaps all the more
deadly for that curbing. But to meet his anger I
summoned will. Somehow I knew that I could
not impress upon this man my desire as I had
upon the sentry—if I had—still will gave me a
shield to arm-sling for my own protection.

"The time for rue is past—or has not yet
come," I tried to choose my words with care,
those best to hold attention and make him think.
"Time is not one of your menie this night, my
lord. Return me to Norstead and you have lost.
Send me back with one of your men, and again
you have lost—for at the Throat of the Hawk

there must be twelve and one, or honor shall be broke."

His arm moved and he shook me to and fro, his strength so that in his grasp I was a straw thing. But my will held and I faced him. Then he flung me away so I slipped in the snow and went to my knees, jarring against the parapet of that walk. And I do not believe in that instant he would have cared had I been hurled over it and down.

I pulled to my feet and I was shaking, my bruised shoulder all pain, the fear of what might have been brushing me still. But I could face him head up and still clear of thought, knowing what I must say.

"You were to provide one of the brides, my lord. I am here, nor will I nay-say that I am here through your will, should witness be needed. And still you have Marimme who is of such beauty as to make a fine match. Have you truly lost aught by this?"

I could hear his breathing, heavy as that of a man who had tried to outrace enemy horse and then been cornered in some rock hole. But, though his passions were hot, I had read him aright as one of those men who had full control when that was needed to further his plans. Now he came to me, moving with deliberation, holding up the lamp. However I knew that the moment of greatest danger was past. Imgry might hate me for my deception, but he was greater than some men, able to swallow that which might have been humilation at being befooled, because it best suited. His mind was already working ahead, chewing upon what I said.

"Gillan." My name was flat from his lips,

sounding harsh and dull. "And you fulfill the condition?"

"I am maid, and I think I am some twenty years of age. I was fosterling to Lord Furlo of Thantop and his wife, having been found as a small child a prisoner of Alizon. Since the Hounds had preserved my life Lord Furlo believed me of some consequence—thus you might deem my birth worthy."

He was surveying me insolently from head to foot and back again. It was shameful, that raking stare, and he knew it, making it so deliberately. I knew anger and kept it leashed, and I think he understood that also. Though what my inner defiance meant to him I could not tell.

"You are right—time presses. Twelve and one brides they shall have. You may not find this will be as you hope, girl."

"She who expects neither good nor ill has an equal chance of either," I replied as sharply as I could.

A faint shadow of expression crossed his face, one I could not read.

"From whence did the Hounds have you?" There was interest in that, in me as a person, not just one of the playpieces he pushed about his private board.

"I know not. I remember only a ship in a storm, and after that the port where Lord Furlo's raiders found me." I gave him the truth.

"The Hounds war also overseas. Estcarp!" He flung that last word at me as if to provoke response, perhaps betrayal.

"Estcarp?" I repeated, for the word meant nothing, though I added a guess as a question.

"That is enemy to Alizon?"

Lord Imgry shrugged. "So they say. But it is of no moment to you now. You have made your choice. You shall abide by it."

"I ask no more than that, my lord."

He smiled and it was not a good smile. "To make sure—just to make sure—"

Thus he brought me back to the sleeping chamber, pushed me inside. I heard him summon the guard to stand outside that door. Then I came back to my pallet and lay down. That which I dreaded since I had left the Abbey was now behind me. I had overleaped the second of the walls between me and what I sought. And the third—now my mind turned to the third—he who might wait for me at the Throat of the Hawk.

Mankind was known only at the Abbey-stead through speech, and now and then, at long intervals, by the kin of those refugee ladies who made visits. At such times I had been classed among the Dames and had seen such visitors only at a distance. I knew of men, but I did not know man. Though, this too was a custom among those of gentle blood.

Marriage is a far off thing which lies in a maid's mind but is not early brought to the surface, unless she is among those to whom it is of importance. Perhaps in this way I was far younger than those, or most of those I rode among. For the Dames marriage had no existence, and they did not discuss it. Now, when I tried to think of what my choice might lead me to, I had little to build upon. Even the fears of my companions were not real to me, since an ordinary man seemed as equally strange as one of the Were Riders with his dark reputation. And I

needs must apply my own advice—that which I
had so easily given to Solfinna—not to seek
trouble until its shadow could not be denied.

There was no mention in the morning between
Lord Imgry and me of our night meeting. I used
my masking veil prudently, lest others in the
company remark that I was not Marimme. But I
believe that the closer we drew to the end of our
journey, the more each turned inwards, dealing
with her own hopes and fears to the best of her
ability, and the less attention they spared for
those about them. We were very quiet during
that day's riding.

As far as I knew the world about us we had
ridden off the map of the Dales. The road was a
track along which two might file, ponies shoulder to shoulder, and it brought us down again
from the heights to a plain, brown with winter.
Dark copses of trees looked smaller than those of
the Dales, as if they were stunted in growth.
There was little underbrush. Sere grass showed
in ragged tuffs through snow which lay thinly
here.

We crossed a river on a bridge, man-built of
timbers rudely cut and set in hardened earth. But
there had been no recent travelers on this way,
no tracks broke the snow. Again we moved
through a deserted world which would lead one
to believe that mankind had long passed away.

Once more we began to climb a slope, a little
steeper than before. And our way led now to a
knotch between two tall cliffs. We came out on a
level space where stones had been built into a
rude half shelter and a pit, lined with rocks, was
marked with the black of past fires. There we
came to a halt. Lord Imgry joined with one of our

guards and the guide before he faced us to say:

"You will rest here."

No more. He was already riding off with those two. Stiff and tired, we dismounted. Two of the escort built a fire in the hold and then shared out trail provisions, but I do not think that any of us ate much. Kildas touched my arm.

"The Throat of the Hawk—" she motioned toward the cut. "It would seem that the brides are more willing than their grooms. There is no sign of any welcome."

As she spoke the gathering dusk was broken, deep inside that cut, by light. Nor the yellow of lamp shine, nor the richer red of fire, but with a greenish glow strange to me. Outlined blackly against it were the three who had left us—just them—no one else appeared in the pass.

"No," Kildas repeated, "one can not name them eager."

"Maybe," there was hope in Solfinna's voice, "maybe they have decided—"

"That they do not want us after all, child? Never think it! In a songsmith's tales such an ending might be granted us—in real life I have found it always goes differently." As on the day previous her face of a sudden had an aged, pinched look. "Do not hope. You will only be dashed the deeper when you know the truth."

We stood within the range of the fire where there was warmth, but perhaps all of us shivered within as we looked upon the Throat of the Hawk and that ever-steady green fire well within it.

# IV UNICORN MORN

"KNOW YOU WHAT night this is?" She who tossed back her veil and loosed her hood so that fair hair strayed limply from beneath its edge was Aldeeth who had lain to my left the night before. From the southlands she had come, and her blazon of salamander curled among leaping flames was one I did not know.

Kildas made answer. "If you mean we stand at year's end, to greet a new one with the dawn—"

"Just so. We pass now into the Year of the Unicorn."

"Which some might take as a good omen," Kildas responded, "since the unicorn is the guardian of maidens and the banner of the innocent."

"Tonight—" Solfinna's voice was very low, "we would gather in the great hall, with ivy and holly on the board so each might have a sprig for wearing—holly for the men, green ivy for us. And we would drink the year's cup together and feed the Strawman and the Flax woman to the flames, burning them with scented grasses, so that the crops would be fair and plentiful and luck would take its abode under our high roof tree—"

I had memories of the household meeting she put tongue to—a simple one, but carrying meaning for those who lived upon the fruits of the soil. Each silent and dark farmstead we had passed would be doing likewise this night, as would they with more revelry in a great hall. Only at the Abbey there would be no feasting nor burning of symbols, as the Dames allowed no such pagan ceremonies within their austere walls.

"I wonder whether our lords-and-masters-to-be welcome in the year's beginning in some such manner," Kildas broke the silence of our memories. "They worship not the Flames, since Those by their very nature are alien to the Riders' world. To what gods do they bow? Or have they any gods at all?"

Solfinna gave a little gasp. "No gods! How may a man live without gods, a power greater than himself to trust upon?"

Aldeeth laughed scornfully. "Who says that they are men? They are not to be judged as we judge. Have you not yet bit full upon that truth, girl? It is time to throw away your cup of memory, since you and we were born under ill-fated stars which have determined we pass so out of one world into another, even as we pass from the old year into the new."

"Why do you deem that that which is unknown must likewise be ill?" I asked. "To look diligently for shadows is to find them. Throwing aside all rumor and story, what evil do we know of the Riders?"

They spoke then, several together, and Kildas, listening to that jumble of speech, laughed.

"'They say'—'they say'—this and that they say! Now give full name and rank to they I'll warrant that this, our sister-comrade has the right of it. What do we know save rumor and ill-wishing? Never have the Were Riders lifted sword or let fly arrow against us—only have they ravaged the enemy in our behalf, after making covenant and bargain with our kin. Because a man grows black hair upon his head, wears a gray cloak, likes to live in a land of his own choosing, is he any different in blood, bone and spirit from he who had fair locks beneath his helm, goes with scarlet about his shoulders, and would ride in company along a port town street? Both have their part to play in the land. What evil of your own knowing has ever been from Rider hand?"

"But they are not men!" Aldeeth wished to make the worst of it.

"How know we that, either? They have powers which are not ours, but do all of us have talents alike? One may set 'broidery on silk so as to make one wish to pluck the stitched flowers and listen to the singing of the birds she has wrought. Another may draw her fingers across lute strings and voice such a song as to set us all a-dreaming. Do we each and every one of us do these things in a like measure? Therefore men may have gifts beyond our knowing and yet be men, apart from those talents."

Whether she believed what she spoke or not, yet she was doing valiant service here against the fear which sucked at us all.

"Lady Aldeeth," I broke in, "you wear upon your tabard a salamander easy among flames. Have you seen such a creature? Or does it not have a different meaning for you and your house—and its friends and enemies—than a lizard encouched on a fiery bed?"

"It means we may be menaced but not consumed," she replied as if by rote.

"And I see a basilisk here, a phoenix, a wyvern—do these exist in truth, or do they stand for ideas which each of your houses have made their guiding spirits? If this is true, then perhaps those we go to, have also symbols which may be misunderstood by those who are not lettered in their form of heraldry." So did I play Kildas' game, if game it was.

But still the green light glowed unchanged in the pass and Lord Imgry and his companions did not return. While waiting always frays the nerves of those who have only time to think.

We were sitting on stones, still huddled around the fire, when he who was Imgry's lieutenant returned with the message that we were to move on, into the Throat. And while I can not answer for the others, I believe that each of them shared what I was feeling, an excitement which was more than half fear.

But we rode not into any camp of men prepared to do us welcome. Rather did we find at the end of the pass a wide ledge and on that set shelter-tents of hide. Within were couches covered with the skins of beasts, and some of them of beasts we had never seen, and the floors were so carpeted also. There was a long, low table in the largest tent and it was spread with food.

I stroked a fine, silver-white fur, beautiful enough to form a mantle for the lady of a great lord. It was dappled with a deeper gray and so well cured that it was as soft in my hands as a silken shift. Though all about us was leather or fur, still there was a magnificence which spoke of honor offered and comfort promised.

Lord Imgry stood at the foot of the table as we finished those viands left for us, a bread with dried fruit baked therein, smoked meat of rich flavor, sweets which had the taste of wild honey and nutmeats. He had a shadow about him, I suddenly thought, as if between him and our company was forming a barrier—that indeed we were already forsaking our kind. But there was this time no fear in that thought, only again did I feel that prick of eagerness to be away—to be doing—where and what? I could not name either.

"Listen well," his voice was unduly harsh, sending us all into silence. "In the morn you shall hear a signal—the calling of a horn. Then will you take the marked path leading from this tent, and you will go down to where your lords await you—"

"But—" Solfinna protested, "there will have been no marriage, no giving by cup and flame."

He smiled at her as if that shaping of the lips came, for him, with vast effort.

"You pass from those who deal by Cup and Flame, my lady. Marriage awaits you true enough, but by other rites. However, they will be as binding. I bid you," he paused and looked at each in turn, coming at last to me, though his gaze did not linger, "good fortune." His hand moved in the green light of the table lamps. He was holding a cup. "As he who stands for all of you as father-kin, do I drink long years, fair life, and easy passing, kin-favor, roof-fortune, child-holding. Thus be it ever!"

So did the Lord Imgry perform for the twelve and one he had brought hither the father-kin farewell. And then he was swiftly gone before any found tongue.

"So be it." I stood up and in that moment of bewilderment their eyes all swung to me. "I do not think we shall see my lord again."

"But to go alone—down to strangers—" one of them made protest.

"Alone?" I asked. Swiftly Kildas came in, as might a shield companion in a sharp skirmish.

"We are twelve and one, not one alone. Look you, girl—this may not be a festive hall, yet I think we have been made good welcome here." She drew to her a lustrous length of block fur, with small diamond sparkles touching the hair tips in the light.

I had half expected trouble after the going of Imgry. But, while there was little talk among them as they prepared for the waiting couches, also there was more a sense of expectancy and content. Almost as if each in truth did wait for a wedding she might have hoped for in the usual passing of time. They were quiet as if their thoughts were turned inward, and, now and again, one had a shadow of smile about her lips. As I drew the silver fur about my shoulders I wondered a little.

But I slept that night deeply dreamless, and knew no waking until the morning sun lay from the tent's entrance as a thin spear.

"Gillan!"

Kildas stood there. She had looped aside the flap to look out, and now she glanced at me, plainly disturbed.

"What make you of this?"

I crawled from my warm nest of furs and joined her. The horses we had ridden the night before were gone from the picket line our escort had set up. The other tent still stood, its flap looped up to show it empty. To all appearances the camp was deserted, save for the brides.

"It would seem they feared some last minute changes of mind," I commented.

She smiled. "I think they need not have harbored such doubts. Is that not true, Gillan?"

With her asking I knew it was true. On this morn, had all the powers that ruled High Hallack stood ranged before me and offered me the greatest desire of my heart's wishing—still would I have chosen to go down the Throat to the north, rather than return to the world I knew.

"At least they were thoughtful enough to leave our bridal fairings, and did not condemn us to make a poor showing over-mountain." She pointed to packs set out in an orderly fashion. "I do not know how long we have before our lords summon us to a bridal, but I think it might be well for us to waste no time. Rouse you!" She raised her voice to summon the others already beginning to stir and murmur on their beds. "Greet the Unicorn and what it has to offer us."

In the deserted tent we found bowls of a substance like unto polished horn and with them ewers of water, still warm and scented with herbs. We washed and then shared out equally the contents of the packs, so that shabbiness was forgotten and each adorned as fairly as might be. Nor did this oneness on property seem strange, though some had come poorly provided for and others, such as Kildas, with the robes due a bride of a noble house.

We ate, too, with good appetite, of what was left from the night before. And it seemed we had timed matters very well. For, as we put down our cups from a toast Kildas had proposed to fortune, there was a sound from beyond our small world in the pass. A horn—such as a hunter might wind—no, rather as the fanfare of one greeting a friendly keep.

I arose and turned to Kildas and to Solfinna.

"Shall we go?"

"There is no need to linger." Kildas put aside her cup. "Let us see what the fortune we have drunk to has in store for us."

We went out into a curling mist, which cloaked that lying below, but not the path ahead as we walked. And the road was neither steep nor difficult. Behind us followed the rest, holding their skirts from sweeping the earth, their bride veils modestly caught across their faces. None faltered, nor hung back, and there was no trace of hesitation or fear as we went silently.

The horn sounded thrice, when we first obeyed its summons, again when we left the pass behind hidden in the mist, and then a third time. On that the mist before us cleared as if drawn aside by a giant hand. We came into a place which was not winter but spring. The soft turf was short and smooth and of a bright and even green color. A wall of bushes made an arc beyond, and on these small flowers hung as white and golden bells, while from them came the scent of bridal wreaths.

Yet no men stood in our sight, but rather was there a strange display. Lying hither and thither, as if tossed aside in sport, were cloaks. And these were wrought of such fine stuff, so bedecked with beautiful embroidery, with glints of small gems in their designs, that they were richer than any I believe any of us had seen in our lifetimes. Also, each varied from his fellow—until one could not believe so many patterns could exist.

We stood and stared. But, as I looked longer at what lay before me there I was twice mazed, for it seemed that I saw two pictures, one fitted above the other. If I fastened my will on any part of that green cup, the flowering bushes, or even the cloaks, then did one of those pictures fade, and I saw something else, very different which lay below.

No green turf, but winter brown earth and ash-hued grass such as had covered the plain across which we had ridden yesterday; and no sweetly flowering bushes, but bare and spiky limbs of brush, lacking either leaf or blossom. While the cloaks—the beauty of the stitchery and gem was a shimmer above darker color, where there were still designs, but these oddly like lines of runes for which I could summon no meaning, and all were alike in that they had the ashen hue of the earth on which they lay.

The longer I looked and willed, so more did the enchantment fade and dim. Glancing to left and right at the rest of my companions I saw that with them this was not so, that they saw only the surface and not that which lay beneath it. And their faces were rapt, bemused, those of mortals caught in a web of glamourie. They looked so happy that I knew no warning of mine could break that spell, nor did I wish to.

They left me, first Kildas and Solfinna, and then all the rest, passing by me swiftly into that enchanted dell. And each was drawn by herself alone, to one of the cloaks which lay beckoning with that semblance of what it was not.

Kildas stooped and gathered up to her breast one of blue, brilliantly rich, with a fabulous beast wrought upon it in small gems—for the double sight came and went for me and it seemed as if I could see now and then through those ensorcelled eyes as well. Holding it to her as a treasure beyond all reckoning, she moved forward as one who saw perfectly her goal and longed only to reach it. She came to the bushes, passed through a space there and was gone, for beyond still held the mist curtain.

Solfinna made her choice and was gone. Aldeeth and all the rest followed. Then with a start I realized I alone remained. My double sight was a thing to fear, and to hesitate now might be a risk of peril. But when I looked at the remaining cloaks, for there was more than one, their beauty was vanished and they were all alike. Still not entirely so, I decided when I studied them more closely—for their bands of rune writing differed in number and width.

There was one cloak lying well away from the rest, almost to the hedge which set the boundary of the dell. The runes did not run on it as an uninterrupted edging, but rather were broken apart. For a moment I strove to see it enchanted—green—or blue—or something of them both—and on it a winged form wrought in crystals. But that glimpse was gone so quickly that I could not have sworn to it a moment later. I was drawn to it—at least it drew my eyes more than did the others. And I must make a choice at once, lest I be suspect—though why I thought that I could not tell.

So I crossed dead and frozen ground, and I picked up the cloak, holding it before me as I went on, through bare bushes and the chill of the mist, leaving yet perhaps a half score cloaks still lying there, their spells fled, their color vanished.

I heard voices in the mist, carefree laughter, joyful sounds. But I saw no one and when I tried to follow any of the sounds, I could not be sure of my direction. In the filmy entrapment my uneasiness grew and all the dark of dread rumor whispered in memory. The cloak between my hands was heavy, lined with the white-gray fur which was harsh to my skin. Also I was chilled, and my borrowed finery dew-wet, little protection against the mist.

A darkness within that cloud, a figure coming towards me. In that moment it was as if I were being stalked, cunningly and with no hope of escape.

Shape changers, that was the cry in one's ears when the Were Riders were named. Man—or beast—or both? What did I face now—a darkish shadow—but it walked on two feet as a man. Did a beast's head rest upon its shoulders? Whatever my companions had met with in that disguising fog, they had not feared, or voices would not continue to rise with so happy a ring, even though the words they spoke I could not distinguish.

I halted, holding still the cloak which grew ever heavier in my hands, dragging them down with its weight. Man, yes, the outline of the head was human, not that of a shaggy beast. And still I had clear sight, for the gray-brown cloak I held proved that.

A last whip of the fog between us was sundered and I looked upon this stranger from another breed who had come a-hunting me. He was tall, though not of the inches of a hill warrior, and slim as any untried boy on his first foraging would be slim. Smooth of face as a boy, also. Yet the green eyes beneath slanting brows were not a boy's eyes, but weary and old, still ageless also.

Those brows slanting upward, made the eyes in turn appear angle-set in a face with a sharply pointed chin, and were matched in outline by his thick black hair which peaked on his forehead. He was neither handsome nor unhandsome by human standard, merely very different.

Though his head was bare of war-helm he wore a byrnie of chain-link, supple by his easy movements within its casing. This reached to midthigh and beneath it breeches, close fitting, of furred hide, a silvery fur shorter in the hair than the pelt which had taken my fancy at the tent though still of the same nature. His feet were booted, but also in furred leather, their color being a shade or two the darker than his breeks. About his slender waist was a belt of some soft material, fastened by a large clasp in which were set odd milky gems.

Thus did I face for the first time Herrel of the Were Riders, whose cast cloak I had gathered to me, though not through the same weave spell as intended.

"My—my lord?" I used the address courteous, since he did not seem disposed to break the silence between us.

He smiled, almost wryly.

"My lady," he returned and there was a kind of mockery in his voice, but I did not feel it was turned upon me. "It would seem that I have woven better than was deemed possible, since that is my cloak you bring."

He reached out and took it from me. "I am Herrel," he named himself as he shook out the folds of cloth and fur.

"I am Gillan," I made answer, and then was at a loss as to what was expected of me. For my planning had not reached, even in fancy, beyond this point.

"Welcome, Gillan—"

Herrel swung out the cloak and brought it smoothly about my shoulders so that it covered me, from throat almost to the ground now lost in the mist.

"Thus do I claim you, Gillan—it being your wish?"

There was no mistaking the question in those last words. If this be some form of ceremony, then he was leaving me a chance of withdrawal. But I was committed now to this course.

"It is my wish, Herrel."

He stood very still as if awaiting something more, I knew not what. And then he leaned a little toward me and asked, more sharply than he had yet spoken:

"What lies about your shoulders, Gillan?"

"A cloak of gray and brown and fur—"

It was as if he caught his breath in a swift gasp.

"And in me what do you see, Gillan?"

"A man young and still not young, wearing chain mail and furred clothing, with a belt about him buckled with silver and milk white stones, with black hair on his head—"

My words dropped one by one into a pool of quiet which was ominous. His hand came out and took from my head the bride's veil, so swiftly and with such a jerk that it dislodged the pinning of my braids, so they loosened and fell upon my back and shoulders over the cloak he had set about me as a seal.

"Who are you?" His demand came with some of the same heat as Lord Imgry had shown at our night meeting.

"I am Gillan, beyond that I do not know." The truth I gave him because even then I knew that the truth was his right. "A war captive from overseas, fostered among the Dales of High Hallack, and come here by my own will."

He had dropped the veil into the mist, now his fingers moved in the air between us, sketching, I believe, some sign. There was a faint trail of light left by their moving so. But the smile was gone from his mouth and now he wore a battle-ready face.

"Cloak-bound we are—and there is no chance in that, only destiny. But this I ask of you, Gillan, if the double sight is yours—see with the outer eyes only for this while—there is danger in any other path."

I did not know how to regain the less from the greater, but I tried fumblingly to see green grass under my feet, color about me. And there was a period of one wavering upon the other, then I stood with rippling splendor about me, green-blue hung with crystal droplets. And Herrel wore a different face more akin to that of humankind and strongly handsome—yet I found it in me to like his other guise the better.

He took my hand without more words and we walked from the never-never land of the mist into more green and flowering trees. There I found my companions, each companied with a man like unto Herrel, and they were seated on the grass, drinking and eating, each couple from a common plate, even as was the custom at bride feasts in the Dales.

To one side there were more men, and these were without companions, nor did the feasters appear to note them. As Herrel drew me onward we passed close to these apart and almost as one they turned to stare at us. One started forward with a muffled exclamation, and it was not a pleasantry I knew. Two of the others shouldered him back into their midst. Nor did they do aught more as we passed and Herrel brought me to a small nook between two sweet flowered bushes and then vanished, to speedily return with food and drink, set out in crystal and gold, or that which had such seeming.

"Laugh," he told me in a low voice, "put on the happiness of a bride, there are those who watch, and there is that which must be said between us which other ears—or minds—or thoughts—must not share."

I broke a cake and held a portion to my lips. From somewhere I summoned a smile and then laughter. But in me there was a sentry now alert.

# V  TRIAL BY SPELL

"I GIVE YOU good fortune," Herrel was smiling too as he raised cup in formal courtesy and sipped of the sparkling amber fluid it held.

"But," I returned, low voice, "that may not be . . . is that what you must say? If so—why?"

He held out the cup to complete the fair-wishing, and I drank in turn, but over its rim my eyes held his.

"For several reasons, my lady. First, this was not meant to be worn, by any of you—" Herrel put his hand to the cloak which still spread a shimmer of glory about my shoulders. "By Pack Right they could not deny any the weave-spell. But neither did Halse, or Hyron, believe that mine would draw a bride. You have chosen ill, Gillan, for in this company I am the least—"

He said that easily, as if no shame or hurt lay behind his words, but as if some sentence had been passed upon him and accepted.

"That I do not believe—"

"Smile!" He broke a bit from a cake. "You speak from courtesy, my lady wife."

"I speak what is mine to say."

And now it was his turn to fall serious, and his eyes searched my face, looked into mine as if he would indeed enter into my mind and shift the thoughts there, both those I knew and what other lay beneath them. He drew a sudden deep breath—

"You are mistaken. I have been wrought in such a way that I fumble where others move easily to their goals. I am of their blood, yet within me something has gone awry so that the powers I use may sometimes be as I wish, and other times fail me. Thus, you have come to a man who is held by his fellows to be less than they."

I smoothed the cloak about my shoulders. "It was this which drew me, thus it would seem that this time your power did not fail."

Herrel nodded. "So have I stepped where I should not tread—"

"And this is a reason to fear disaster?" But I did not think he feared, this was no rear-line warrior, whatever else he might deem himself.

"You know not." He did not say that sharply. "But I would have you learn at this first hour that there may not be a clear road for our riding. Twelve and one brides did we bargain for, but near twice that number are in this war band. We left it to the spell that our destiny be read, but there are those who will not accept what does not match with their desire. Also—war captive from overseas you have named yourself, and then fosterling in the Dales. But you are not of High Hallack blood, none of them have the true sights. Therefore you may be far kin to us—"

And not of humankind therefore? questioned that within me which had awakened and thirsted to grow.

"I know not who I am, Herrel, save that my memory is of being captive on a vessel of Alizon, thereafter being taken by raiders from the port. I came here of my own choice, replacing one who dreaded it—"

"Let no one else suspect that you possess the true sight. In these late years that which is not of us is mistrusted—perhaps doubly so for one who took up my cloak." He looked down into the wine in the cup as if some picture of the future might be mirrored there. "Walk softly in the night when the enemy sleeps nearby. Do I fright you with raider talk, Gillan?"

"Not greatly. I do not think I need hold a mirror before you for my protection."

"A mirror?"

"A mirror to kill demons. Seeing themselves their fright kills or repells them. See, I am learned in the ancient lore."

And this time his laugh was no matter of study and need, but came lightly.

"Perhaps I should have the mirror, my lady. But I think not, for one so fair need only look in such to learn how much she pleases."

"Is this—" I was warm of cheek from such a speech as had not ever been made me before, "your camp?"

"For an hour or two." Still he smiled and I knew he read my discomfiture—which added to it. But courteously he spoke now of other things.

"If you look for a snug keep to sit between you and the air, or the walls of a great hall, then you will search in vain, my lady—for the while. We have now no home save the waste—"

"But you go from here—that was part of the Bargain! Where then do we ride?"

"North—yet farther north—and east." His hand was on his belt, fingers upon the milky gems of its buckle. "We are exiles, now we are minded to turn homeward once again."

"Exiles? From what land? Overseas?" It might

be true then that we were distantly of one blood.

"No. Afar perhaps in space and time, but not sundered from this land. We come from a very old people, and those of High Hallack from a new. Once we had no boundaries on our far-faring. All men and women held a sway over powers which could build, or serve according to their wishes. If one wished to savor the freedom of a horse running before the wind, then one could be that horse. Or a hawk or eagle in the heavens. If one wished raiment soft and silken for one's wearing, jewels for the bedecking, under will they were his, to vanish when he tired of such. Only, to have such power and use it ever brings with it a great weariness, so that in time there is naught left to wish for, no new delight for one's eyes and heart and mind.

"This then is a time of danger, when those who grow restless turn from the known to the unknown. Then may doors be opened on forbidden things and that loosed which can not be controlled. We grew older, and more weary of mind. And some of the restless and yet curious tried other ways of amusement. Indeed did they loose what they could not rule, and death, and worse then clean death, stalked the land. Men who have been brethren now looked upon their fellows with suspicion, or hate. There was killing, sword-blooding and with it another kind of killing which was worse.

"Until, after one great battle there was set upon us all a bond. Those who were born among us from that time forward with a restless spirit, they must issue out of the land to which our kin withdrew and become wanderers. Not by choice—though some did choose so—but because they were deemed to be disturbing to a peace which must be kept or our breed would perish. And they must wander for a set number of years, until the stars moved into new patterns. When that was accomplished, then once more they might seek out the gate and ask for admittance. And if they could pass the testing there— then they would know again the homeland of their kind."

"But the men of High Hallack say that always since they have pushed into this country have they known the Riders—"

"The years of man and our years are not one and the same. But now the day comes when we may essay the gate. And whether we win or fail, we shall not let our breed die. Thus we take brides from among men, that there will be those after us."

"Half blood is not always as great as full blood."

"True. But, my lady, you forget that we do have powers and arts. Not all the changes we can make are to confuse the eye only."

"But will their eyes continue to be confused?" I glanced about me. Those who had preceded me were rapt, ensorcelled, so that they looked only upon those with whom they shared cup and plate. Whether this was for good or ill, I could not tell.

"For now," he said, "they see what they are designed to see, according to the desires of those whose cloaks they wear."

"And I?"

"And you? Perhaps, if more than one will was bent to the task, you might see at another's bidding—but that I do not know. I only say, with all my cunning as a warrior, it is best that you pretend to see. There are those within this company who would not welcome a will they believed they could not dominate. Fortune, my lady—"

His change of tone and word were so abrupt that I was startled and then alerted. Someone approached us from behind. But taking my cue from those about me, I showed no sign of knowing this, and I looked only to Herrel as if he alone meant anything in a narrow world.

He who had come up behind me stood silently, but from his very presence there flowed a vast, disquieting cloud of—hate? No, this emotion was too contemptuous, too self confident for hate. That we save for those who are our equals or superiors. This was the kind of anger one directs at lesser things which have crossed a will which believes it should have no limits. And how I knew this I could not have said, save that within this enchanted place perhaps emotions were made keener by design, and mine, not having been snared in the set trap, thus scented out the stranger's.

"Ah, Halse, come to drink bride cup?" Herrel looked up to the one who stood behind me. There was no unease open in him. But once in Norstead village at a feasting I had watched a wrestling match. And it was said that those who pitted their strength against one another so bore ill will, so the battle was not in sport or play. Then I had witnessed that small narrowing of the eyes, that stiffness of shoulder for the instant before they sprang at one another. And so was I sure that this Halse was no good friend to Herrel, but one of those whom he expected might show anger that his cloak-spell had succeeded. But still I schooled myself to watch only Herrel, with the bemusement of the other girls.

"Bride cup?" Derision on that, laid over anger. "For once it would seem, Herrel the Wrong-handed, you set a spell aright. Let us see how well you set it—what kind of a bride came to your cloak!"

In one fluid motion Herrel was on his feet. He was weaponless yet it was as if he stood with bared steel to take up the challenge the other had so plainly flung at him.

"My lord?" Had I put into that the proper amount of wonder? It would appear that I must continue to play the part of one I was not. Putting forth my hand I caught at Herrel's where it hung by his side. Under my touch his flesh was cool and smooth. "My lord, what's to do?"

Exerting unusual strength he drew me up and then I was at last able to turn and face the other. He was perhaps a finger taller than Herrel, and, of the same slim and wiry breed. Yet his shoulders were the wider. In general appearance though he differed only from his troop-mate in that his breeches and boots had been fashioned from a rusty brown fur and the belt around him had small red stones to its clasp. But beneath the general resemblance of one to the other—for they might have been brothers, or at least close kinsmen—there was a parting of spirit. Here indeed, I thought for a moment almost wildly, I might well raise my demon repelling mirror. Anger, arrogance, a self-belief so great that he deemed naught in the wide world could withstand his will were Halse's. And to me he was one whom I would have fled as a small

frightened mousething would flee the strike of a
hunting owl. But that very fear worked within
me to build ramparts for defense.

"My lady," Herrel's hand still held mine in a
warm, sustaining grip. "I would make known to
you this my fellow Rider. He is Halse, the
Strongarmed."

"My lord," I strove valiantly to play well my
role, "friends and comrades of yours are high in
my sight and regard—" The words were formal
but perhaps that was not wrong.

Halse's eyes glowed not green but red. And his
smile was like a whip laid upon bare skin for
those who could see.

"A fair lady indeed, Herrel. Luck has played
you good wisher this time. And what think you,
my lady, of luck's efforts?"

"Luck, my lord? I do not know what you mean.
But by the Flame," thus did I retreat upon the
language of the Dales, "I have grasped great
happiness this hour!"

Now I had aimed whip lash, though I had not
intended so. He continued to smile, but under
that stretching of skin and lip boiled emotion he
kept in check—so much emotion that I began to
wonder if more lay behind his exchange with
Herrel than that explanation given me.

"May it continue, my lady." He bowed and
stepped aside, going with no more farewell.

"So be it," commented Herrel. "Now, I think,
we face war. And for your own sake, Gillan,
guard your tongue, your smiles, your frowns,
your very thoughts! Never did Halse believe that
he would be one to ride hence unaccompanied
by a cloak-mate, and to have me succeed where
he failed sets him doubly afire."

He held out his hand again and I noted that those about us were also rising, their feasting done.

"It is time to go?"

"Yes. Come—" He set his arm about my waist and drew me with him, walking as all those other couples under the flowering trees and out of the bower, to a place where horses stood.

A shaggy pony of the hills, sure footed and yet slow of pace, had carried me here. But these mounts were far different. They were strangely dappled of coat, gray and black so intermingled that unless they made some movement they were hidden in plain sight because of their melting into the winter landscape, for we had passed once more from spring to winter.

Tall were these horses of the Riders, thinner of body, longer of leg than any I had seen in the Dales. Their saddle cloths were furred and the saddles smaller, less cumbersome. All suggested a need for speed. Some wore packs, though I noted that, just as we had left behind all that had been in the tents, so also we appeared to abandon that which had refreshed us in the bridal valley.

Herrel brought me to one of the mounts and it swung its head about, surveying me as if it were no mere beast, but carried intelligence akin to mine in its narrow head.

"This is Rathkas, and she will serve you well," Herrel told me.

Still the mare looked upon me in that measuring fashion. I stepped forward and laid hand upon her shoulder. She shivered throughout her body, then throwing up her head she whinnied. Around the other horses looked at me.

Herrel moved quickly, laying his hand above

mine on the mare's neck. She dropped her head and looked no more at me, while the others also lost interest. But I saw Herrel's lips were tight set, and once again his eyes held the wrestler's watchfulness.

"Guard," he made a whisper of that word as he aided me to the saddle. And he glanced over his shoulder, but it would seem that none of those near us had marked that small happening.

Thus we rode from our wedding. Though I did not feel that I was truly bride, nor Herrel groom. It was plain that such doubts were not shared elsewhere in that company. So once again I was set apart from those whose life I was destined to share.

This was no amble of a pony in the hills, this was a swift, tireless covering of ground at a pace I had not thought possible for any four-footed creature. Though none of the mounts showed any signs of distress at holding to it as time passed. Time, also, took on a different rhythm—hours—what hour held us now? I could not truly answer that. It had been morning when we had come to the place of the cloaks— was it even the same day? For I had the feeling that the Riders might, with their bedazzlement also alter time at their pleasure.

Perhaps there was that in the food and drink which we had shared that banished both fatigue and hunger for a space as we did not rest nor eat. We rode—through the night, and into the day, and again into night. Horses did not tire and the hours were part of a dream, flowing together. I do not believe that any of the others marked any passing of time, for they rode with tranced faces in which a kind of delight had frozen. And this also I tried to maintain, though it was hard, for I could not hold long to the surface sight, my will not being equal to my desire.

Those such as Halse, who had gone unpartnered from the wedding, mustered at the head and rear of our party, as if set on guard against danger. But though the land was wild and barren, we saw no life through the miles.

Bleak though that country was, I saw so little difference between it and the lesser dales, that I wondered why it was spoken of always as "the waste," a word which brought to mind desert unfriendly and sealed to man. Here were open plains with the brittle brown grass of yesteryear covering them, showing in hillocks through light snow. And there were tree copses and brush.

No, it was not the land itself which did not welcome man, it was rather what brooded over that territory. For as we rode I knew a heaviness of spirit, a fear, of what I did not know. This grew the more with every mile, until I had to summon power of will against crying out, that my voice might break that shadow spell.

We came at last to higher ground and here I saw first the handiwork of man, for a wall of boulders had been set up, standing perhaps the height of two men or a little more, roofed above with an untidy thatching of tree limbs and brush. Or so I saw it. For I heard Kildas say:

"My lord, fair indeed in this hall!"

Then once more I put will to the task of seeing as the Riders would have me see. Thus I, too, rode into a courtyard where stone was cunningly wrought and finely carved wood roofed the buildings set around. Herrel turned to me, saying:

"This is our biding place until we go hence, my lady."

As I dismounted all the fatigue which should have been mine from the hours behind me, struck, and I think I would have fallen had Herrel's arm not been there to steady me. Of the rest, it was a dream of which I could not sort out true or false, a dream which became sleep indeed . . .

Until I awoke in the dark! And beside me there was quiet breathing so that I knew I had a bedfellow. I lay taut and tense to listen. Save for that come and go of breath there was no sound. Only I had come from sleep at some summons, the call was still clear.

It was very dark, I could see only denser shadows against the lighter. Moving with caution I sat up in bed, harking ever for any change in that small sound to my left. The room was warm as if a fire blazed on a hearth where there was neither flame nor fireplace. I wore my shift only yet I was not chilled—not outwardly. But in my body there was a spreading cold. All of a sudden it was very necessary to see—to see not only the room, the bed, but most of all what lay upon that bed and slept so soundly.

My bare feet were on deep fur, skins must make a carpet. I moved on one step at a time, sweeping my hands before me lest I stumble against some piece of furniture. How did I know that somewhere before me lay a source of light and that would satisfy my desperate need?

A wall—across its surface my hands moved

with haste which was not of my conscious willing. A window—surely this was a window—
shuttered and with a bar across. My fingers
tugged at the bar. I thrust at the shutters, sending
them flying open. Moonlight—it was very
clear and brighter than I had ever seen it before,
so bright as to dazzle my eyes for a moment.

"Ahh—" Voice—or snarl?

I turned to look to the bed I had left. What
lifted heavy head and looked at me green-eyed?
Fur, sleek and shining fur, the fanged mask of
awakening fury— A mountain cat, yet not a
cat—but also death. The lips wrinkled, showing
even more the fangs meant to tear, to devour—
It was horror beyond any horror I had ever
dreamed upon.

This—this you have chosen!—

In that moment by the words which rang in my
head, did evil defeat itself. Mayhap with another
it would have succeeded—but for me that broke
the spell. And what I looked upon now was two,
one over lying the other, furred hide above
smooth skin, a beast mask over a face—only the
green eyes were not two but one. And if they had
flashed battle on their opening, now did they
show intelligence and knowledge.

I went towards that thing which was now
beast, now man. But because I could see the man
I was no longer afraid of what shared my
chamber. Though of that which had awakened
me, sent me to the window—of that I was
frightened.

"You are Herrel—" I said to the beast-man.
And with my speech he became wholly man, the
beast vanishing as if it had never been.

"But you saw me—otherwise—" He made a statement, he did not question.

"In the moonlight—I did."

He moved, out of the bed until he stood at its foot. Faced towards the door I could now see, he moved his hands in the air, at the same time uttering words in a tongue I did not understand.

There was a glow by the door which was not silver clear as the moon, but carried the green tinge of the Rider lamps, and from that glow were two small runnels of light, one to the bed where he had lain, the other to my feet.

Once again I witnessed the mergence of man and beast, this time because of anger burning in him. But control won and he was man again. Herrel caught up a cloak and threw it about his shoulders, went to the door. Then, his hand already set to the latch, he looked back at me.

"Perhaps it is just as well—" he could have been arguing with himself. "Yes, it is better—Only," now he did speak to me, "let them see that you have had a fright. Can you scream?"

What play he intended I could not guess, but I had faith in his wisdom for us both. Summoning up what art I could, I screamed, and surprised myself with the shrill note of terror I put into that cry.

No longer was the building silent. Herrel threw open the door and then ran back to me. His arms drew me close as one who would comfort and his whisper in my ear suggested further display of terror on my part.

There was more outcries, running feet, and then lamp light. Hyron was there, looking at us. Captain of the Riders I had seen him only at a distance, now he wore the face of a man wanting a satisfactory explanation.

"What chances here?"

Herrel's moment of counciling aided me. "I awoke and was warm—too warm. I thought I must open wide the window—" Now I raised my hand uncertainly to my head as if I felt faint. "Then I turned and saw a great beast—"

There was a moment of silence and Herrel had the breaking of it.

"Look you—" that was more order than request. He pointed before me to where that green line crawled across the floor. Faded now from our first sighting though it was, it was still visible.

Hyron looked, and then, grim faced, he raised his eyes again to Herrel.

"You want sword right?"

"Against whom, Captain? I have no proof."

"True enough. And it would be well not to seek it—in these hours."

"Do you lay that upon me?" Herrel's voice was very cool and remote.

"You know where we must ride and why. Is this the time for private quarrels?"

"The quarrel is none of my provoking."

Hyron nodded, but I felt that his assent was given reluctantly, that he had taken the matter ill, as though this was some trouble pushed upon him which only duty made him consider seriously.

"This game or others like it must not be played again," Herrel continued. "There is no naysaying cloak-spell. Did we not all swear to that, weapon-oath?"

Again Hyron nodded. "There will be no trouble." And that also rang like an oath.

When we were again alone I faced Herrel in the moonlight.

"What arrow was aimed at us this night?"

But he did not answer that, rather did he look at me very searchingly and ask:

"You saw a beast, yet you did not flee?"

"I saw a beast and a man, and of the man I had no fear. But tell me, for this was clearly sent by malice, what chanced?"

"A spell was set, to disgust you with me, perhaps to send you running to another who waited. Tell me. Why did you seek the window?"

"Because I was—ordered—" That was it! I had been ordered from my sleep to do just that. "Is it Halse?"

"It might well be. Or there are others—I told you, none believed that you or any woman would choose my cloak. Having accomplished this, I have in a little belittled their power in their own eyes. Thus, they would like to see me fail now. By frightening you with shape change they would drive you away."

"Shape change— Then you *do* wear this guise when it is needed?"

But to that he did not answer at once. He went to the window and looked out into the silence of the night.

"Does it give you fear of me to know this?"

"I do not know. I feared, yes, when I first saw— But with the undersight perhaps you will always be a man to me."

He turned back to me, but his face was now in

shadow. "I promise you this weapon-oath, Gillan, willingly never will I fright you!"

For an instant only did I see fur on his shoulders, a mountain cat's muzzle in place of his face? But I willed to see a man, and I thereafter did.

# VI    TRIAL BY SWORD

"ARE THERE no mirrors in your household? Does demon lore speak true thereof?" I strove to rebraid my hair. By touch alone that was an unhandy business.

A laugh behind me, and then, swept over my head and down, held for my convenience, a mirror indeed. But this of shining metal, meant rather to ward battle stroke than to provide an aid for adornment. Wan and strange did my reflection look back at me from that shield surface; still it did guide my hands in the ordering of my hair. My pins were half missing and the final coiling looser than I wished.

"You have taken up rough housing, Gillan—unless you wish to see it as the others do—" There was question in that.

"Matters as they are suit me very well indeed," I made quick reply. "I have a liking for facing what I must with a clear head. Herrel what do we have to fear?"

"Most of all discovery." He had slung sword on a shoulder baldric which was set with the same milky gems as those of his belt buckle. And now he held in his two hands a helm, wrought of silver, or so it looked. For a crest it had no plume such as those worn by the fighting lords of High Hallack, but a small figure, marvelously made, a thing of rare beauty, in the form of a crouching, snarling mountain cat, preparing to launch in attack-spring.

Discovery, he said. And the burden of escaping such discovery fell largely on me. Herrel must have read my dawning knowledge in my face for he came to me swiftly.

"I do not think we have aught to fear this day, for the trickery in the night will make them wary. But if you again sense anything strange tell me. There is this," beneath his helm his eyes had the same cold glitter of the jewels in the eye sockets of the silver cat, "perhaps you have chosen ill after all, Gillan. I can not stand against Halse, or the others in spell weaving. But should I learn which one would attack so, then I may challenge sword battle, and they can not nay-say me. Only, to so speak I must have proof that he who I would meet is indeed guilty. I can lay no wall about you—"

"Perhaps I have another safeguard—I had forgotten it."

It was so slender a thread, but one about to fall will clutch any rope. I pulled aside the cloak on the bed, the one which had plunged me into this. Under that lay the one thing I had brought out of Norstead for my own, the bag of simples. Why I had clung to it, I could not tell, but now perhaps I could be glad.

Healing salves and balms, most of them. But in the last pocket a small amulet which I had made for an experiment and which I had never shown to Dame Alousan, lest she turn on me for following the country beliefs in a fashion unbefitting one who dwelt in a holy place.

Wild angelicea, and the dried flowers of purple mallow, with a pressed ivy leaf or two, and also the berries of rowan, sewn into a tiny packet, with certain runes stitched on it. All lore coming from records, yet never so combined before.

There was a cord to it, and I looped that about my throat where it could not be seen under the high collar of the tabard. Dame Alousan herself had admitted that some old lore had a foundation of truth, the which she had proved by her own experiments. But this was from tradition older than her religion and alien to it.

Against my skin it felt warm, almost as if some heat generated within it. I turned to face Herrel. His hand went up as if he could ward me off.

"What is it?" he demanded.

"Herbs, leaves, berries from the field."

His hands moved in gestures and then he gave a sharp exclamation and the fingers of one went to his lips, his tongue licking as if he would so cool them against some heat.

" 'Tis a bane, right enough." He smiled. "And perhaps not a thing they will be expecting. Or, if they find it, they will deem it a safeguard natural. I do not know how that will hold against any determined sorcery. Let us hope it will not be put to any such test."

Our company rode forth from the hold of the Riders, and this time there were more horses with packs, for there would be no returning. We were bound for the gate of their vanished homeland. Our pace was less demanding on our mounts, but the land through which we traveled repudiated us as it had the day before, inimical to man, and perhaps to the Riders also. Or was that aura some defense they had set against those not of their blood and kin?

The heights on which the hold had been set was only the beginning of land which climbed. It did not snow, but the wind cut coldly. And we were glad when the unmarked trail we followed wound through woods shelter which kept off the worst of the blasts.

Herrel rode at my left hand, but he spoke little. Now and then he held high his head, his nostrils expanding as if he would scent something in the air which might be the odor of danger. As I looked cautiously about me, I saw that others of his company did likewise, though the girls were still deep in their contented bemusement. Herrel's crest was that of the mountain cat, but that of the man who rode with Kildas was a bird—an eagle perhaps—its wings outstretched a little as if it were about to launch into the air. And beyond him was one who wore the semblance of a bear, the viciously tempered, red-brown coated dweller in the mountain forests, wily and cunning so that hunters dreaded it almost beyond any other beast.

Bear-helm turned his head, and I recognized him for Halse. Bear, cat, eagle, I strove to identify the others—finding, without making too obviously my eye-search, a boar, tusked and head lowered for the charge—a wolf— Shape changers, sorcerers, were they also beast and bird at will? Or was what I had seen last night merely part of a spell sent to disgust me with Herrel?

I felt no disgust, however fear, a little, as the unknown always awakens first the emotion of fear. How had the Were Riders proved so formidable in war? As men bearing swords and bows, fighting as the men of High Hallack fought, or as beasts with the brains of men, tearing, stalking, leaping as the furred and the feathered? Before the day was out I was to have my answer.

Our ride was not steady, though it was undoubtedly ground covering. We paused in a small clearing to break our fast when a pale sun marked a nooning. And I thought we were swinging farther to the east than our track had been heretofore. Herrel was uneasy, that I noted first. His testing of the wind increased. And I saw that others of the Riders moved restlessly about, their pacing almost being that of animals scenting a danger yet afar.

Those without brides gathered to Hyron by the picket line and three of them rode out. None of the girls appeared to note any of this so was I restrained to be likewise unheeding. But when Herrel brought me a cup of the amber-hued wine, I dared to whisper:

"What has gone amiss?"

He did not fence with me. "There is danger—to the east. Men—"

"High Hallack?" But I could not believe they were so honor-broke, for the code binding the High Lords to certain customs was not easily shattered.

"We do not know. It may be Alizon—"

"But Alizon is finished on these shores! There are no more—" I could not at once tame my surprise.

"Alizon was broke. But there might be those who fled. Desperate would they be with their ships gone and no path left for their returning home. Such a band under an able leader would try to turn Hallack's tricks upon her lords and live in the wilderness to raid. They are not soft men, the Hounds, nor ones to throw down sword and call for peace because the tide turns against them."

"But this far north—"

"One of their long boats could slip along the coast, that would take them away from the ports fallen to their enemies. And they would come north because they know that High Hallack does not patrol in this direction—leaving the waste to us—"

"But surely they also know—"

"That the Riders bide here?" His lips drew back, and for a second did I see a faint shadow form across his face? "Do not misjudge the Hounds, Gillan. Long did the Lords of High Hallack fight them. But all men are not formed the same. Oh, they have two arms, two legs, a head, a body, a heart, a mind— But what lies within to animate all that—that may differ much. There were those of the coast lands, of Dales' blood, who did lay down sword and accept Alizon's overyoke years ago. Many were hunted down and put to the sword when we finished off the invaders. Still perhaps not all such turncoats were so finished. And do you not think that there has not been much talk through these years just past the Great Bargain? What better stroke might a band of desperate men deliver than to cut us off now, leaving dead whom they could, perhaps making us believe that Hallack broke faith, so in turn we would return to rend the Dales?"

"You believe this?"

"It is a suggestion we do not throw away without question."

"But to attack the Riders—" So deeply had I been schooled in the beliefs of the Dales that I had come to accept the common opinion that those I now rode among were invincible, and no man, lest he be bereft of his sense, would go up against them willingly.

"Gillan," Herrel was smiling a little, "you do us too much honor! Powers we have which those of other races do not use. But we bleed when a sword pierces, we die when it cuts deeply enough. And we are now only as many as you see. Also, we can not detour too far from our chosen trail lest we do not reach the gate we seek in the appointed time, and so must rove on unsatisfied."

Thus once more was I caught in another race against time. Only I could not credit that the Were Riders were not as all powerful as their reputations made them. Perhaps my face mirrored my doubt for Herrel then fitted another portion of the puzzle into place for me.

"Do you not understand that to maintain an illusion or bind a spell on another's mind wears upon a man? Twelve in this company ride in spell. More than just the will of he who companies with each holds steady that illusion. You asked me last night—was I as you saw? Yes. I am that, at times—in battle. For our own sakes in fighting we are all shape changers. But to put on one shape or another is an effort of mind and will. These maids from High Hallack see as it is laid upon them to see. Should we be attacked then they would see what you have witnessed. From that true seeing could come an end to all we sought in the Bargain. Speak now the full truth, Gillan—which of those who rode hither with you would accept such a full sight and have it make no difference?"

"I do not know them well, I can not say—"

"But you can venture a guess, and what is that?"

"Very few." Perhaps I was misspeaking the

maids of Hallack, but remembering their murmuring on the ride to the Throat, and the stark fear which some showed then, I did not think I was so far in error.

"So. Thus are we now crippled. And those who might attack us have the courage of men who have been stripped of all—who have nothing left to lose. So would they come into battle with the advantage."

"What will you do?"

He shrugged. Just such a gesture as I would have expected from Lord Imgry in such a strait. "What do we do? We send out scouts to spy us a trail, we strive to find a swift passage, we hope that we do not have to fight for it."

But his hopes were in vain. We struck a fast pace leaving that halting place. Within the hour we split into two parties. Those who were unpaired, save for three of their number, took a branching way yet farther east and rode from us at a gallop. While for the remainder we had a trail straight ahead. One of our three guards, who ranged up and down the line, as I had seen men of the Dales ride herd while moving cattle, was Halse. Each time he swung past it seemed to me that he turned his head, so that the baleful gems in that bear topped helm flickered, the ornament almost appearing a small living creature fully aware of all it saw.

In winter, twilight comes early. Shadows crept across our way which was now clear of forest or many trees, but which wound about to avoid outcrops of snow-crowned rock. Herrel's mount was dropping behind and I reined back. The last of the party were now out of sight and we were alone.

"What is the matter?"

He shook his head. "I do not know. There is no reason—" He had stopped, now his head went up, his nostrils expanded, as he half turned in the saddle to look back along our trail. His hand moved in an imperative gesture for quiet.

I could hear the clop-clop of hooves ahead, the creak of saddles, growing fainter by the moment. Surely Halse or one of the others would come pounding back to see what delayed us.

Herrel dismounted. He looked up at me, his face a blur not easily read beneath the shadow of his helm.

"Ride!"

He went down on one knee to examine the forefeet of his mount, not looking at the hooves but rather in the longish hair above them. His fingers stilled and his whole body tensed.

"What is it?" I asked for the second time.

But there was no answer—only singing in the air, shrill, ear-piercing in high notes. Herrel's mount reared, screamed, striking out, and sending the man at its feet rolling.

There was no controlling my mare either. She dashed ahead so wildly that she might have been blind. I fought against her terror with hands on reins and my will—that same will which lept ever to my defense when there was need. Then, when it seemed she was truly mad, I leaned forward in the saddle, grasping her mane. Against my breast I felt a burning coal, eating into my flesh. The amulet—but why? I dared loose hold with one hand, clutched for that packet. Why I did then what I did I had no knowing, any more than why I had performed many actions these past days.

Jerking the cord until it broke, I pressed the amulet between my palm and the mare's foam spattered neck. She ceased the terrible neighing which had been bursting from her as a woman might scream; her wild run slackened. My will caught her—we turned back. I was sure that what had moved her and Herrel's horse had been no freak of nature but a deliberately planned blow.

Almost I feared I could not find my way back. The rocky outcrops all looked the same. But I urged the mare on, my amulet still pressed on her sweating hide. And I could feel the shivering which racked her. Fear was a stench in the air, and mine a part of it.

Behind me the pounding of hooves. Halse drew even, his cloak swept back on his shoulders. I could see sparks of fire . . . man's eyes . . . bear's eyes. He leaned forward as if to grasp at my rein, bring me to a halt. And I flung out my hand to ward off his. The amulet swung forward on its broken cord, struck across his bare wrist.

"Ahhh—" A cry of pain, as if I had laid a whip there in earnest. He jerked back and his horse reared with a startled neigh. Then I was out of his reach, riding on to where I had seen Herrel roll away from his mount's striking feet.

His horse stood there, spraddled of leg, muzzle close to the ground. It shivered, plunged once as I moved up, yet did not run. While on a rock ledge of the outcrop crouched that which I had last seen by moonlight on a bed.

"Man—man!" My mind fought fear. But this time my will did not dislodge a phantom. The great cat was silent, it did not even look at me. Those green, glowing eyes were turned elsewhere, down slope, and above its head was a flicker of slender green flame.

"Herrel?" So intent was I on winning man back from cat that I forgot all caution. I slid from the saddle, ran to the rock. As I called the cat's stare broke, it arose in a great bound to clear the fear striken horse and reach the ground beyond.

The hair along its spine arose, its ear flattened against the skull, and the long tail quivered at tip. Still it looked back down our trail. Then for the first time it yowled.

Herrel's horse plunged and screamed. My mare bolted. Now the cat growled, slinking into a crevice between two rocks, belly to the ground. Seeing that hunter's creep I shrank back against the outcrop, losing touch with the reality of the world I had always known.

I still held the amulet, though I did not remember that until once more in my hand it was burning hot. When I snatched away my fingers I saw, standing out from a crack in the stone, a strange thing. It was perhaps as long as my forearm, and it glowed when the amulet approached it. There was such an effluvium of evil exuding from it that before I thought clearly I pulled it free and flung it to the ground, setting my boot heel upon it as I might upon some noxious insect, grinding against the stone until it splintered.

"Harroooo!" Echoed, changed by the rock walls and the wind, but still that was no animal cry. It had come from a human throat, and with it other shouts and a beast's growling.

By me, with more speed than I could have thought possible for such a clumsy seeming body, raced a bear, on its way down trail. A whistle of wings in the sky and a bird, beyond my reckoning large, followed after. A great gray wolf, another cat—this one with fur spotted black on tawny-red, a second wolf, black—the company of the Riders on their way to battle. But that struggle I did not see. Perhaps that was well, for there came a cry so horrible that my hands went to my ears and I crouched against the outcrop with no courage left, only filled with a desire not to see, hear, or think, of what passed where men met beasts in the twilight.

I found myself then, me, who had never believed in the service of the Abbey, muttering prayers I had heard there years on end, as if those words could build a wall between me and terror unleashed to walk the earth. And I strove to concentrate upon the words and their meanings, using them as a shield.

Hands upon my shoulders—I tried to free myself as if they had been claw-set paws. Still I would not open my eyes. For how could I bear now to look upon a man who was also a beast?

"Gillan!" The grasp which held me tightened. I was shaken to and fro, not in punishing anger as my Lord Imgry had used me, but as one would awaken another caught in a nightmare.

I looked—into green eyes, but they were not set in a beast head. Only, still could I see them so. And above them was that helm on which crouched a cat—a stark reminder. I was too weak to pull away from Herrel's hold, yet my flesh shrank from it.

"She saw us—she knows—" Words from beyond the narrow world which was mine, in which only the twain of us stood.

"She knows more than you think, pack

brothers. Look upon what she has in her hand!"

Anger rising about me. Almost I could see that with my eyes as a dull red mist. I stood on a high and open place and they would stone me with rocks of their hate.

"Doubtless sent to lead us into some trap—"

There was an arm about me, holding me close, promising security. Once I thought I could accept that with open eyes. Now there was such a revulsion working in me that I had to force my will to stand fast, lest I run screaming into the wilderness. And the anger continued to thrust spears of rage at me.

"Cease! Look you well, this is what she holds within her hands. Take it—you, Harl, Hisin, Hulor—Magic, yes, but where is there any evil in it, unless evil was intended in return? Harl, say the Seven words while it rests in your fingers."

Words—or sounds—so sharp they hurt ears, rang into one's skull—words of alien power.

"Well?"

"It is a charm, but only against the powers of darkness."

"Now—look yonder!"

The red wall of anger was gone. I saw again with my eyes and not my emotions. From where I had trampled and broken that shaft I had found in the rock arose a line of oily black smoke, as if from a fire feeding on rottenness. And there was a sickly smell from it. The smoke swirled, formed into a rod which had the likeness of the unbroken shaft.

"A screamer, and one under a dark power!"

Again they spoke words, this time several voices together. The rod swayed back and forth, was gone in a puff.

"You have seen," Herrel said, "you know what kind of a spell that bore. One who wears such an amulet as Gillan can not dabble in dark learning. And there was another charm here also. Harl, I ask of you, look to the fetlock of Roshan's left forefoot."

I saw him who wore the eagle go to Herrel's mount, kneel to feel about the hoof. Then he arose with a thread between his fingers.

"A hinder-cord!"

"Just so. And this also do you say is of the enemy, or of my lady's doing? Perhaps," Herrel looked at each of them for a long instant, "it was a trick for amusement. But almost it worked to my bane, and likewise to those of you who came hither. Or was it more than a trick, a hope that I fall behind to some undoing by fate or enemy?"

"You have the right to ask sword-battle then!" flashed Halse.

"So I do, as I shall call upon you all to witness—when I find the one who tried to serve me so."

"This is one thing," boar-crest broke in, "but she—" he pointed to me. "is yet another. She who deals in outland charms, who and what is she?"

"All peoples have their wise women and healers. We know well the skill of those of High Hallack. Gillan had for mistress one who was well learned in such arts. To each race its own powers—"

"But such a one has no place in our company!"

"Do you speak for all the pack, Hulor? Gillan," Herrel spoke to me, far more softly, as one who would win words from a sorely frightened child, "what know you of this other thing—this shaft?"

And as simple as a child I made answer. "The Amulet burned my hand when I rested it on the rock. There was a break in the stone and that stood within it. I—I pulled it loose and broke it with my foot."

"Thus," he swung back to the others, "it would seem, pack brothers, that we owe herewise a debt. With that still potent what might have happened had we gone into battle shape changed and then returned, unable to be men, to face so these we would shield from the truth?"

I heard murmurs among them.

"Upon this matter the whole company must have their say," Halse spoke first.

"So be it—with you witnessing as to what happened here," Herrel replied evenly. His arm tightened around me. I fought against the shudders with which my body would have resisted that hold. "Now, we have no threat left behind, but that does not mean it has vanished from the land. Only, hold in mind, pack brothers, that you return now to those whom you cherish as men this night because of the courage and wit of this my lady."

If he expected any outward assent from the others he did not get it. They drew away. Herrel lifted me into the saddle and climbed up behind, the circle of his arms holding me. Yet I was alone, alone in a company who had let me feel the fire and storm of their hate, and in arms which now I thought of as wholly alien.

# VII   NIGHT TERRORS AND DAY DREAMS

OF THAT NIGHT I remember very little, waking, but of sleeping— Even now my mind shrinks from that memory. Dreams seldom linger in the mind far past the waking hour, but such dreams as haunted me that night were not the normal ones.

I ran through a forest, leaved and yet not green—but a sere and faded gray, as if the trees had died in an instant and had not thereafter lost their leaves, but only become rigid ghosts of themselves. And from behind their charred black trunks things spied upon and hunted me—never visible, yet ever there, malignant and dreadful beyond the power of words to make plain.

There was no end to that forest, nor the hunters, nor to my anguish. And there grew in me the knowledge that they were driving me to some trap or selected spot of their own wherein I would be utterly lost. I can yet feel beneath finger tips the rough bark of trees against which I leaned panting, pain a sword in my side, listening—oh, how I listened!—for any noise from those who followed. But there was no sound, just ever the knowledge they existed.

A wild hunt—though the hounds, the hunters I never saw—only the fear which preceded them drove me.

Time and time again I strove to hold to courage, to turn and face them, telling myself that fear faced is sometimes less than fear fled, but never was my courage great enough to suffer me to hold, past a quivering moment or two. And always the dead-alive trees closed about me.

Growing in me was the knowledge that the end would be horrible past all bearing—

And when I broke then and screamed madly, beating upon the trunk of the tree where I had paused, there was a murmur in my head, a murmur which was first sound and then words, and finally a message I could understand:

"Throw it away—throw it away—all will be well—"

It? What was it? Sobbing with breaths which hurt, I looked first to my hands. They were scratched, bleeding, the nails torn—but they were empty.

It? What was it?

Then I looked down at my body. It was bare, no clothing left me. And it was so wasted that the bones showed clearly beneath scarred and scratched skin. But on my breast rested a small bag patterned with runes stitched on in black. Memory stirred faintly, fading before it really told me aught. I caught at the bag. That which stuffed it crunched, and from it rose a faint odor to sting my nose.

"Throw it away!" A command.

There was sound now and not only in my head. With the bag between my fingers I turned to look upon the masks of beasts—standing man-like on their hind legs. Bear, boar, cat, wolf—beasts—and yet more, far more—far worse!

I ran, witlessly, with a pain in me which seemed to burst the ribs about my heart. From the beasts I ran, back towards that which had hunted me. And behind I heard a cat's yowl.

Perhaps I might have died, caught in the horror of that dream. But the pressure of the bag in my clenched hand, from that spread—what? Courage? No, I was too far past the point where courage could return. I was only an animal—or less—filled with fear and a terror beyond what we call fear. But there came a kind of new energy and then an awareness that I had outrun the beasts. And after that, a small ray of hope that there would come an end to all this and perhaps it was better to face that end than go mad with terror.

I did not run any longer. I dropped, my breast heaving, under one of the dead trees, and I pressed both hands with the bag to me.

So—thus was it? Knowledge and then anger, then purpose which in turn drew upon the depths of will. My enemies were blind masks behind which men hid. Masks could be torn away.

They had overreached themselves this time, not knowing the temper of the metal they had striven to destory. In me that metal hardened. They had not yet the breaking of me. Will—I must will myself out of here—

But so little was I used to that weapon that I fumbled. The trees—they were evil—they should be cut away— An axe lay gleaming at my feet.

No wish-axe was the answer. No—that lay elsewhere. Will—I was me—Gillan! At that naming the trees wavered. Gillan—me—I flung that thought at them. I have a will, a power—if the bag I held was in someway a key—then I would turn it. Light routes dark, I held the bag to my dry, cracked lips. Light—I will light!

The gloom beneath the shadow trees thinned. I am Gillan and elsewhere do I have a place which is mine—mine! I will it!

Green of a lamp. In my nostrils the smell of aromatic wood burning, the odor of food. Sounds—of voices, of people moving not too far away. This was the sane world, the world of which I, Gillan, was a part. I was back!

Yet I was so weary that I found it hard to raise my hand, run it along my body, which was clothed as always, under the cover of a fur lined cloak. There was the light of a cloudy winter morning about us. Outside a shelter of skins, not as formal as a tent, I saw Riders moving. Men—or beasts such as I had seen in the dead forest?

I struggled to lever myself up on my hands, straining to see those men. But between me and them came Kildas. Kildas—how long ago had it been since we had eaten together on another morning and wished each other fortune with a formal toast before answering the summons which had brought us here? I found I could not name the days, they mingled one with the other.

"Gillan." She did not look as bemused as she had since her bridal in the field of cloaks, "how do you feel? You are fortunate that you came from such a fall with no broken bones—"

"Fall?" I repeated and stared, stupidly I am sure, into her face.

She steadied my swimming head against her shoulder, raised a brimming drinking horn to my lips, and perforce I swallowed a mouthful of its contents. Hot and spicy, yet the heat did not warm me and I shivered as if never again would my body be shielded from any icy wind.

"Do you not remember? Your mount took fright upon the slope and threw you. Since you have lain unheeding through the night."

But what she said was so at variance with the memories now crowding in upon me, that I shook my head from side to side, awaking in it an aching. Were—were those memories born of some hurt I had taken? Evil dreams could come from fever, as well I knew—though my body was cold, not hot. A blow on the head—from that came my beast-men? No, I had seen the cat before—before we had ridden into these wastes. And I could look now and see—I raised my shaking hand to cover my eyes.

Perhaps the Riders had their own heal craft; they must have had since Herrel had said they, too, knew wounds and hurt. As Kildas urged upon me again the contents of the horn, I grew stronger. My shaking was stilled. But I was cold—so cold—and that cold was fear—

"My lord," Kildas looked beyond my shoulder to one who had come to us. "She has wakened and, I believe, mends—"

"My gratitude to you, Lady Kildas. Ah, Gillan, how is it now with you, dear heart?"

Hands again on my shoulders. I stiffened . . . afraid to turn . . . to look. His words meant nothing. What had happened to me? cried one inner voice. I had not feared before, I had not shrunk from his touch, I had—

I had stood apart, answered something within my mind. All this had been action I watched, which had not engulfed me in its pattern. I had now stepped from one path where I knew, or thought I knew, the trail, into another running on into darkness and fear.

"I mend—from my fall, I mend," I answered dully.

"It was a sorry one."

Not yet did I look to him; it was all I could do to not flinch from his hands upon me. "Do you think you can ride," he continued, and now there was a difference, a more formal note, in his voice.

"Kildas—" That voice also I knew. He who called wore an eagle crested helm. Or did he sprout a bird's cruel beak, feathers and claws?

"I am called," she laughed joyfully. "Take good care, Gillan. I hope you will meet no more ill fortune." She left us and when she was gone I summoned will and stood away from Herrel, daring to face him.

"So I fell, and struck my head upon a stone," I said swiftly, making myself look. But he was a man, and I was safe. Safe? Would I ever be safe again?

Herrel did not answer me with words. He lifted his hand to my cheek. And this time I could not control my aversion. I dodged his touch as I might have eluded a blow. His eyes narrowed as a cat's might. I waited for furred mask to appear. But it did not and when he spoke again his voice was very remote.

"So you are now using another sight, my lady. What illusion—"

"Illusion?" I cried. "I am seeing with eyes which are freed, shape changer! Tell what tale you need. I shall not nay-say it. Perhaps I could not. You and your pack brothers have woven too well your spells. Only they do not blind me—any more than you can conquer me with night fears—"

"Night fears—?"

"Hunting me through the forest of ashes—but you did not have your will there."

"Forest of ashes?"

"Can you do naught but repeat my words, shape changer? I have run before fear. But be warned, dreaming or waking, Lord Herrel, there comes a time when the whip of fear breaks. One can learn to live under it, which is the first step towards making it servant, not master. Haunt my sleep as you will—"

Now he caught me again in his grip, holding me so I must meet his eye stare directly and in the full. Green—vast green—pool—sea into which I was falling—falling—falling—

"Gillan!"

Eyes only, but not human eyes. Below them a mouth straight set, a face hard as if carved from some white gem stone.

"Not of my doing. Do you understand, Gillan? Not of my doing!"

Not quite coherent those words, yet their meaning reached me. He was denying what I had thrown at him in accusation, not quite believing it all myself. And his denial had an effect. That had been no vivid nightmare; it had been an attack, delivered in a different time and space, but aimed at me.

"Then whose?" I demanded of him.

"Could I point the sword, then I would in this instant! Until I can—"

"I must run haunted and— What was that they spoke of last night—the hinder-cord?" For now memory supplied another bit.

"Something which could have been named a trick if discovered, or be my undoing if it had been aided by fate. A spell laid to slow and perhaps lame a horse. But night terrors are not one man's trick, they are a flight of arrows from more than one bow."

"They would be rid of me, wouldn't they? The bear, the eagle, the boar—"

"They must abide by the covenant—or be shape spelled! And I do not think they will try to strike again—"

"Because, warned, you may strike back?"

"I? The least of them? I think they do not deem that possible." He had no shame in that saying. "They may not know me yet, however. Now— can you ride?"

"I think that I had better—"

He nodded. "It will not be for more than a day. We draw near to gate. But, I ask of you, keep in mind that still we deal in illusions and it is best not to fight before we must—"

Herrel spoke as if together we faced danger. Yet in me I was alone, all alone. There was no Herrel I could depend upon, there was a man and a beast, and neither dared I cling to. But that I would not dispute upon now, not when I was so tired in mind and body.

"I fell and hit my head on a stone," I said as one repeating a well learned lesson. "There was no battle?"

"No battle," he agreed.

"In my dream battle then," I pursued the question, "what force trailed us and what weapon did they use which might have destroyed your illusions?"

"You remember it all?"

"I remember—"

"They were Hounds of Alizon. But some one

of them must have been schooled in the knowledge they make such a parade of abhoring. What they sent to confuse us was a power of the dark to shape change and then enforce that change to continue. In this they heaped their own grave mounds—better would they have wrought to keep us men."

"How many of them were there? And why did they attack?"

"Twenty—that we found. It was cleverly planned for they split our party with a false trail and then struck at what they deemed the weaker portion. As for why? They carried Hallack shields and blazons—thus they wished to embroil us with the Dales. It is only the dark arrow we do not understand, that has no place in their armament."

"Herrel—" Hyron, his crest of a rearing stallion plain in the growing daylight, stood at the open end of the leanto. "Lady—" he sketched a hand salute to me, but I noted that he did not really look in my direction. "It is time we ride. You are able to, lady?"

I wanted to say no, that I could not cling to a saddle, that I had no desire, nor strength to face a day's ride across this land which was enemy to my kind. But I could not say those words; instead I found myself nodding as if what he willed could only be my heart's desire also.

We rode, but in a different pattern from that which we had followed before. Now woman companied woman; the men threw out advance scouts and set a rear guard. I looked to Kildas at my left, Solfinna at my right. Neither seemed apprehensive, nor did they remark upon this division.

"Hisin says that this night shall we bide in the outer way," Solfinna's words broke my absorption. "Soon there will be an end to this journeying, though we are still two days from the appointed hour. Very fair must be the land beyond the Safekeep—" She smiled happily.

"Gillan, you have said so little. Does your head still ache?" Kildas shifted a little in the saddle to look at me more closely.

"It aches, yes, and I dreamed ill in the night."

To my surprise she nodded. "Yes, Herrel was in great concern when you cried out. He strove to wake you, but when he touched you, Hyron bade him cease for you seemed in even greater distress. Then he put something into your hand, and thereafter you quieted."

"Why did that so anger Hyron?" Solfinna broke in. "I could not see that it did harm, rather good."

"Hyron was angered?"

"Yes—" Solfinna began but Kildas broke in:

"I do not think angered, rather concerned. We all were, Gillan, for you cried out strange things we could not understand, which frightened, as if you were caught in a very evil dream."

"I do not remember," I lied. "One may do such after a head blow, that much I know from healcraft. And this land is so dreary it puts phantoms into one's mind—"

My first real error. Kildas looked at me oddly.

"The land lies under winter, but it is like unto the Dales. Why men speak of it as a waste. I do not understand. Look you how the sun touches all to diamond snow and crystal ice?"

Sun? Where shown any sun? We moved under a leaded sky. And the diamond snow was rimed drifts. Icy coated branches spoke only of frozen death. Illusion— Now I wanted to share that illusion for my own comfort. But this time, for all my willing, I could not see the land under the beneficent haze through which my companions moved. All was gray, grim, stark, with branches reaching for us like the misshapen hands of monsters, while every shadow could be granted evil and alien life of its own, lying in wait for the unwary.

I closed my eyes against what was real to me, summoned my will, desired to see . . . only to open sight once more on the same forbidding countryside. Also—the rush of power I had come to associate with my will-summons did not answer—save as a weak and quickly ebbing ripple. And with that discovery self-distrust awoke in me, weakening me yet farther. But I needs must guard my tongue and strive to fight my fears.

Now and again one of the Riders came to bear us company for a short while—always the mate of one of the brides. Then I noted that Herrel did not come so, nor had I seen him since we rode out of camp, though Halse passed twice down the line. Once when the bear-man slacked pace and Solfinna jogged ahead, I spoke, perhaps recklessly, but as I thought was only natural.

"My lord, where rides Herrel?"

There was that derisive smile on his face as he made answer courteously enough, but with such under mockery as to be an unseen blow.

"He rides rear guard, my lady. Shall I tell him you wish words with him? Doubtless some message of importance?"

"No. Just tell him all is well—"

Those red eyes searching me, trying to read my thoughts. Could these sorcerers in truth read thoughts? I did not believe so.

"You are wise not to draw him from his duty. Hyron believes him now best employed for the service of the company. And we must rest upon the best defenses we can muster—"

Words innocent enough, but so delivered that a threat ran beneath their smooth surface. And now Halse, in a low voice, added more:

"I would have nay-said Herrel could gain a bride. Has he told you that in this company he is the wrong-handed, the limper? But destiny is right after all, now we consider him well matched—" Still he smiled, and it was enough to make one dread all smiles.

"I thank you, my lord." From some last bulwark of pride and defiance I summoned those words. "Can any one truly say what a man is, or may come to be? If cloak-spell united us, then you will not miscall your own power. I am content, if my lord is also." A lie, and a lie he knew, yet one I would continue to cling to.

The method of our pairing from the bridal dale had been such that we knew only he whose cloak we had chosen—knew him? That was not my case certainly. But as to his fellow Riders, what did any of us know? My companions were so bound in illusion woven to hold them apart from the truth, that they would accept any seeing. Me—I was so torn with fear and suspicion that perhaps I saw awry also. Yet Halse I did not like, nor did I take kindly to the gaze Hyron turned upon me. And I had felt the animosity of those others last night.

What of Herrel? Yes, what of Herrel? Our first

meeting when he had taken me to wife, in name, by the cloak about my shoulders . . . the night when I had been willed by another's ill wishing to wake and see him as he could be and was, upon occasion. Last night when I had watched him go into battle and heard the horror of that fight—

I had come to our first meeting prepared to accept an alien—or had I really? Can anyone accept what they do not know? Now after testing I was as faint-hearted as Marimme, if able to conceal it better. Was Herrel a beast who could put on the semblance of a man for his purposes, or a man putting on the beast? It was this question ever seesawing at the back of my mind which made my flesh shiver and cringe from his touch, made me rejoice he was not my mate in truth. Kildas, Solfinna, the rest, they harbored no doubts. I believed they were all wives as I was not. But which husbanded them—beast and bird—or human body?

"To have the true sight, my lady," Halse's mount crowded closer to my mare; his voice dropped lower still, "can be a grievous thing. You do not belong here."

"If I do not, my lord, this is a very late hour to make such a discovery. And I think you do not give me much credit—"

He shrugged. "It may be, my lady, that we do you wrong. At least you have not spilled your doubts to these, your sisters. For that we give you due credit. And I shall give your message to Herrel." He wheeled his horse and was gone, leaving me with the feeling that I had done very ill to give him any reason to seek out Herrel.

I urged my mare on and caught up with Kildas, suddenly having a dislike for riding alone.

"Harl says that Halse is sharp tongued," she commented. "Though he does not seem to lack in proper courtesy. He resents it that he did not win a bride."

"Perhaps his cloak was not eye-catching enough."

She laughed. "Do not tell him that! He is one who fancies that in most companies he is the first to be noted. It is true he is very handsome—"

Handsome? To me he was the bear, danger covered with a deceptively clumsy skin.

"A fine face is not everything."

"Yes. And I do not care much for Halse. He ever smiles and looks content, but I do not think he is. Gillan, I know not what Herrel has told you, but do not speak freely—too freely—with Halse. Harl has said that there is old trouble between him and Herrel, and since the bridals it has grown worse. For Herrel obtained what he would have—"

"Me?" I laughed, startled by her speech which was so far from the truth I knew.

"Perhaps not you, but a bride. He spoke much before our coming as to what his luck would be, and then to have it dashed so, it has been as a burr within his tunic. The other Riders, they have not forgotten his boasts, and they lead him to remember them from time to time. It is odd," she glanced at me, "before we came I thought of the Riders as all alike, gathered into a pack which thought and acted as one. Instead they are as all men, each having thoughts, faults, dreams and fears of his own."

"Harl taught you thus?"

She smiled, a very different smile from that which curved Halse's lips, deeply happy. "Harl has taught me many things—" She was lost in a dream again, a dream which I could not enter.

And so the long day passed and I saw naught of Herrel—thought whether that was by his own design or the will of others. I did not know. We came at last to a long and narrow valley. Its entrance was masked with trees and brush, so thick that I would have believed there was no opening, yet he who was our guide wound a serpent's route through which we filed in a long line. The wall of vegetation gave way to an open space walled with steep rock cliffs. Down one was a lace of ice marking the passage of water flowing away in an ice encased brook. Before us the defile was a slit which was half choked by rock falls from above.

There were journey tents standing—those before us in the advance guard had made good use of time. Twilight was fast falling, but green lamps winked at us and there was a fire. At that moment it all looked as welcoming to me as the safe interior of any great hall—rough though that might be.

But when we would dismount the man who came to aid me wore a wolf helm.

"Herrel?"

"The rear guard has not yet come in, my lady." A smooth answer, aptly given.

And the truth was that I could not have honestly said that it would have lightened the burden of my fear had the cunningly wrought body of a cat over-topped the face looking up to mine.

That weariness which appeared always to

hold off while one was in a Rider's saddle, fell
upon me as I made my way, stiff limbed, to the
warmth of the fire. Loneliness closed me off from
the others, the loneliness of knowledge. I could
no longer hold off the thought that I had been left
no return. A choice, made too lightly and in
overconfidence had long since wiped away a
bridge between present and past—the future my
mind flinched from considering.

Night—sleep—but I dared not sleep! Sleep
held dreams—not as Kildas and the others
dreamed by day, but the other, the dark side of
that shield.

"Gillan?"

I turned my head stiffly. Herrel was coming
from the picket line. And in my loneliness I saw
a man, a man to whom I might have some small
meaning. My hands went out as I answered:

"Herrel!"

## VIII   POWER OF THE PACK

"IT IS WELL with you?"

"A day in the saddle is not like unto one spent in a bower," I fenced. The impulse of welcome which had made me move a step forward was a break in the wall of my fortress, imperiling me.

"We shall not drive you further, Gillan. And do not build up your defenses; to yield will be more to your profit, I promise you." His hand enfolded mine past my strength to free my fingers unless we struggled in good earnest.

And his touch built illusion. We stood not in a steep walled, dark cut, but in a place of spring time. Night was about us, yes, but a spring night. Small pale flowers gave sweet perfume to the night, blooming in a turf carpet, a thick cushion for our feet. Ripples of green and gold ran free from lamps along the edges of the tents, outlining them. There was a low table set with a multitude of plates and goblets, with mats for the diners. Those who were not partnered were gone. Only the twelve and one of us who had come out of the Dales and those of our choice remained.

Herrel drew me to the feasting table, and I went without question, as much bemused in that moment as any of the others. It was a relief to push aside reality, to plunge into the illusion, as one might dive into a pool of cooling water when one's body was fevered with summer heat.

I ate from the plate we shared in the courtly fashion. I could not have named the food, only knew that never before in my life had I tasted such viands, so subtle of flavor, so beguiling to the senses, so satisfying of hunger. There was drink in the goblet before me. Not the amber liquid Herrel had brought me in the marriage dell, but darkly red. And from it arose an aroma like the first fruits of bounteous autumn, rich, freighted with the sunlight of summer past.

"To you, my lady," Herrel raised that cup.

That which lay within me stirred, the lull of illusion was troubled, a ripple across the surface of a pool. Did he drink, or did it only appear so? He held out the cup to me. And I no more than wet my lips as I bowed my head in return.

"Can this then be journey's end, my lord?" I asked as I put away the scarce tasted wine.

"In one fashion. But it is also a beginning. Tonight we feast to that. Yes, a beginning—" He looked down at the table rather than to me.

Alone were we sober in that company. Around us there was soft, fond laughter, the murmur of voices, a kind of beatitude. But that part of the illusion was not ours.

"Ahead lies the gate you must storm?"

"Storm? No, we can not force a way here. Either the path is freely open, or it remains closed. And if it is closed—" He paused so long I dared to question:

"What then?"

"Why, once more we go a-wandering—"

"By the Bargain you can not return to the waste—"

"This land is very wide, larger than you of the Dales know. There are other portions in which we may live."

"But you hope not—"

Now he did turn to me, and what I read in his face struck all other questions from my lips. Yet when he answered, the words came evenly, as if he read them from some often conned book.

"We hope wandering is past."

"When and how will you know?"

"When?—tomorrow. How?—that I can not tell you."

But his "can not" was plainly "will not."

"And if we pass this gate, what then shall we find waiting us beyond?"

Herrel drew a deep breath. Always his man face had been that of a youth with the eyes of age, but now when he looked upon me the eyes were young also. And of the beast—had I ever seen the beast?

"How can I tell you? It is far beyond the words we share. Truly life there is different; it is another world!"

"And you came from there—how long ago?"

Once more his eyes were weary with years of looking at what he must see. "I came from there—how long? I—we—do not reckon times save when we must deal with those of this world. I do not know. We were granted one favor when we came forth, that our memories would be dimmed and dulled, that we would only dream, and that infrequently—"

Dreams! I shivered. The table before me, the feast, the lights, shimmered, lost substance. I wanted no dream memories. I reached forward, lifted the goblet to my lips. I was cold—cold— Perhaps the wine would warm me. Yet when it was on my tongue I paused, again within me that warning.

About us one by one the couples arose, arms

entwined, going to the tents. What I had uncon-
sciously feared was now before me.

"Dear heart, shall we go?" His voice had
changed, he was soft-spoken, not as he had been
when telling of the gate.

NO! shrilled my mind. But my body did not
elude the pressure of his arm about my waist. To
any onlooker we would have been another lan-
gorously amorous couple.

"A Toast," he glanced at the cup I still held,
"to our happiness, Gillan—drink to our happiness!"

No lover's request—an order. And his eyes
compelled me to it. I drank. My vision wavered,
the illusion mended—could it indeed be illusion? I went with him, for a moment unheeding
save that this was ordained.

Lips—gentle, seeking, then demanding, to
which demand I responded. And then hands—

Sharp as a sword thrust the awakening in me
of denial. No—no—this was not for me! This was
an end to the Gillan that was, a small death. And
against that death all the will and what I termed
"power" arose in savage defense. I crouched on
the far side of the pallet, my hands crooked to
claw. Herrel's white face I saw and across it a
band of bleeding scratches.

Herrel's smooth skin—or was it furred,
blurred with fur—and his mouth fanged? Man or
beast? I think I cried out and flung up my hand
before my eyes.

"Witch—"

I heard him move away. That word he had
flung at me—

"So—that is it—witch," he added. "Gillan!"
I dropped my hand shield to look at him. He

made no move. Only his face, truly a man's face, was set as it had been when he had fronted his pack brothers after the battle.

"I did not know—" he spoke, not to me, but as one seeking support or assurance from a source greater than he, "I did not know."

He moved and I shrank instinctively.

"Be not afraid. I lay no hand on you this night, nor like to any other night either!" There was bitterness in that. "Indeed Fortune is crossgrained to me. Another—Halse—would force you—to your good and the company's. But that is not in my birthright. Very well, Gillan, you have chosen—upon you be the consequences—"

He seemed to think I understood, yet his words were riddles past my reading. Now he drew the sword from the sheath he had thrown aside, laying the naked blade in the center of the pallet. So doing he laughed without mirth.

"A convention of the Dales, my lady. I shall honor it this night, you may rest without fear—that fear. But perhaps later you will discover that your choice was not altogether a wise one."

He stretched himself beside the sword and closed his eyes. Why? Why? I had so many whys swelling in my mind, but his face was closed. It was as if, though he lay only a hand's distance from me, we were separated by miles of a haunted waste. And I dared not break the silence.

I thought to lie sleepless. But when I came to the other side of that sword barrier I was straightway plunged into dark where there was not thought nor feeling. Nor did I dream.

From sleep to wakefulness I passed in an instant. I have heard that soldiers in the field sleep so, with an inner alert which walks sentry go for their protection. Around me—what could I name it—a quickening?

Though I listened there was naught but silence. Yet it was a silence which was alive. Herrel? My hand went out—there was no cold steel—

"Herrel?" Did I whisper that or only think it?

I opened my eyes. There was a faint gray light—perhaps that of very early morning. And I was alone in the tent. But in me that surging need to be out—about—I had known it back in the hillkeep when it had brought me to the discovery of Lord Imgry, but not as greatly as I did now. I was summoned—summoned! By whom and to what?

Swiftly I ordered my clothes and then pushed out into the morning. The enchantment was gone—cold stone cliffs, a dying fire— No movement, save now and then at the picket line a mount pawed the ground. I felt as if I alone were awake when all else slept. And the need for knowing I was not alone swept me.

I came to the next tent, moved by that need. Kildas lay there, covered by a cloak, sleeping. I looked farther, the Riders were gone! Returning to Kildas I strove to rouse her, but I could not. Perhaps she dreamed happily for there was a smile on her lips. Nor were my efforts more fruitful with the rest.

The restlessness possessing me until to sit still was beyond my power, I fed the dying fire. My flesh tingled; I was eaten by a rising excitement I did not, could not understand. Somewhere action was in progress, and it drew me—

Drew me! That was the answer. Not my mind—I must blank out my mind and the here and now as I had sought to do to preserve the illusion—the other sight. Let that drawing force take over, it must if I would ease this torment within.

Clumsily I strove to do that. Closing my eyes against the reality of the camp, trying to shut out what I knew and yield to that tugging I felt. I swayed, as one in a wind too great to breast, and then turned to the rubble filled end of the valley. There—somewhere there—!

Danger—I forgot danger—I was aware of nothing save the drawing. I scrambled through the rubble of the fallen rocks, impatient at the hindrance of my skirts. On and up—on and up!

It was like blood beating in the regular pound of my heart, yet also was it a throb in the air which was not as loud as the pound of a drum—waves beating, becoming a part of my body as I labored up the path to the Safekeep gate.

Sound now, and the tingling in me responded to that sound. But within a growing frustration. I should know—I should! And yet I did not. I was shut outside some door on which I could beat with my fists until they ran blood, yet I could not enter for the knowledge which controlled the door was not mine.

I reached the top of one of the mounds and looked down. I had found the Riders.

They stood in a triple line, facing the end of the valley, and it was indeed an end—a wall of solid rock without break, smooth past any climbing. They were bare of head, their helms and their arms, all laid behind, immediately below my perch. They faced that wall with empty hands.

And they were calling, not with voices, but from their hearts. It tore at me, that calling. I put my hands to my ears to shut it out. But that gesture was nothing against the evocation rising from below. Hunger, sorrow, loneliness—and a small spark of hope. They hurled emotions against the stone as besiegers would swing rams to batter down a keep gate.

One of them came forth from the line—Hyron, I believed, though I could not see his face. He went forward to the wall, laid the palms of his hands against its surface and stood so, while still they cried silently their desire for admittance. He stepped aside and another took his place, and another, each in turn. Time passed and I was no more aware of that than the Riders. The first line were done with that touching, the second, one by one, and now the third and last. Halse led them. He came to the barrier with an air of confidence, as if it must open for him.

On and on—and now the last—Herrel—wall. I remembered his face as I had seen it the night before, naked, scored by loss and longing. They were not willing down there, they were pleading, humbling themselves, against the nature of their kind.

Answer— Did they expect an answer now? Herrel came away from the wall to his place in the last line. And the beat, beat of their plea was unchecked. Almost I could believe that they had mistaken their gate. That stone must have stood unriven from the beginnings of time. Or had madness, born out of their wanderings in the waste, tainted their minds so they expected the very mountains to break— Was there any lost land?

I was accustomed now to the beat in my own body. Now that I knew what they strove to do here perhaps prudence would argue that I make my way back to camp. But when I tried to move from my vantage point I could not. I was one bound to the rock on which I half lay. And the fright that realization gave me brought a cry from my throat.

They would know—would find me here! Only not a head turned, no eyes moved from their steady fix upon the wall. I struggled the more, summoned all my will—and could not break those invisible bonds. On and on the Were Riders called upon whatever power they sought to reason with, and I lay there helplessly.

Now it seemed endless and I found my fear of the trap which held me broke through my preoccupation with what passed. Will—I would not lie here helpless! I could move— My fingers stretched across a stone before my eyes. Those I would move—narrow my world and my will to my fingers—

Move, fingers! Flesh and bone arched up in answer, free of the flesh held in prison. My hand curved into a fist, thrust against the rock to push away. Arm—next—arm!

Beat—beat—open gate— NO! Doggedly I pulled will and mind back to me—me! Arm—raise—

I tasted the salt of my sweat running across my lips, into the corners of my lips. Arm—raise!

Slowly—with such painful slowness— obedience. I could set hand on rock, arm as a brace, lever myself up a little. But the rest of me was unstirring weight. Foot—knee—

Beat—beat—the gate—that was important—the gate—

"No!" Perhaps I flung that denial down upon the heads of those below in an outburst of fury and frustration. Their gate meant nothing to me. They had receded from my life. What was needful was to move a foot, bend a knee, break out of a web I could not see.

I lay back, my shoulders supported by the cliff wall, panting as I drew great gasps of air into my laboring lungs. So far—in this small way I had broken free. Now—on my feet—I must get to my feet! From this new position I could no longer see the Riders, though their wall, still unbreached, was in my line of vision. As it would doubtless continue. They had failed. Why would they not accept that fact?

No—do not think of them! To do so was to lose the small ground I had gained, again it was hard to turn my head. There was nothing, nothing beyond this pocket of stone and earth which held my disobedient body, feet, legs, arms, hands— Will their coming alive!

Now I stood, stiffly, unsteadily, afraid that any attempt at a step would plunge me from my perch. Once more I could look down upon the Riders. And from them now arose no disturbing beat of supplication. But still they stood facing the wall. And it came to me that they awaited their answer.

I edged around. It no longer mattered to me what that answer would be. My world now held only Gillan and her concerns. I was encased in a hardening shell in which I could depend upon myself alone. And, when I thought that, there flashed a vivid picture out of memory, of Herrel setting between us a drawn sword—not of custom, but of severence.

As I managed to drag myself away from the rock where I had lain to watch the Riders my movements became freer. I had to expend less effort of will on making each limb do as I wished it to.

And sunlight found its way down into the valley. It was warm on my face, my hands, scraped raw and bruised. By the time I had turned my back fully on the slide of rock which walled the Riders from me I was moving normally, but with the fatigue which had punished me after my flight through the dream forest. There was on me now another kind of need, to reach the camp—to find there anchorage.

But I was only a few steps upon my way when my isolation was broken. I had heard the mellow gong notes they sound in the Abbey chapel to tell the hours proscribed for prayer. More rounded than the voice of any bell, richer, deeper. But this note came as if from the rock about me, the sky overhead, the rough ground under foot. And with it all that was stable moved, shook, was stirred. Stones toppled and fell. I threw myself back against the cliff side. My arm was numb as one struck against flesh and bone.

The echo of that note rolled, now growing fainter and fainter down the chain of the hills, seemed louder, more imperative, than the sound from which it was born. No war trumpet's ring, no temple gong, no sound I had ever heard could compare with it.

So—they had succeeded in opening their long closed door. Their homeland was before them. Theirs—theirs! Not mine—

A further rattling of rocks—I looked around. Slavering boar eyeing me, and behind its shoulder the narrow muzzle of a wolf, and the beat of eagle's wings. The Weremen—or beasts— coming to me. It was my vision from the dead forest brought into the sunlight of open day. And this time I could not flee.

"Gillan!"

A weaving, watering of the pattern. Men now and not beasts. Herrel had pushed to the front of the pack.

"Kill!"

Did that come from the wolf's jaws, or in the scream of the eagle, or the wild neighing of a stallion? Did I hear it at all, or only read it in their eyes?

"You can not kill—" that was Herrel, "she is sister stock—"

Their heads swung so they looked upon me, and then to him, and again to me.

"Do you not understand what we have netted by chance? She is wise-stock—witch by blood!"

Hyron had come to the fore, was looking upon me with narrowed eyes, noting my disheveled clothing, the wounds on my hands.

"Why came you here?" His voice was quiet, too quiet.

"I woke—I was—called—" Out of somewhere I chose that word to describe the uneasiness which had impelled me here.

"Did I not tell you?" broke in Herrel. "All of the true blood would answer when we—"

"Silence!" That carried the force of a blow in the face. I saw Herrel's body tense, his eyes glitter. He obeyed, but only just.

"And you came where?" Hyron continued.

"Up there." At that moment I could not have raised hand to point. I used my eyes to indicate the rise from which I had viewed their calling.

"Yet—" Hyron said slowly, "you did not fall, you climbed down in return—"

"Kill!"

Halse? Or another? But Hyron was shaking his head. "She is no meat for our rending, pack brothers. Like draws like." He raised his hand and lined a symbol in the air between us. Green it was as if traced in the faintest curl of mist, and then that green became blue which was gray at its dying.

"So be it." Hyron spoke those three words as if he pronounced some sentence. "Now we know—"

He did not move towards me, but Herrel did. And I yielded to his hand. Together we walked slowly, none of the Riders following closely behind, letting the distance grow between us.

"Your gate is open?"

"It is open."

"But—"

"Now is not the time for talking. We shall have many hours for that ahead of us—"

Then he broke the moment of new silence. "I wish—" he began but did not continue, looking never at me but at the way ahead, picking out ever the easiest footing for me.

"What do you wish?" I did not really care

much. I was so tired I wanted nothing but to slip into some dark place and there rest content.

"That there was more—or less—"

More or less what? I wondered mistily, not that it mattered. But to that he made no reply.

We came to the tents. The fire was dead, and there were no signs of life—the others must still sleep. Why had I not been able to share that? Since we had passed through the Throat of the Hawk I had shared nothing—nothing—

Herrel brought me back to the bed where the sword had lain between us. Weary I lay down upon it and closed my eyes. I think that I slept— or swooned—because of my great weariness of body and mind.

Had I been adept in the power born in me, but which I used only as a clumsy child would play with a weapon which could either save or harm, then I would have been armed, warned, perhaps able to defend myself against what the new night brought. But Hyron, in that testing, knew me for what I was, witch blood right enough, but unskilled, so no foe to stand against what he could summon and aim.

I had thrown away the one defense Herrel might have set between me and what they intended. Though I was not to know that for long to come.

Hyron moved quickly, and he had the backing of all the pack but one in that moving. Illusions they dealt in—but illusions may be common, or very complex. And the opening of the gate allowed them to draw upon sources of energy which had been dammed from their use for a long time.

I roused as Herrel knelt beside me, cup in his

hand, concern in his face, his touch tender. He would have me drink—it was the reviving fluid which had restored me before. I could recall its taste, its spicy scent. Herrel—I put out my hand—it was so heavy—so hard to lift. Herrel's cheek bearing my nail brand—Why had I so misused one who—one who—?

But that cheek wore no brand! Herrel—cat— Or *was* it a cat's green eyes watching me? Cat— bear—? My eyelids were so heavy I could not hold them open.

But though I could not see, yet still it would seem that hearing had not foresaken me, the dregs of my power leaving open that small channel to the outer world. I could hear movement in the tent about me. Then I was lifted, carried—

I was aloof, apart from what my ears reported.

"—fear him—"

"*Him?*" Laughter. "Look upon him, brothers! Can he move to raise his hand, does he even know what we now would do?"

"Yes, he will be content enough to ride with us in the morning."

It was like that beat of their desire in the valley, but now it formed a huge, stifling cloud of will—their will—pushing me down into darkness—with no hope of struggling against it.

## IX  THE HOUNDS OF DEATH

THE ASHEN FOREST about me again—and the hunt!
But this was, in its way, worse than it had been
before. I looked down upon my breast for that
amulet which had been my safety in a sea of
terror. This time it did not warm my flesh. I was
bare of any defense. Yet I did not run. As once I
had said, when fear comes too often, then it loses
its sharp edge. I braced my back against one of
the dead trees and waited.

Wind—no, not wind, but a purpose so great it
sent its force before it as a wind—stirred the
leaves which were pallid skeletons of their living brothers. Still did I make myself stand and
wait.

There were shadows—but not dark—these
were pale and gray and they flitted about, their
misshapen outlines hinting of monstrous
things. But, as I continued to stand my ground,
they only gathered behind the trees, menacing,
not attacking.

A wail to follow on that wind of purpose, so
high and shrill as to hurt the ears. The shadows
swayed and fluttered. Now down the forest
aisles moved those who had substance. Bear,
wolves, birds of prey, boar, and others I could
not name. They walked erect which somehow
made them more formidable to my eyes than if
they hunted four-footedly.

The need for speech struggled in my throat.
Let me but call aloud their names! Only that

relief was denied me, and it was as if I suffocated in the need to scream.

Behind the beasts the shadows gathered thickly, their outlines melting, reforming, melting again, so all that I knew was they were things of terror, utterly inimical to my form of life. Now the pack of beasts split apart and gave wide room to the leader of their company. A long horse head, the wildness of an untamed stallion gleaming in the eyes. And in its human-hands a weapon—a bow of gray-white tipped with silver, a cord which gave off a green gleam.

He who wore the bear's mask held out an arrow. It, too, was green. A spear of light might have been forged into that splinter shaft.

"By the bone of death, the power of silver, the force of our desire—" No spoken words, the invocation rang in my head as a pain thrust, "Thus do we loose one of three, never to be knotted together again!"

The shaft of light set to the cord of light. Now had I desired in that last moment to seek a small and doomed moment of safety in flight, yet I would not have succeeded, for their united wills held me as fast as if I were bound to the tree. And the cord twanged, or else that small sound was sensed rather than heard.

Cold—a bite of frost so bitter and so deep that it was worse than any pain I had ever known. I stood still again the tree—or did I? For in strange double vision now I looked upon the scene as one who had no part in it. There was she who stood, and another she who lay upon the ground. Then she who stood moved forward to that company of beasts, and they ringed her around and vanished among the trees. But she who lay did not move. And now I was she who lay—and the shadows were drawing in to—

I had said fear could become so familiar it no longer was a goad. But there was that in those shadows which caused such a revulsion and terror in me that I answered with a frantic denial of them, of what I saw— And was answered by dark and no knowledge at all—

Cold—piercing cold—I had never known such cold. But cold was my portion now—cold, cold, cold—

I opened my eyes. Over me a leaden sky and from it the falling of snow. Tent—surely there was a tent—?

Slowly I moved, struggled to sit up. Memory also awoke. Those cliffs I had seen before—this was the valley which led to the gate of the Riders' lost land. But it was empty. No tents stood, no mounts in a picket line. Snow drifted a little, but it had not quite yet hidden a ring of fire blackened stones. Fire—heat to banish this body aching cold! Fire!

I crept to those stones on hands and knees, thrust my fingers into the ashes. But they were long dead, as cold as the flesh and bone which probed them.

"Herrel—Kildas—Herrel!" I cried those names and had them echoed ghost-fashion back to me. There came no other answer. The camp, all those who had been within it—gone—utterly gone!

That this was another dream I never believed. This was the truth, and one my mind flinched from accepting. It seemed that the Riders had indeed rid themselves of one they did not want, and by the simplest of methods—leaving me behind in the wilderness.

I had two feet—I could walk—I could follow—

Swaying I got to those feet, staggered along. Only to return again to hands and knees, to crawling. And then—there it was—that unbroken cliff wall. Had there ever been a gate? After all I had not seen it. If there had it was firmly closed once more.

Cold—it was so cold—I would lie in the snow and sleep again and from that sleep there would come no waking. But sleep—sleep perhaps meant an ashen forest and the shadow that crept in to—feed! Painfully I made my way back down over the rubble. There, already powdered with snow was the furred rug on which I had lain. I shuffled to it, to find something else—my bag of simples.

My hands were so cold I could hardly feel anything my fingers handled, but somehow I brought out one of the vials, got it to my lips, sipped, waited for inner warmth to follow.

No warmth—cold—cold—As if some part of me had been frozen for all time, or else drawn out to leave an empty void into which ice had moulded. But my head cleared, my hands answered the commands of my brain with more skill.

I had the rug on which I had lain, and my bag, the travel stained clothing I wore. There was naught else—no weapon, no food. I might have been left for dead on some battle field where the victor cared not to honor the remains of the vanquished.

Cold—so cold—

Wood, some wood left. And they had not been wise to discard my simple bag—no, that had been a grievous mistake on their part. I was better learned in the worth of what I carried so far than they might guess.

I dragged the wood to the fire stones, laid it as best I could, and then smeared on some twigs a finger tip of salve, to which I added drops from another vial. My hands were steady. They moved easily now. Flame answered, caught easily at the branches around. I drew as close as I might to its warmth.

Warm—on my hands, my face, my body, yes, there was warmth. But inside me, cold, cold, cold emptiness! At last I found the right word for that sense of loss. I was empty—or had been emptied! Of what? Not life, for I moved, breathed, knew not hunger and thirst, which I assuaged with handsful of snow. The cordial from my bag had quieted the pangs of physical hunger. Still I was empty—and never would I be whole again until I was filled.

That me which the beasts had taken with them—that was what I must find again. But a dream—? No, not wholly dream, they had wrought some sorcery of their own over me when—last night—many nights ago? By all accounts sorcery could alter the wave of time itself. They had left me to the shadows in the dream world—perchance thus, they believed, to one form of death. And if that failed, as it had, then to this other death in the wilderness. Why had they so feared—or hated—me? Because I could not be ensorcelled or shaped, controlled as those others from the Dales?

"Witch," Herrel had named me. And he had

spoken as one who knew well of what he spoke.

Dame Alousan was a Wise Woman. She had known more of things outside the beliefs of the Abbey than she had ever said. In her library of old knowledge there were books, books I had understood only in part. Sorcery existed. All men knew that. It was remnants of a kind of learning from a very old day and from other peoples who lived in the Dales before the men of High Hallack came from the south to spread out among the hills. And the Were Riders—all men knew that they controlled powers and forces beyond human ken.

Some such powers were for the good of those who sought them, or they could be shaped for good or ill. And a third sort were neither good nor evil. But beyond the bonds laid by men, yea or nay. There was a flaw in the use even of good powers. That had been early impressed on me until I learned it as an undeniable lesson. For the sense of mastery such use gave the one who practiced it led to a desire for more and more. And finally, unless one was strong willed enough to put aside temptation, one ventured from light into shadow, and into the dark from which there was no return.

No return—there might have been no return from that ashen wood for me. And—also there had been something rift from me there. Cold— cold—I pressed my hands tight to my breasts— so cold! Never would I be warm again, filled again—until I won back from those who had taken it that other self of mine. Won back? What chance had I of that? I would die here in the wilderness, or this part of me would die— Oh, I could keep life in me for a short period using those simples and my knowledge—but it would only stave off an inevitable end.

Cold—would I never be warm again? Never?

If only I knew a little more! If I have not been denied my birthright—birthright? Who was Gillan? Witch, Herrel had laid name to me—witch? But one who could not perform her witchery, who had power of a sort but could not use it to any great purpose—a witch who was maimed, even as Herrel had claimed to be maimed, unable to be whole. Whole?

I found myself laughing then, and that laughter was so ill a thing to hear that I covered my mouth with both hands, though my shoulders still shook with the force of those convulsions which were not mirth, were very far from human mirth.

Whole? The laughter which had torn me subsided. I must—I would be whole. Slowly I turned my body until I faced the gate which was no longer a gate. What would make me whole had vanished—behind that. But—it pulled me—it did, it did! As my body grew stronger, my mind more alert, so did I feel that pull, as well as if I could actually see a cord trailing away, leading into the stone.

The snow had stopped and the firewood was almost consumed. I could not take the back trail; that which dragged at me would not allow it. Thus I must find some way through the barrier—or over it—

"Stand!"

My head jerked on my shoulders.

Men coming up the valley. As the Riders, these were helmed. But their head covering bore ragged crests and were equipped with eye pieces

which fitted down over their eyes mask fashion.
They had short coats of furred hide and their
boots arose on the outer side of the leg in a sharp
point.

Hounds of Alizon!

When they had first come to this continent as
invaders they had been armed with weapons
strange to the Dales, one of which had shot a
searing beam of fire. But when their supply ships
had ceased to arrive, some two years ago, these
had grown fewer and fewer among them. Now
they rode as did the other fighting men of this
land with bow, sword, spear, and I saw arrows
on cord—

I did not move. It would seem prospective
danger was now real. For the fate of any woman
in the hands of the Hounds was not good to think
upon. I had that in my bag which would give
me a last freedom, had I chance to use it.

"A woman!" One of them rode past the
archers, slid from his saddle and ran towards the
fire. Wearing his mask helm he was more
alien even than the beasts.

I had no road of escape. Should I try to scramble over the rocks I could be pulled down with
ease, or caught when I came up against the barrier of the gate.

Because I did not flee I surprised him. He
slackened pace, looked from the fire to me,
glanced about—

"So your friends have left you, wench?"

"'Ware, Smarkle," an order snapped from the
others, "have you never heard of baited traps?"

He halted almost in mid-stride, and dodged
behind a rock. There was a long period of silence

wherein the archers sat their saddles, their arrows centered on me.

"You there," a man stepped out from between the horsemen, his shield well up to cover his body, a captured shield since its surface bore a much defaced bearing of the Dales. "Come out—to us! Come or be shot where you stand!"

Perhaps the best choice would be to disobey, to go down now in clean death with the arrows reaching into that emptiness. But there was a need in me greater than any other, to regain that which I had lost, and it would not let me turn away from life so easily. I walked past the fire, to the rock behind which Smarkle crouched.

"She is one of the Dale wenches right enough, Captain!" His voice rang out.

Still with his shield before him the Captain dodged from one bit of cover to the next in a zig-zag course.

"Come, you, on!"

Slowly I went. There were four archers, the two men behind the rocks—how many more might be in the valley I could not guess. Plainly they had trailed our party here, which showed strong determination on the part of these hunted men, since the course brought them deep into the waste and away from the sea which was their path homeward, could they ever find a ship. As Herrel had said, these were desperate, with naught to lose which counted longer, even their lives. And so they were also beasts, perhaps much worse than the Riders.

"Who are you?" The Captain fired a second demand at me.

"One of the Dale brides," I made answer with

the truth, knowing now that these men were not as they had been weeks, or even days ago. Even as I they had lost some part of them, worn away by hardship and the abiding loneliness and despair which dwelt in the waste.

"Where are the rest then?" That was Smarkle.

"Gone on—"

"Gone on? Leaving you behind? We are not fools—"

Small inspiration came to me. "Neither are they, men of Alizon. I fell ill of hill fever—to them it is doubly dangerous. Do you not know that the Were Riders are not as we? What ails us is sometimes doubly fatal to them—"

"What do you think, Captain?" Smarkle asked. "If this be a trap, they would have cut us down by now—"

"Not and risk her. You—go back, beyond that fire, against the rocks! Keep your arrows on her as she goes."

I returned, passing the dying fire, setting at last my shoulders against the stone.

"You—back there—" Now the Captain did not address me, now his own men, but the debris in the valley which masked the gate wall. "Move, and we arrow slit this dainty piece of yours!"

His words echoed about the walls as they waited tensely. And when the last sound died away, he spoke to Smarkle.

"Take her!"

He came at me in a run, dodging about the smouldering fire, slamming his body against mine, pinning me to the rock by his weight. His breath was hot and foul in my face, and through the eye slits of his helm I could see his eyes, a-glitter with a vicious hunger.

"Got her!"

They moved, still cautiously, towards us. Smarkle contented himself for the present with whispers, the obscenity of which I could guess, though most of the words he used I had never heard. Then he pulled me away from the rock and held me with my arms clamped to my sides, though I had made no struggle.

"She's no Dale wench." One of the archers leaned forward in the saddle to stare at me. "Did you ever see such hair on one of them, now did you?"

My braids had loosened and fallen, and against the snow their black hue was startlingly dark. The Hounds looked me up and down as Smarkle held me for their inspection, and now I thought I saw a wariness in their eyes. Not as if they feared me to be bait in some baffling trap they had not yet uncovered, but that something in my appearance alone made them uneasy.

"By the Horns of Khather!" swore the archer. "Look upon her, Captain—have you not heard of her like?"

Beneath the half mask of his helm the Captain's lips curled in an evil leer. "Yes, Thacomer, I have heard of her like. Though in this land—no. But have you not heard there is a way to disarm such sorceresses, a very pleasant way—"

Smarkle laughed, his grip tightening painfully on my arms.

"Let us not look into her eyes, Captain. It is so a man is held in spell. Those hags of Estcarp know how to bewitch mortal men."

"So they may. Yet they are also mortal. We have caught us some fine sport."

The sun had come from behind clouds, its

westerning rays struck full in my face. Of what they spoke I had no clue. Though that they believed me of a race of old enemies of theirs I could guess.

"Build up the fire," the Captain flung the order to the archers. "It is cold here—these walls hold out the sun."

"Captain," Thacmor asked. "Why would she stay here—unless she means us harm—"

"Harm to us? Perhaps. But rather do I think she was found out for what she is, and so left—"

"But those devils also deal in magic—"

"True. But wolves of a pack turn upon one another when hunger bites deep. There may be some quarrel we do not know. Perhaps even these Dale sheep laid plans and planted her among the rest to bring their 'Bargain' to naught. If so, she has failed or been found out. At any rate they have left her to us. And we shall not nay-say them!"

As yet Smarkle held me, and his touch was an offense it would shame me to put into words. Feeling was left me, like a dim memory of something which had once been alive—and good.

They gathered more wood. At one time this valley must have been a channel for a stream of size and storm drift was still caught among the boulders. They stirred the fire I had kindled into higher blaze. Smarkle threw a loop of hide thong about my shoulders and arms, another about my ankles, making me prisoner.

But with them one kind of hunger seemed greater than the other, for one brought a brace of birds, a large rabbit to the fire side, and these they cleaned and spitted for broiling. One of the archers had a leathern flask. He unstoppered it, strove to drink, and then hurled it from him with a curse.

"Witch," the Captain stood straddle-legged before me. "Where did they go—the Were Riders?"

"On."

"And they left you because they found you out for what you are?"

"Yes." That might or might not be true, but I thought he guessed rightly.

"Therefore their magic was greater than yours—"

"I can not judge their power."

He thought on that, and I do not think he relished his thoughts.

"What awaits ahead?"

Again I gave him the truth. "Now—nothing."

"Did they become thin air and float away?" Smarkle twitched the cord about my ankles in a cruel pull. "The same you will not, witch wench!"

"They passed a barrier, it closed behind them."

The Captain glanced up at the sun, now almost gone from this shadowed valley, and then at the choked passage ahead. He did not appear to like its looks, but he was a seasoned warrior and prepared to make sure of his ground. At a gesture from him two of the archers laid aside their bows, drew swords, and worked their way up the piles of slide debris.

To one side lay the fur rug which had been left with me. Smarkle advanced a hand to it, and then lifted it higher with the toe of his boot, scudding across the frozen ground.

"Stupid fool!" The Captain turned on him.

"That is a shape changer's hide. Would you touch it?"

Smarkle shivered, his leering grin gone. He grabbed a branch from those laid ready for the fire and lifted the finely dressed hide, thrusting it yet farther away. A rug—they so feared a fur rug? But these men must have faced the fur of the Riders in their battle guise, to them it was indeed an animal's pelt.

My bag of simples—I could see the end of its carrying strap lying in the shadow of a rock. Doubtless they would deal the same with that should they find it, mistrusting the "magic" it might contain. Were I free and had it in my hands, then I might indeed work "magic"—

But they did not sight it, not yet. And now the Captain came back to his interrogation of me.

"Where did they go? What lies behind this barrier?"

"I do not know—save that they sought another land—"

The Captain snapped up the eye piece of his helm, took off the head covering. His hair was very fair—not the warm yellow, or light red-brown of a Dalesman—but rather almost white, as if he were an old man—yet that he was not. He had a sharp and jutting nose, not unlike an eagle's beak (an eagle's beak . . . would I ever now look for such signs on a man's face?) and high cheekbones set wide apart—though his eyes were small and narrow lidded so that he appeared to ever squint.

He ran his hand from one temple back up his head. There were marks of fatigue on his face, and that kind of tautness shown by a man driven to the edge of endurance, perhaps beyond. He sat down on a stone, no longer looking at me, but staring into the fire.

Moments later the scouts returned.

"Well?"

"Much fallen rock and then just cliff—they could not have gone that way."

"They came in here," the other scout said, a thin, unsteadiness in his voice. "They could not have doubled back past us. They came in here—but now they are gone!"

The Captain's gaze swung once more to me. "How?" his voice rasped that one word demand.

"To each his own sorcery. They asked a gate to open—it did."

It had opened for them—not me. But that would not stop me, any more than this remnant of broken, fleeing men would stop me. Somewhere beyond that wall was a part of me. It would draw me on, guide me, and I would be whole once again!

"She—she can get us by—" Thacmor nodded at me. "The witches—they say wind and wave, earth and sky, obey them."

"One witch alone, who could not use her power before?" The Captain shook his head. "Do you think she would have been here, waiting for us, had she been able to break their spells? No, the hunt's lost now—"

Smarkle licked his lips, the others shifted uneasily.

"What do we do now, Captain?"

He shrugged. "We eat, we—" He paused to grin at me, "amuse ourselves. On the morrow we lay plans again."

Some one of them laughed. Another slapped his near companion on the shoulder. They were pushing aside tomorrow, living for the hour as was customary with fighting men whose lives were long forfeit. I glanced at the meat by the fire. It would soon be done, then they would eat and then—after—

So far my passiveness had appeared to serve me. I was bound but they had not otherwise misused me. However my respite was very close to an end. They would eat and then—

If I only had the knowledge. There was that in me, I was sure, which might act as shield and sword at this hour could I release it. Will—I had always thought of it as power of will. Will—power— Could I channel will to make of it a weapon?

# X   NO SHADOW!

THE SIMPLE BAG, my desperate thoughts kept coming back to that. They had scooped up snow, dumped it by the fistful into a small pot now shoved close to the flames. A few drops from a certain small bottle into that and—

But I was as far from achieving that as I was from finding the vanished gate. What I did not know was so much more than what I did.

They ate and the smell of the roasting meat, as they tore it with teeth or sawed chunks off with the belt knives, aroused the hunger the cordial had allayed. They offered me none and I knew their purpose. Whatever use they planned to make of me this night, I would not go hence with them in the morning. Why should they wish to burden their troop with a woman who was also a feared witch?

The simple bag. I tried to keep my eyes from it, lest one of them follow my gaze and find it. But when I stole another look I saw, doubtless by some trick of firelight, it was now in the open, could be sighted by any who turned his head. In the open—but how? It had been between two rocks—those two—and now it was inches away!

That shook me—so simple a thing among all the greater. However it is such that tugs at reason when greater shocks will not. The bag had lain there, now it was by so much the nearer to me. As if my desire and will had lent it legs on which to answer my unvoiced summoning. Legs—will? Almost I dared not believe—but I had to.

The flap-cover of the bag—it was fastened so and so. Not daring to look I stared into the flames of my captors' fire and concentrated on building a picture in my mind of that latching. So easy to finger, but for the mind—ah, that was different. How many times can one accurately and minutely describe some well known possession we handle a hundred times a day? It is so familiar to us that the eye takes no record of its details. To try to recall without looking at it now becomes strange and alien.

Thus and thus—rod into metal loop, turned down—so! I had it correctly pictured, or hoped that I had. Now—to reverse that locking—turn up—slide out— Dared I look to the bag once more to see if it had obeyed my will? Better not—though not to know—

Now—within—how were ranked those contents? I put myself back in the night filled room of Dame Alousan, the cupboards I had opened, drawers which had yielded to my pull. In what order had I filled those pockets and loops? So deeply did I search memory that the fire and the scene before me blurred. I dared not think on how much time I might have left, as one by one I used memory as a pointer as to what lay now in the shadows. The fifth pocket—it was the fifth pocket! If memory had not foresaken me utterly when I needed it most.

Slender tube, not of glass, but of bone, hollowed and then capped with a stopper of black stone. Out—tube! Greatly daring I dropped my head forward on my knee, face turned to the darkness. They might well believe me sunk in despair, but now I could see what I wrought, or tried to do—

The tube—out! Movement under the flap of the bag. I do not think it was until that moment, in spite of hope, I dared to believe that I was accomplishing anything. And the sight of my small success almost defeated my efforts by surprise. Again my will steadied, I saw the bone tube work from beneath the leather cover, lay open to sight on the ground.

Tube—pot—one into the other. The meat they were eating was hot and greasy; they would thirst. Tube—into pot. The small bone stirred, arose, pointed for the direction in which I would aim it. I put into that all the force I could muster.

It had no arrow swiftness. Now and then it swayed groundward and my will failed, my concentration broke. But I did it, toppled it into the melting snow water and none of the Hounds had noticed it.

Last of all—the stopper—that black stone. Out—out—! Trickles of moisture from my temples, runnels of it from my armpits. Stopper—out! I kept on the battle, having no way of knowing of my success or failure.

A hand reached for the pot. I held my breath to see a small drinking horn dipped into the contents. Would that archer see what lay within— had it done its purpose? He drank thirstily from the horn, and so did the one next to him. Three—four—now Smarkle. The Captain? So far he had not.

Time—would time serve me now? I knew what the effect of that liquid was under certain controlled conditions. How it might answer this night was something else.

They had finished eating; clean picked bones cast out among the rocks. I had had my respite.

Now it was coming to an end. The Captain—one other—had not drunk. And of those who had—I could see no signs they were affected. Perhaps the stopper—but it was too late to regret now—

Smarkle stood up, wiping his hands down his thighs, grinning.

"Do we go to the sport, Captain?"

Now—he was turning to the water pot! Just as I had used my will on the bone vial, so did I now fasten it upon him, urging the need for drink. And he did, deeply, before he made answer to Smarkle's question. Beyond—the other holdout did also.

"If you wish—"

Smarkle gave an obscene crow and strode towards me while laughter and calls of encouragement came from his fellows. He reached down to drag me up against him, thrusting his face into mine, pulling at my clothing—though I struggled as best I could.

"Smarkle—!" A loud cry, but he laughed, blowing foulness into my face.

"You will have your turn, Macik. We will do it fair, turn and turn about."

"Captain—Smarkle—" One of the archers came in a leap to tug at his fellow. "Look you—fool!"

His grasp had loosened Smarkle's hold on me, pulled the other a little away from where I fell against a rock. Smarkle mouthed an oath and turned, but something in the other's excitement stopped the blow he had raised his hand to strike.

"Look you!" The archer pointed to the ground. "She—she throws no shadow!"

As the rest I stared down. The fire was bright

and the shadows seemed clear and dark, thrown as they were by the men. But—there was none for me. I moved, and no answering black appeared on rock or ground.

Smarkle shook off the other's hold. "She is real enough, I had hands on her—she is real, I tell you! Try her for yourself if you do not believe that!"

But the archer he ordered to that action stepped back and shook his head.

"Captain, you know about the hags," Smarkle appealed. "They can make a man see what is not. She is real, we can break all her magic easy enough—and have a good time doing it."

"They can make you feel as well as see, do they wish it," the archer replied. "Perhaps she is no woman at all, but a shape changer set here to hold us until his devil pack can come to our blooding. Shoot—prove her real or shadow. Use one of the cursed shafts—"

"If we had one left, Yacmik, do not doubt I would use it," the Captain cut into the argument. "But we do not. Hag or shape changer she has powers. Now we shall see if they can stand against cold steel." He drew his sword and the others fell back as he came to me.

"Ahhhhh—" That sound began as a startled cry and ended as a sigh. He who had first drunk from the pail of snow water lurched back, clutching for support of the man beside him. Then he went down, dragging the other with him. A second man wavered, fell.

"Witch!" The Captain thrust with his sword. But the blade went between my arm and my side, scoring the flesh along my ribs, but not the fatal wound he intended, jarring its tip against the rock which backed me. He blinked at me, his face creasing in a grimace of hatred and fear, and made ready to strike again.

But smothered cries from those about the fire made him turn his head. Some of his men lay prone and still, and others strove to keep on their feet but wavered drunkenly, with manifestly little control over their bodies. The Captain put his hand to his head, brushed across his eyes as if to clear them from some vision. Then he thrust at me a second time, his blade tearing a long rip in my robe, and he went to his knees, to crash forward on his face.

I pressed my hand to my side, feeling the damp of my blood, not yet daring to move for there were some still stumbling about. Two tried to reach me with drawn weapons, but in the end I alone stood among the fallen.

They were not dead, and how long the drug would hold, so diluted and used, I did not know. Before they woke I must be gone. And where was I to go? When I was sure they were all unconscious I went to the bag my will had opened and searched for that which would aid my hurt. That salved and bound, I passed among my sleeping enemies, looking for aught which might aid me in the struggle to keep life in my body.

A long hunting knife was in my belt, and I found some food—the compact rations known to the forces of Alizon, which they must have been saving, trying to live off the country when they could. Swords, bows, arrow-full quivers I gathered and threw upon the fire—which might not harm the blades but would finish the rest. Their horses I freed from the picket line and sent down the valley, flapping a blanket to frighten them.

With the knife I cut away the long skirt of my divided robe, binding what was left to my legs so that I would not be burdened in my climb. For only climbing would take me where I must go. And, even though it was now night, I must be on my way, lest the sleepers rouse to find me still within their reach.

There was no use in attempting the barrier which masked the Riders' "gate"; not so much as a finger or toe hold could be found on its surface. So—there remained the valley walls. And the danger of such a road was marked by the debris of past slides.

Only in me one purpose had grown so great that it filled even the emptiness. The pull which drew me north had strengthened during the passing of hours, not become lesser. I was no longer a creature of flesh and blood alone. That flesh and blood was rather an envelope for something now more acute and desirous than any ordinary human might know. It was as if my ordeal in escaping from the Hounds had awakened, or shaped, yet farther that unknown which I had always possessed but been unable to bind to my service.

I began to climb. This much favored me, I had never found it hard to walk high places. And I had heard it said many times by the hunters from the mountains who came to trade their fur take in the Dale towns, that one must never look down or back. Though it seemed to me now that my advance was the journey of an ant compared to the stride of a tall man, as I looked ahead to what still way before me. Also, I had no lessoning in this, and was ever fearful of a wrong move plunging me down, while I never knew at what moment those I had left might rouse and take to the hunt.

Up and up, moments lengthened until they weighed upon me as full hours. Twice I clung in stark terror as rocks did crash, missing me by very little. At last I came upon a fault in the rock which had better holds within it. So, venturing inside that break, I went on and on until, at last, I pulled out upon a bare and open space which must mark the top of the cliff. There I tumbled forward into a pocket of snow, my body weak and trembling, no longer able to obey my will.

At length I recovered enough to crawl between two pinnacles of rock, and from my back I loosed the fur rug which I had knotted to me with strips of my robe. This I wrapped about me and so huddled in the poor shelter I had found.

There was a moon that night. It had ridden high in the sky as I climbed but now it paled, and so did the glittering stars. I had reached the crest of the guardian cliff, so I must now be on a level with the top of the gate barrier. What I had to face I did not try to guess. I was so fired my mind seemed to float away, out from my aching body.

I did not sleep, I drifted in an odd state of double awareness which was puzzling. At times I could see me huddled between my rocks, a bundle of furred robe, as if another Gillan crouched on one of the pinnacles, detached, uncaring. And at other times I was in another place where there was warmth, light, and people whom I tried to see more clearly but could not. The scratch on my side had stopped bleeding,

the salve had done its duty, and the rug kept out
the major part of the cold. But finally I stirred
uneasily, the pull on me urging me on. It was
past dawn and the rising sun streaked the sky
with red. We would have a fair day—we?
I—I—I—Gillan who was alone—unless Fortune
turned her face utterly from me and the Hounds
came baying up my scent.

Beyond the pinnacles which had protected me
during the last hours of the dark was a broken
country, such a maze of wind worn rock in
toothy outcrops as could utterly bemuse and
confuse the would-be traveler. The cliff must be
my guide and I should keep to its lip in order not
to become lost.

The wall which was a barrier was perhaps
twelve feet or more thick—beyond it the same
narrow valley continued—no different from the
one out of which I had climbed—save that here
the walls were sheer past any hope of descent. I
must move along the edge hoping to find more
favorable territory beyond.

Here in the heights the sun was not veiled and
struck fair across the stone, bringing with it
warmth, fleeting though that might be. And now
I noticed a difference in the rocks about me.
Whereas they had been gray, brown or buff-tan,
here they were a slatey blue-green. But as I
paused by one and let my eyes move to the next
outcrop and the next, I perceived that these col-
orful pieces, many of them taller than my head,
were not natural to the terrain they rested on.
And also that, tumbled as they were, they yet
followed a given course, as if some titanic wall
had long since tumbled into rubble. They grew
to be taller and taller and more thickly set to-

gether, so that many times I had to detour and backtrail to find a path among them. Which course in time drew me farther from the edge of the cliff which was my guide.

I rested and ate of the rations I had plundered from the Hounds. The stuff was dry and taste-less, and it did not give the satisfaction of food, but I thought it would renew the energy I had lost. As I sat there I studied those blue-green rocks and their piling. They were not finished, bore no signs of ever having been dressed or worked; yet they did not arrive here by natural chance, of that I was sure.

Now that I stared at them, I shook my head, closed and opened my eyes. As in the wedding dell of the Riders, I again faced two kinds of sight, melting and running together until I was utterly confused, made dizzy by that flowing and ebbing before me. One moment there was an open pathway a little to my right. But as I watched that closed, rocks rising to bar it. I was sure this was not born from my fatigue, but rather of a shadowing and clouding of mind. If it continued to last I would hardly dare move, lest my eyes betray me into dangerous misstep.

This time my will could not control it, except for very short snatches of time. And each attempt to do so wore on me heavily. Also any prolonged survey of that changing landscape made me giddy and ill. In me the tie urged forward— now—with no delay. But to obey—I could not.

I was on my feet again but the shifting before my eyes made me cling to the rocks. For it seemed that the ground under my feet was no longer stable. I was trapped in this place and there was no escape.

Then I closed my eyes and stood very still. Gradually the dizziness subsided. When I pushed one foot cautiously forward it slid over solid, unchanging ground. I felt before me, grasped rock and drew myself to its reassuring solidity.

Perhaps the trouble was now past. I opened my eyes and cried out—for the whirl about me was worse than it had been, giving no promise of any end. With my eyes closed the world was solid, when I looked upon it there was only chaos. And I must go on.

Shouldering the bag of simples and the rug, I stood for a moment trying to summon logic and reason. I did not believe that my eyes were to blame for this confusion, but that some spell or hallucination was in force. It did not confuse touch, but only sight. Therefore I ought to be able to advance by feeling my way, but to do so would lose me my guide—of the rim of the cliff, the landmarks I had set upon. I could wander about in circles until either I fell or wasted away.

Lacking a guide—but did I lack a guide? It was so thin a cord to which to trust one's life—that which drew me ever onward after the Riders. Could that bring me, blind, through this maze? I did not see that I had aught else to try.

Resolutely I closed my eyes, put out my hands, started in the direction which beckoned me. It was not easy and my progress was very slow. In spite of my hands before me I crashed against rocks, to stagger on, bruised and shaken. Many times I paused to try sight, only to sicken from the vision which was not only double now, but triple, quadruple, and maddening.

I could not be sure if I were making any prog-

ress; my fears might be very well founded and I
might be wandering in a circle, utterly lost. only
the tugging at me continued, and I believe, as
time passed, I was growing more alert to its
direction, found it easier to answer. My hands
grazed rocks on either side. But then my outstretched palms flattened against a hard surface.
Not harsh contact with rough stone—I slid them
back and forth across smoothness. And that was
so foreign I dared to open my eyes.

Light, dazzling, threatening to engulf me, to
burn me to ashes. Yet no heat against my hands.
It was blinding and I dared not look upon it.

Back and forth I examined it by touch, up and
down. It filled a gap between two walls through
which I had come, stretching from beyond a
point above as high as I could reach, down to the
ground. There was no break, or even rough spot
on the whole invisible surface.

I edged back, tried to find some other way past.
But there was none, and my guide pulled me
ever into the defile which was so stoppered. At
last I dropped to the ground. This, then, must be
the end. No way forward except one barred, and
no guide back if I strove to retrace my steps. I
dropped my head to rest on my hunched knees—

But—I sat not on stone—I rode a horse. Daring
to open my eyes because this I could not
believe—I saw Rathkas' tossing mane, her small
ear. We were in a green and golden land, fair to
look upon. Kildas—there was Kildas—and Solfinna. They wore flower wreaths on their heads
and white blossoms were twisted into their
reins. Also they were singing, the whole company sang—as did I.

And I also knew that this was one side of the

coin of truth, just as the twisted rock maze and the barrier of light was the other. I wanted to shout aloud—but my lips shaped only the words of the song.

"Herrel!" In me rose the cry I could not voice—"Herrel!" If he knew, he could unite the whole—I would not be Gillan ahorse with the brides of the Dales, nor Gillan lost among the rocks—but whole again!

I looked about me and saw the company strung out along a green banked lane. And the Riders, too, wore flowers upon their helms. They had the seeming of handsome men, not unlike those of the Dales, with the beast quite hidden and gone. And very joyful was that company— yet he I sought was not among them.

"Ah, Gillan," Kildas spoke to me, "have you ever seen so fair a day? It would seem that spring and summer have wedded and that we have the best of both to welcome us to this land."

"It is so," my lips answered for the one who was not wholly Gillan.

"It is odd," Kildas laughed, "but I have been trying to remember what it was like, back in the Dales. And it is like a dream which fades from one's waking hour. Nor is there any reason for us to remember—"

But there is! cried my inner self. For I am of the Dales yet and must be united—

There came a rider up beside me, holding out a branch which flowered with waxy white blooms, giving off such perfume as to make the senses swim.

"Sweet, my lady," he said. "Yet not as sweet as she who would accept my gift—"

My hand went to the branch— "Herrel—"

But as I raised my eyes from the flowers to he who offered them I saw a bear's red eyes on his helm. And beneath that his own narrowed, holding mine in a tight gaze. Then his hand flashed up between us, and in its palm was a small, glittering thing which pulled my attention so that I could not look away.

I raised my head from my knees. Shadows, darkness about me in a pool which denied that green and gold had ever been. I rode not with flowers and spring about me, I crouched along among enchanted stones in the cold of winter. But this I brought with me—the knowledge that there were indeed two Gillans—one who strove to reach the other side of these heights in painful weariness, and one who still companied with those from the Dales. And until those two were one again there was no true life for me.

It had been Halse beside me on that ride, and he had recognized my return to the other Gillan, had driven me back here. But Herrel—where had he been, what had he to do with that other Gillan?

Now I was also aware that in the dark the dizzy many-sight had ceased, that I could look about me without meeting that giddy whirl of landscape. Had the barrier also vanished?

I crept back between the rocks to face—not the blinding light which had been there earlier, but a glow—a wall of green light. I approached it, put my hands to its surface. Yes, it was as firm as ever. And it was sorcery, of that I was certain. Whether of Rider brewing, or merely some long set safeguard, I did not know. But I must find a way through it, or past it.

Here I could not climb the walls as I had in the valley. And surely I had nothing to dig underneath, I thought a little wildly. With the fading of its day-glare I could see through it.

Beyond lay an open space, an end to the tumble of rocks which had choked my back trail. Perhaps with those behind I need not fear any longer the bewildering of my sight. But how to pass the barrier—

I leaned back against the rock and stared at it hopelessly. It could not be too thick; I could see through it so easily. If I might shape change as easily as those I trailed—wear an eagle's body for a space, this would be no more than a stride. But that was not my magic.

What was my magic—the will which had served me. How could I apply that one poor weapon here? I could see no way—yet find one I must!

## XI   THAT WHICH RUNS THE RIDGES

I WAS COLD, I hungered, both for that which I might take into my mouth and swallow, and that which had been rift from me. And I was caged, for there was no return, nor, it would seem, no going forward from this place.

Down in the Dales I had gone afield with Dame Alousan and some of the village women upon occasion, seeking out herbs, and their roots. And in the summer I had seen webs of field spiders spun between two small bushes or tussocks of grass to form a barrier—

Why did I now have such a memory picture? A web set up between two more solid anchors—? As this wall of light confronting me between stones—

I raised my head, looked more closely at those stones. There was no climbing them—twice my height and a little more, they were sleek and had no handholds. For they were a part of this ancient wall or fortification. Yet those portions between which hung the curtain of light were not a part of the bulk, rather posts of a sort, separate from the rest as the supports of a doorway. Creeping forward I discovered I was able to push fingers knuckle deep between them and the other rocks.

A spider's web— Eluding the danger of the sticky cords it could be brought to naught by the breaking of its supports. So wild a thought yet my mind fastened on it, perhaps because I could see no other way. I had brought the bone vial out of the bag by will. But these were no light bottle, these were weighty stones, such as many men might labor to dislodge. And how could I be sure that moving one would break the curtain?

I covered my eyes, leaned back against the stone of the wall. Though the fur rug was about me, still I could feel its chill, its denial of what that wild thought urged me to try. And always on me that pull from beyond—

Now I looked again to the curtain pillars. To my sight they seemed equally deep set, not to be tumbled from that planting. So I turned my eyes upon that one which stood to the left, and I called upon my power of will.

Fall! Fall! I beat my desire upon it as I would have beat body, hands, all my physical strength had such been able to serve me. Fall! Tremble and fall! I did not have to think of time as I had in the camp of the Hounds. Time here was meaningless—there was only the pillar—and the curtain—and the need for passing it. Fall—tremble and fall!

World without vanished, fading from me. I saw now only a tall, dark shadow, and against it thrust small spurts of blue. First at its crown, and then, with better aimed determination, at its ground rooting. Soil—loosen, roots tremble—I was wholly the will I used—

Tremble—fall!

The dark pillar wavered. That was it! The foot—work upon its foot. Blue shafts in the murk which was none of my world, yet one I should know. Tremble—fall—

Slowly the stone was nodding—away from me—outward—

There was a sound—sound which shook

through my body—was pain so intense it conquered mind and will—drove me into nothingness.

I turned my head which lay on a hard and punishing surface. On my face was the spatter of cold rain or sleet. I opened my eyes. In my nostrils was a strong smell, on which I did not remember ever having met before. Weakly I raised myself.

Black scars on the stone. One of those pillars askew, leaning well away as if pointing my way on. And between it and its fellow—nothing. I crawled on. My hand touched the blackened portion of the stone. I snatched it back, fingers burned by heat. Waveringly I got to my feet, lurched through the charred space, came into the open.

It was day—but thick clouds made that twilight. And from the overcast poured moisture which was a mixture of rain and snow, the frigid touch of which pierced to the bones. But I could see clearly, there were no more shifting rocks ahead—only the natural stones of the mountains, familiar to me all my life. And also there was something else—a way cut into the rock.

But weariness dragged at me as I staggered on to that road. I had only taken a few steps along it when I needs must sit down again. And this time I allayed my hunger with some of the rations from the Hounds' supplies.

There were lichens upon the stones about me, whereas among the blue-green walls there had been no growing things. Also, as I breathed deeply I found a taste in the air, a freshness unknown before.

Since I had come from the place of the curtain

of light the bond which drew me was stronger, and in a way more urgent. As if the need for uniting was far more important and necessary.

Having swallowed my dry mouthfuls, I arose once more. It was lucky that the forgotten road I followed was a smoother path, for in my present unsteadiness I could not have managed as I had the day before. It was not a wide road, that very ancient cut now paved with splotches of red and pale green lichens. And through some oddity of this country, my sight was limited by a mist, which did not naturally accompany rain in the Dales, but did hang here.

I descended gradually, and now the road was banked with walls of rock. Too narrow for a troop of horse that way. If it had served a vanished fortress, then those who had manned the rubbled walls were all footmen. Stunted trees, wind crippled, grew here and there, with tangles of brush and dried grass in pockets. I turned a curve and came down a last rise into a great open space, how large I could not tell, for about it hung the veils of mist.

The road led under an arch into an area which was walled, but not roofed—nor had it ever been roofed, I believed. And I stood in an oval enclosure. At regular intervals along those walls were niches which had been closed up for three quarters or more of their height, leaving only a small portion at the top still open. On each of those was deep set a symbol carved in the walling stone. Worn they were, and most past any tracing— those at the other end so smooth that only a thin shadow of a design was hinted at, though some, to my right, were more deeply defined. None had any meaning for me.

It was dark within the open portion of those niches. As I paused before the first I staggered. From that space came against me—what? A blow of some unseen force? No—as I swung to face that small opening the sensation was clearer. This was an inquiry, a demanding of who?, and what?, and why? There was an intelligent presence there.

And I did not find it odd to speak aloud my answer into the silence which held that questioning beneath its surface:

"I am Gillan, out of the Dales of High Hallack, and I come to claim that which is the other part of me. No more—no less, do I seek."

Outwardly, to my eyes, my ears, there was no change. But I felt a waking of some thing—or things—which had stood guardian here for years past human telling, all of whom now stirred, centered their regard upon me. Perhaps my words meant nothing, perhaps they were not of those who deal in words. But that I was sifted, examined, pondered upon, that I knew. And I moved along the center way of that place, turning from one niche to its fellow across the way, each in order, facing that which weighed me.

From those niches with the clearer symbols it came no stronger than from those so age worn. These were guardians, and I was perhaps a threat to that which they had been set to guard. How long had it been since they had last been summoned to this duty?

I reached the end of that oval, stood before the arched way which carried on the road. Now I turned to face back along the path I had come. I waited, for what I did not know— Was it recognition of some kind, a permission to go as I would, good will towards the fulfilling of my quest? If I expected aught, I was disappointed. I was free of that questioning, that was all. And perhaps that was all that was necessary. Still I felt a kind of loneliness, wished for more.

Once again the rock chiseled road ran on, to descend another long slope. More trees showed and brown grass. The rain held, but now it was not so cold. I found a pool hollowed in a block beside the road and drank from my cupped hands. The water was very chill, but it held a trace of sweet taste. As the air—it refreshed.

Now my trail led along the side of a rise, with a drop to my right, the depths of which were hidden by the mist, for that I had not left behind. And in all this time the only sounds I heard were born from the activity of the rain. If any animal or bird made home in this land, then it was snug in den or nest against the fall of water.

My limbs seemed weighted; I was afraid that I could not go much farther, yet the sharp pull was now a pain inside me. I came to the end of that cliff-side walk and found a grove of trees. Though they were winter stripped, yet their tangled branches gave some shelter. I settled myself at the foot of one, pulling the rug closely about me. Though the fur was matted with moisture, yet the hide was water proof and kept out the rain. From the place I had chosen I could still look upon the road, coming out of the mist above where lay the plateau of the Guardians, continuing on into more mist and a future I could not hope to read. I curled up, pulled a flap of the rug closer so I was completely covered.

This extreme weariness worried me. I had that cordial in my bag; sips of it could strengthen me for a space. Still if I wasted it at the beginning of what might be a long journey, then later I might discover myself helpless in a time of greater need. If I were no stronger in the morning, then I must risk it. Cold—would I always be so cold?

No—not cold—warm— Sun and warmth, and the scent of flowers. Not a horse this time— I opened my eyes and looked out of a tent. The light was that of late afternoon—outside a brook made music. This was the green-gold land of that other Gillan. I saw a man come, his face half-averted from me. But no one could hide him—not by any shaping!

"Herrel!"

His head snapped around, he was staring at me with those green eyes. There was that in his face which was steel-hard, closed—and so it was with his eyes at first. Then they changed as they entered deeply into me.

"Herrel!" I did what I had never done before in my life, I asked aid of another, reached out in need—

He came to me, almost with the leap of a hunting cat, was on his knees before me; our eyes locked.

All that I wanted to say was imprisoned in my throat. Only could I utter his name. His hands were on me; he was demanding in a rush of speech answers—yet I could not hear nor speak. Only my need was so great it was an unvoiced screaming in my head.

There was shouting. Men burst in upon us, fell upon Herrel and dragged him away despite his struggles. Again I looked at Halse. His mouth was ugly with hate, his eyes fire—fire burning me. Once more he held between us that which drove me away—back to the woods and the rain—and the knowledge that I was again in exile.

"Herrel!" I whispered slowly, softly. Somehow I had nursed in me—to learn now it was truth—the thought—the hope—that Herrel had not been one with those who had left me alone in the wilderness. Could he, too, have been deceived by that part of Gillan now riding with the company? Halse had brought that Gillan flowers, as if in wooing. Had that Gillan been turned by their sorcery to favor Halse? How—how far could she have turned?

The chill which was never gone from me was an icy sword in my breast. Halse had the power to exile me from that other Gillan, he used it at once when he knew that we were one—to drive me forth again. Halse—or someone—but I thought it Halse—had striven to part me from Herrel by showing me him as his shape change made him. And then he had turned on me readily when the Riders had discovered that I had some power of my own. This being so—why would he now woo me? Fragments of what Herrel had told me made a pattern of sorts.

Herrel had named himself the least of the Riders, one who lacked the fullness of the talents the others shared, and thus was not reckoned of much account in their company. Because of custom he had set his cloak enchantment that it would draw no bride. But it had me—why?

For the first time I thought back to that moment when I had stood at the edge of the wedding dell, looking upon those cloaks, seeing them with the double vision. Why had I taken up Herrel's? I had not been caught by any enchantment through its beauty. But I had gone to it, passing other cloaks spread there—taken it up in my hands with the same single minded action as displayed by all the other maids of High Hallack.

Thus—Herrel had succeeded where they wished him failure. And I did not know to this moment why I had chosen his cloak—and so him. But Halse had been passed by, came forth from that bridal morn riding alone, and that had bitten into him. It would seem that he alone of those unmated had deemed Herrel fair game, planning to take what was his. Perhaps any more save towards Herrel would have brought retaliation from the pack, and Halse's determination was greater than the rest.

If—when they had rift that other Gillan from me—Halse had fastened on that other self, dividing her from Herrel— How much life did that other Gillan have? There were old tales in the Dales—good telling for the winter nights, when a small shiver up the back added to one's feeling of comfort, the hearth fire blazing before, snug company around. I had heard snatches of stories concerning "fetches"—the simulacrum of the living appearing to those away, generally foretelling death. Did a fetch now ride at Halse's side?

No, that Gillan had more substance, or else the appearance of it. Appearance—hallucination—did Halse actually create—with aid—a bride for himself, or merely the appearance of one to assuage his esteem and deceive those who might be led to question my disappearance—say—Kildas? Or had that other Gillan been used to punish Herrel in some manner, he not knowing her real nature? If so, that short meeting in the tent must have awakened him to the true facts. I did not doubt that Herrel had been made aware in those short moments before the others had come upon us, that there was a difference in Gillans.

Now, with that same urge which I had summoned to topple the pillar, I tried to reach that other Gillan—to be reunited. The cord between us still held, but draw along it to her in this fashion I could not. Warned, they must have set up a barrier to that.

The rain had stopped. But there was no lightening of the clouds, and around me the woods were very quiet, save for the drip of water from the branches. But with the coming of night, there were breaks in the silence which had held by day. I heard a cry which might have been the scream of some winged hunter, and farther away, faintly, a baying—

In my belt was the knife I had brought from the Hound camp. Save for that I was weaponless. And even in the Dales there were four footed hunters not to be faced unshielded and alone. For me fear suddenly peopled this wood, this country, with a multitude of moving shadows, owing no allegiance to any stable thing. Almost I might have been plunged back into the nightmare wood of my dreams.

`Move on, run—down the road—in the open—cried one part of my mind. Stay hid in the dark, under the rug I was but one more shadow— Stay—go—they buffeted me. Back to the oval of the Guardians—the mere thought of walls was steadying. But that which held me to the forward trail would not allow retreat. And if I broke that tie—and could not find it again—I would have no guide—

Stay—Go—

Weariness made my eyelids heavy, pushed my head down upon my knees. That argument which had no end was lost in sleep.

The scent reached me first, for I came to my senses gasping, choking at the foulness of a fog which came in gathering intensity from the road. The stench was throat-clogging, lung-searing—

This was not the mist which still cloaked the distances from my eyes, but a yellowish cloud of corruption which held a faint phosphorescence in its swirls. I retched, coughed. Nothing so foul had ever polluted any world I knew.

Under my body was the ground, and through that came a vibration. Something moved out there, along that road, with force enough to send those waves through the earth. The time for retreat was gone. I could only hope that stillness, the robe shadow—something—would keep me from discovery. I put my palm flat on the wet and muddy ground, since I dared not so bend my head, hoping that thus I might better read the vibrations. And it seemed to me that it was not the ponderous slow step such as one might assign to some great bulk, but rather a rapid beat as from a company running—

The muddy fog was thick. If it hid the road from me, then certainly it should in turn hide me from what passed that way! But that was only a small hope, such as we are wont to cling to in times of great peril.

That this was such a time, I doubted not. I shrank inside and out from the fog and what it held—so alien to my flesh and spirit that to come even this close to it was befoulment beyond the finding of words.

Now the passage of what the fog hid was not only vibration through the ground to my touch; it was sound for my ears. The beat of steps, and of more than one pair of feet—but whether of beast or things two footed and running in company I could not tell.

The phosphorescent quality of that evil cloud grew stronger, its yellow taking on a sickly, red tinge, as of watered blood. And with that a low droning noise, which one's ears strained to break down into the tones of many voices chanting together, but which ever eluded that struggle for clarity. It was coming up the road, not down from the place of the Guardians.

I bit hard upon my knuckles, scoring them with my teeth until I tasted blood, so keeping from the outcry my panic held ready in my throat to voice. Was it better to see—or far, far better to be blinded against this runner, or runners in the night? Flecks of darker red in the fog. And the drone so loud it filled my head, shook my body. I think my very terror worked on my behalf to save me that night, for it held me in a mindless, motionless state very close to the end of life itself. Fear can kill, and I had never met such fear as this before. For this did not lurk in any dream, but in the world I had always believed to be sane and understandable.

Blood on my hands and in my mouth, and that stench about me so that I would never feel clean again unless I could flee it. But I no longer saw those red flecks, and the drone was easing —it was past me.

Still I could not move. All strength had seeped out of my body as it might have drained from an open and deadly wound. I sat there, terror bound, under the leafless tree.

Vibration now, rather than sound, told me it was still on its mysterious way. Where? Up to the place of the Guardians then on to the shifting stones—

With the greatest effort I had forced upon my body since I had ridden out of Norstead, I dragged myself to my feet. To leave the shadow of the trees, go out to the edge of the road, was torture. But neither dared I remain here, to perhaps face the return of that which ran the ridges in the night. I had nigh reached the end of all my strength and beyond that lay death—of that I was sure.

To go out on the road itself I did not dare. I stumbled along under the edge of the trees, heading away from what had passed me. The mist seemed thicker, closing about me at times so I could see only a few steps ahead; there lingered, too, the noisome smell of the fog.

For awhile I had the wood on my right hand and that small promise of shelter. Then once again I had to take to the road for the ground fell on one side and climbed on the other. Always must I listen for what might come behind—

The slope of the road grew steeper. I slowed my pace even more. And I was panting heavily as I paused to rest for a few moments. Then— away and afar—behind—came a cry—a screech which, faint as it was, made me gasp and cry out. For the alien malignancy which frightened it was that of some utterly unbelievable nightmare.

Faint and far, yes, but that did not mean it was not returning this way—

I began to run down hill, weaving from side to side, blindly, without caution, only knowing that I must as long as I could stand on my feet. Then I must crawl, or roll, or claw my way as long as I continued to live.

This was dream panic relived in reality. I caught at stones, at the cliff side, to steady myself. A mud patch on the road—I slipped, went to my knees. Gasping I was up again, staggering on. Always did I fear to hear that cry repeated—closer—

I had not realized that the mist was thinning until I saw farther ahead. And there was light—light? I pressed my hands to my aching side and stared stupidly as I reeled back against the cliff wall. Light—but no lamp—no star—no fire—nothing I could relate it to. Yellowwhite, streaking here and there as if it flashed at random from widely separated sources. Not beams of light, but small sparks, winging here and there—

Winging! Lights which flew, detached from any source of burning, dancing sometimes together, sometimes racing far apart or circling one after the other—in no set pattern which would suggest any purpose. One settled for a moment on a tree below, gleamed brightly, vanished— In and out, up and down, to watch them made me almost as dizzy as it had to watch the shifting stones.

They did not warn me of danger, and after a moment or two of watching them I went on. One sped apart from its fellows towards me. I flinched and then saw it was well over my head.

There was a buzzing and I made out beating wings, many faceted eyes which were also sparks of fire. An insect or flying thing—I did not believe it a bird—perhaps as large as my hand and equipped with a rounded body which glowed brightly—

It continued to fly well above my head, but made no move to draw closer, and I gathered the remnants of my tattered courage to go on. Two more of the lightbearers joined the one who escorted me, and with their combined light I no longer had to pick my way with care. The road became level once again. Here were trees but I could see leaves and smell the scent of growing things. I had come from winter into spring or summer. Was this the green-gold land of the other Gillan?

At least our bond led me forward. And my light bearing companions continued with me. Here the trees grew back from the road, leaving a grassy verge on either side of its surface and there was a welcome which was as soothing as an ointment laid upon a deep burn. I could not conceive that that from which I fled could walk through such a land as this. But it had come from this direction and I dared not allowed myself to be so lulled.

The road no longer ran so straight, it curved and dipped and came out at last by a river. There was a bridge, or had been a bridge, for the centerspan was gone. Under that water rushed with some force. To cross here, unless driven, in the night was madness. I dropped down on the entrance to the bridge and half lay, half sat, content for the moment just to have come so far unharmed.

Scent turned my head to the left. One of the light creatures settled on a beflowered branch which swung under its weight. The waxen flowers—those were the kind Halse had offered Gillan on the road. In this much had I come on my journey; I had reached the land behind the gate—that which the Riders had so longed for during their years of exile. Fair it was—but what of that which ran the ridges in the night? Could this land be also greatly foul? I was not spell-entranced, one ensorcelled as that other Gillan and her companions. Would my clear sight here serve to warn and protect—or hinder?

## XII  LAND OF WRAITHS

DAWN CAME gently, and with color; not in the grayness of the waste and the peaks. The light-bearers flitted away before the first lighting of the world about me, and now birds began to sing. I no longer was lonely in a country which rejected my kind. Or so I thought on that first morn in the forbidden land.

In me blood ran more swiftly. I had drawn back my fled courage, my wanning strength. That which ran the ridges haunted a former life far behind.

Though the river ran swiftly enough to delay my passage yet there was a small backwater below where I rested, having the calm of a pool. Over this leaned trees with withy branches which bent to the water's surface and those were laced with pink flowers from which each small breeze brought a shower of golden pollen sifting down, to lie like yellow snow upon the water. Slender reeds of brilliant green grew along the bank, save for where a broad stone was deep set, projecting a little into the water, as if meant as a wharf for some miniature fleet.

Stiffly I found my feet and climbed down to that stone, skimming some of the pollen from the water with my hand, letting the clear drops run down my skin. Cool and yet not too cool. My fingers went to buckles, clasps and ties and I dropped from me the travel stained clothing, with all its tears and the mustiness of too long wearing, to wade out into that back eddy of the

stream, washing my body. The wound on my
side was a pink weal—already more than half
healed. Some of the blossomed withes rubbed
my head and shoulders, and the perfume of the
flowers lingered on my skin and hair. I
luxuriated in that freedom, not wanting to return
to my clothing, to that urge which sent me on. If I
moved in illusion, then it was so strong as to
entrap me utterly—nor did I want to break the
spell.

But at length I returned to the bank and pulled
on garments the more distasteful for my own
cleanliness. Having eaten I again studied the
bridge. It looked as old as time, its gray stones
patterned with moss and lichen. The centerspan
must have vanished years ago. No, the only way
to cross the river must be to—

I stared at the gap in the bridge. Then, tenuous
as a spider's transport thread—there was something there. Illusion? I willed for true sight.
There was the dizziness of one picture fitted over
another. But I could see it. The old, old bridge,
half gone and another intact, with no break!
And—the intact bridge was the true one. But it
still remained, for all my concentration, a
shadowy, ghostly thing. I glanced away to the
pool where I had bathed, to the flowering shrubs
and trees, the green generosity of this smiling
country. But that showed no ghosts of over-fitted
illusion—only the bridge did so. Another
safeguard of this land, set up to delay, to warn off
those who had not its secret?

Slowly I stepped upon the stone I could see
well, heading towards that ghost. Or was it
another and more subtle illusion, beckoning the
wayfarer on for a disastrous fall into the flood

below. As I closed upon the broken gap mended by that dim rise, I went down on hands and knees, creeping forward, warily testing each stone before me, lest a dislodged block turn and precipitate me down. It was very hard to believe in—that shadow portion.

I reached the end of the solid stone, or what one sight reported solid stone. My hand moved out, expecting to thrust into nothingness, but the shadow was firm substance. I crept on, hardly daring to look about me. For my eyes said that I was coming onto a span of mist, too ephemeral a thing to support my weight. And below the water boiled and frothed about the support pillars. My touch told me that the mist was real, the break was not. Almost it was as confusing as the shifting stones on the heights.

Across what I could see only as a shadow I went, still on hands and knees until I came to the solid stone. As I stood upright, supported by one hand on the parapet, breathing hard, I knew that once again I must ever be on guard, not disarmed by the smiling peace of this land, so that my double sight could aid and warn.

The road wound on, now through fields. No cattle nor sheep grazed there, nor were any crops sown. At intervals I called upon my double sight, but no hazy outlines formed. There were birds in plenty, and they showed no wariness of me, scratching in the dust near my feet, soaring within a hand's distance, or swinging on some bush limb eyeing me curiously. They were brighter plumaged than the ones I knew from the Dales, and of different species. There was one with stiffly curled tail feathers of red and gold, wings of rust-red, that did not fly at all, but ran beside me for a space in company, calling out at intervals a small questing note as if it expected some coherent answer. It was larger than a barnyard fowl and more assured.

Twice I saw furred things watching me as unafraid. A fox surveyed my passing, sitting up as might a hound. Almost I expected it to bark a greeting. And two squirrels, these a red-gold, rather than the gray that lived in Norstead gardens, chattered together, manifestly exchanging opinions concerning me. Were it not for that cord ever drawing me onward, that sense of necessity and need, I would have traveled with a light and joyous heart.

Still caution walked with me and I did not forget to use the sight as a check upon the countryside. The sun arose, was warm, so that the fur rug which had been such a boone in the hills was now a sorry drag upon my arm. I was folding it for the fourth time when I chanced to look upon the ground and a small chill froze me in midgesture.

I threw no shadow—that dark mark of any standing or moving thing in a lighted world was no longer mine! Smarkle had accused me of that in the Hound camp, but I had been too intent upon escape for it to make much impression on my mind. But I *was* real—solid—flesh and bone! Around me trees, bushes, tall clumps of grass all had their proper patch of corresponding shade to mark their presence. But it was as if I were as unsubstantial as that piece of bridge had been in my sight.

Was I only real to myself? But the Hounds had seen me, laid hands upon me, had thought to do even more. To them I had been solid, had had

life. That I hugged to me, though I had never
thought to be thankful for my meeting with those
ravagers and outlaws.

Now I moved my hands, striving to win an
answer to that movement on the ground. And the
confidence built up during my morning's wanderings ebbed somewhat. So small a shadow,
something we seldom think on. But to lack
it—ah, that was another matter. Suddenly it became one of the most important possessions, as
needful as a hand, a limb—as needful to one's
sense of sanity.

Even the double sight gave me no shadow. But
I used it on the surrounding country and saw—

I was no longer in a world empty of inhabitants. Mist formed grew more visible as I concentrated, stiffened, became opaque and solid seeming. To my left there was a lane turning from the
road, and at the end of that lane a farm garth. An
old house with a sharply gabled roof, outbuild-
ings, a walled enclosure which might mark a
special garden. It was unlike the holdings of the
Dales with that steeply pitched roof, with the
carvings scalloped around the eaves and dormer
window. The front faced a paved yard in which I
saw figures passing. And the more I studied it,
the clearer my sight came to be. This was the true
sight, the empty fields the illusion.

Without making any real decision I turned
into that lane, hurried my steps to the paved
yard. And the closer I came the more imposing
the house. The roof was covered with slates, the
house itself was of stone—that same blue-green
stone I had found on the heights. But the carvings were touched with gold and a richer green.
Over the main door was set a panel bearing a

device like unto the arms of the Dales, yet different, since it made use of intertwined symbols and not the signs of heraldry. And about it was the feeling of age, not an age which drains and exhausts by the passing of years, but an age which adds and enriches.

Those who went about their business outside were two, a man who led horses from the stable to drink at a trough, and a capped maid shooing fowls before her—fowls of brilliant feathers and long slender legs.

I could not see their faces clearly, but plainly they were made like unto me and human seeming. The man wore silver-gray hosen, and an over-jerkin of gray leather, clipped in at the waist with a belt on which gleamed metal. And the maid had a gown of russet, warm as a hearth fire and over it a long, apron-shift of yellow, the same color as her cap.

The pavement of the yard was solid under my boots. And the maid approached me, sowing grain for the birds from a shallow basket on her arm.

"Please—" Suddenly I needed contact, for her to see me, answer—I had spoke aloud but she did not glance at me, even turn her head in my direction.

"Please—" My voice was thin but loud. In my own ears it rang above the sounds made by the fowls. Still she did not look to me. And the man, having watered the horses, returned with them to the stables, passing close by. He looked, yes, but manifestly he did not see. There was no change of expression on his thin face with its slanted brows and pointed chin—like in that much to the Riders' features.

I could stand their indifference no longer.
Reaching out I caught the maid's sleeve. She
gave a little cry, jerked back and stared about her
as one bewildered and a little afraid. At her
ejaculation the man turned and called query in a
tongue I did not know. Though both of them
looked to where I stood, yet they did not show
that they saw me.

My concentration broke. They began to fade,
that age-old house, man and maid, buildings,
fowls, horses—thinner and thinner—until they
were gone and I stood in the middle of one of the
fields utterly alone again. Still in me I knew that
my sight was reversed—where once I had seen
good slicked over ill, now I saw ill slicked over
good. To me this was a land of wraiths—and to
them I was the wraith!

I stumbled back to the road and sat down on its
verge, my spinning head in my hands. Would I
ever be real in this land? Or not so until I found
the other Gillan? Was she real here?

The Hound rations were only a few crumbs
now. Where would I find sustenance, this wraith
who was me? Perhaps I could break the illusion
long enough at some garth or manor to find food,
though I might have to take it without asking, if
those who dwelt there could not see me. Let me
only reach that other Gillan, I prayed—to what
power might rule in this land—let me be one
again—and real—complete!

For a while I no longer tried to see what lay
beneath the overriding cover to emptiness. How
well these people had chosen their various skins
of protection—the Guardians—that horror on
the mountain road, and this new blanket to meet
the eyes of any invader. A company of Hounds

might ride here, mile after mile, and see naught to raid. How much had I passed by chance without knowing that it was there? Keeps, manors, towns?

More food I must have, and if I must raid for it, then it would be necessary to see. Two manors I sighted dimly as I went on were too far from the road, and I clung to that because it was real. And it led, my invisible guide told me, in the right direction.

It was mid-afternoon when I saw the village. Again it lay on a side way. And I speculated as to why all the dwellings I had seen did not abut on this highway but stood always some distance from it. Was the road itself a trap of sorts, to lead an invader across open country well apart from any inhabited place where blundering chance might inform him that all fields were not as they appeared?

A small village, perhaps a score of houses, with a towered structure in their midst. The people in its two streets were shadows to me. I did not try to see them better. It was enough that I could distinguish them and avoid their movements. But the houses I concentrated upon.

The nearest I dared not approach, for a woman sat on the stoop spinning. The next, children ran about the yard engaged in a vigorous game. And the third showed a closed door which might be latched against all comers. But the fourth was a larger building and a signboard with a painted symbol swung out over its main door—it could well be an inn.

I strained my power to keep it real and visible as I went in the half open door beneath that board. There was a short passage, a door in it to

my left, giving upon a long room in which were
trestle tables and benches. Set out on one of
those tables a plate with a brown loaf, next to it a
round of deep yellow cheese from which had
been cut a wedge. Almost I thought they might
fade into nothingness as my fingers closed about
them. But they did not. I bundled both into a fold
of the rug and turned to go, well content.

A figure flickered in the doorway—one of the
misty people of the village. I backed to the wall.
But the newcomer came no farther in. A little
alarmed, I strove to build that wavering outline
into a solid person. A man—he wore leather
breeks, boots, chainmail under a short surcoat of
silky fabric, like in fashion to that of the Riders,
save his were not furred. Instead of a helm a cap
covered his head, its front turned up and fastened with a gemmed brooch.

He was looking intently into the room, searching, once his eyes swept across me without pausing. Still I read suspicion in his manner. Though
he had not drawn it, there was a sword in his
baldric, and, being of this land, perhaps he had
also other guards and weapons which did not
show as openly.

There was another door to the chamber, but it
was closed, and to open it might instantly betray
me. If he would only come farther into the room,
I could slip along the wall and be out— But that
helpful move he did not seem inclined to make.

It was a struggle to keep him so sharply in my
sight. I was fast discovering that it was easier to
"see" the buildings than the people who inhabited them.

I saw his nostrils expand, as if he would sniff

me out. Always his eyes searched the room, his head turned from side to side. Then he spoke, in the language I did not understand.

His words had the rising inflection of a question. I tried to hold my breath, lest the sound of the quickened breathing I could not control would reach his ears.

Again he asked his question, if question it was. Then at last, to my great relief, he took several steps into the room. I began my sidewise creep to reach the door, afraid my bootheels would scrape. But the floor was carpeted with a woven stuff which had been, in turn, needleworked in a sprawling design and that deadened any sound. I was in a foot of escape when the stranger, who by now reached the table from which I had taken the bread and cheese, tensed, swung around. At first I thought that by some illhap he had seen me. But, though he was now staring straight into my face, there was no change in his listening, wary expression. Only—he was coming for the door.

With a last effort I was at it, through, intent on leaving the hall behind me. He shouted. There was an answer from the road. I saw another figure before me. Desperately I threw myself forward, one arm held out stiffly. That met solid flesh and bone, though what I saw was a faded blur. There was a cry of surprise as the newcomer reeled back. Then I was out, running in the street, away from the village, back to the road which I was beginning to consider a haven of safety.

Sounds of cries, of pounding feet behind me. Did they see me, or was I safe by that much? I dared not look back. And I let my defense against illusion drop, saving all my energy for that dash across field.

On the verge I stumbled, sprawled forward, to lie for a few seconds to quiet my racing heart and laboring lungs. When I at last sat up and turned my head it was to face nothing but meadow and sky. But I could hear. There was still shouting back there, and now the sound of a horse galloping, nearer and nearer. I caught up my booty bundled in the rug and began to run, along the road, away from the vanished lane. When at last I paused, breathless, there was nothing to be heard, save the twittering of a bird. I had aroused suspicion but they had not really seen me. I had nothing to fear, at least for now.

But still I put more distance behind me before I sat down on a grassy hillock beside the road and tasted my spoils. Better than any feast the Riders had spread for their brides it was on the tongue—that bread pulled apart in ragged chunks, the cheese I crumbled in my fingers. The Hound rations had given me energy, but this food was more than that—it was life itself. After my first ravenous attack I curbed my appetite. Perhaps a second such raid could not be carried out and I must hoard my supplies.

A bird hopped out of the bushes to pick up crumbs, chirped at me as if asking for more. I dropped some bits to watch their reception. There was no doubt that the bird saw me, as had the fox, the squirrels, the other birds during my day's travel. Why then was I a wraith to those made in the form of humankind? Was it the other side of their defense? For now I was convinced that this coating of illusion was their defense.

Already the sun was well west. Night was coming and I must find some kind of shelter. Ahead I could see a darker patch which might mark a wood. Perhaps I should try to reach that.

I was so intent upon my goal that only gradually did I become aware of a change in the atmosphere about me. Whereas I had felt at ease and light of spirit all day, so now there was a kind of darkening which did not come from the fading of the day, but within me. I began to remember, in spite of my struggle to shut such mind pictures away, the terror of the night before, and all the other shocks of mind and body which had come upon me since I left the Dales. The openness of the land beyond the borders of the road no longer meant light and freedom, but plagued me with what might lie hidden in illusion.

Also—the sensation of being followed became so acute that I turned time and time again, sometimes pausing for minutes altogether, to survey what lay behind me. There were more birds fluttering and calling, doing so in increasing numbers along the verges of the road, or flying low about me. And I had an idea that things peered and spied from farther back.

So far this was no more than a kind of haunting uneasiness. But now I did not like the idea of night in this land. And the trees ahead which had promised shelter at my first thinking threatened now.

It was a wood of considerable size, spreading from north to south across the horizon. Almost did I decide to halt where I was, lie to rest on the

verge of the road apart from fields which could
hold so much more than I saw. But I did not—I
walked on.

These trees were leafed, though the green of
those leaves had a golden cast, particularly to be
marked along their rib divisions and their ser-
rated edges so that the effect of the woods was
not one of dark, but of light. The road continued
to run, though the verge vanished and boughs
hung across as if the trees strove to catch hands
above. It was narrower here, more like the track
in the heights. I dared not allow my thoughts to
stray in that direction.

There was a lot of rustling among those leaved
branches and around the roots of the trees.
Though I sighted squirrels, birds, another fox,
yet I was not satisfied as to an innocent cause for
all that activity. To me it was rather that I was
being carefully escorted by a woodland guard of
bird and beast—and not for my protection!

Though I kept watch for anything which
might promise shelter for the coming night, I
saw no place which tempted me to turn aside
from the road. And I had come to think it might
be well to settle in its center, hard though the
pavement promised to be, rather than trust to the
unknown under the trees.

It was then that the road split into two ways,
each as narrow as a foot path. In the center between those was a diamond shaped island of
earth on which was based a mound, following
the same outline as the portion of ground and
leveled on its top. Set equidistant down there
were three pillars of stone, that in the middle
being several hands' taller than the two flanking
it.

They bore no carving, no indication that they were aught but rocks, save that their setting was so plainly the work of man, or some intelligence, and not natural chance. Oddly, once I had sighted them much of my uneasiness fled. And, though the position was exposed, I was drawn to that earthy platform beneath the central pillar's long shadow.

Slowly I climbed and unrolled the rug, sitting on it so that I could pull the flaps up about me when I wished. The pillar was at my back and I leaned against its support, while before me stretched the road, uniting beyond the point of the islet, to run on and on, though it was hidden by the trees not too far away.

Once more I ate from the bounty the inn had supplied, far less than I wanted. I was thirsty and it was hard to chew the bread, but the cheese had a measure of moisture and went down more easily.

It was past sunset now. I pulled the rug about my shoulders. The voices of the wood were many, a kind of murmur which kept me straining to identify just one sound and so bring a measure of the familiar past to comfort me in this strange present. But sleep was heavy on me, a burden weighting my tired body.

I awoke in the dark, my heart pounding, my breath fast and gasping. Yet it was no dream terror that shook me into wakefulness. My head lay against the pillar's foot. There were streaks of moon on the road. But around me the light was very full and bright. Under its touch the pillars glowed silver.

Again I was as one blindfolded, stumbling about a room which held a treasure of great importance. Only I could not guess what that was. That I had unwittingly been drawn to a place of real power, I was sure. But the nature of that power—for good or ill—was past my reading.

There was no fear in me, just a kind of awe, a despair because I could not receive the messages which flowed about me, which might mean so much—

How long did I sit there, entranced, striving to break the bonds of my ignorance and reach out for riches, the nature of which I could not name?

Then it broke, failed. And another emotion swept in, a need for awareness, for being prepared— A warning which again I could not read past its general alerting.

Sound—the pound of hooves on the road. That did not come from behind, but from ahead. Someone rode toward me at reckless speed. Around my island the forest stirred. A multitude of small, unseen things fled away from the road and from me who they had been watching with set purpose.

Yet under my silver pillar no fear touched me . . . only the need to be ready, an expectancy. The rider must be very close—

Out into the moon came a horse, flecks of white foam on its chest and shoulders. The rider reined in so suddenly the animal reared, beat the air with forefeet.

A Were Rider!

The horse neighed and again beat with forefeet. But the rider had full mastery. Then I saw clearly the crest of his helm and I was on my feet, the rug falling from about me. It tripped my feet as I would have run to the end of the mound, and I kicked at its folds. I shook free. My hands were out as I called—called?—rather shouted:

"Herrel!"

He swung from the saddle, started to me, his cloak flung back, his head lifted so that his eyes might seek mine, or so I believed. But his face was still overshadowed by the helm.

# XIII BEAST INTO MAN

THIS WAS LIKE journeying down a dark way in the cold of a winter's night, making a turn, and seeing before one the open door of an inn from which streamed warmth and light, the promise of companionship with one's kind. So did I scramble down from the safety of my moonlit mound-island and run to meet him who had ridden in such haste.

"Herrel!" Even as I had called to him from the tent when I was for a short space that other Gillan, so did I now reach out to him, voice and hand—

But a swirl of that green light which was the Riders' mark coiled between us serpent-wise, threatening—and when it vanished—

I had seen the beast which had crouched on the ledge before it leaped to go hunting the Hounds of Alizon. But then I had not fronted it—only watched it in lithe action. Now beast eyes were on me, lips raised in a snarl over cruel fangs—and there was nothing left I could reach.

"Herrel!" I do not know why I named that name—the man had gone.

Stumbling I tried to back away as that long, silver furred shape stooped low to the ground in a threatening crouch and I knew that I looked upon death. The firm earth of the mound was hard behind my shoulders, but I dared not turn my back upon that death to climb to what small safety its summit might offer.

There was a knife at my belt, but my hand did

not go to it. This I could not meet with steel. Nor perhaps would my other weapon be any more than a reed countering a sword stroke. Still it was all I had left me.

Deep did I stare into those green eyes which now held nothing of man in them, were only alien pools of threat. Within the beast was still Herrel—hiding, submerged, yet there. Or else man could not rise again from cat. And if my will—my power—could find the hidden man, then perhaps I could draw him once more to the surface. For to front an angry man was far, far better than to be hunted by a beast.

—Herrel—Herrel— I besought him by mind rather than voice. —Herrel!

But there was no change, only a small, muted sound from that furred throat, of anticipation— hunger— And from that thought my mind recoiled sickened, and my will nearly broke. But I fought our battle as best I could.

Suddenly that round head with the ears flattened back against the skull arose a little and from the beast bubbled a yowl such as it had voiced before the Hound attack.

—Herrel!—

Its head waved from side to side. Then it shook it vigorously, as if to throw off some irritating touch. One paw, claws unsheathed was outstretched in the first step of a stealthy advance which could only end in a hunting spring.

—Man not beast—you are a man!—

I hurled that at him—or it. For now was leaving me the conviction that man did lie within the cat. This was its own land. What new power or source of power lay open to it here?

—Herrel!—

Long ago I had lost the talisman I had brought out of the Dales. I knew no power which might lie over this land to which I could raise voice in appeal—in protest—against this ghastly thing which was to pull me down. It is very daunting to stand alone with riven shield and broken sword as I did then.

I cried out—no longer his name—for what or who I had known as Herrel was gone as surely as if death had severed our worlds one from the other. I closed my eyes as my small power was swept away in a rush of hate. The beast sprang.

Pain raking along the arm which I had flung across my face in that last instant. A weight pinning me against the mound so that I might not move. I would not look upon what held me, I could not.

"Gillan! Gillan!"

A man's arms about me, surely—not the claws of a beast rending my flesh. A voice strained and hoarse with fear and pain, not the snarling of a cat.

"Gillan!"

I opened my eyes. His head was bent above me, and such was the agony in his face that I knew first a kind of wonder. Held me in a grip to leave bruises on my arms and back, and his breath came in small gasps.

"Gillan, what have I done?"

Then he swung me up as if my weight was nothing, and we were on the platform on the mound where the moon was very bright. I lying on my robe while, with a gentleness I had not thought in him, Herrel stretched out my arm. The torn cloth fell away in two great rents and revealed dripping furrows.

He gave a sharp cry when he saw them clearly, and then looked about him wildly, as if in search of something his will could summon to him.

"Herrel?"

Now his eyes met mine again and he nodded. "Yes, Herrel—now! May yellow rot eat their bones, and That Which Runs The Ridges feed upon their spirits! To have done this to you—to you! There are herbs in the forest—I will fetch—"

"In my bag there are also cures—" The pain was molten metal running up my arm, into my shoulder, heavy so that I could not breathe easily, and around me the moonlight swirled, the pillars nodded to and fro—I closed my eyes. I felt him pull the bag from beneath the rug and I tried to control my wits so that I might tell him how to use the balms within it. But then he laid hands upon my arm again and I cried out, to be utterly lost in depths where there was neither pain nor thought.

"Gillan! Gillan!"

I stirred, reluctant to leave the healing dark—yet that voice pulled at me.

"Gillan! By the Ash, the Maul, the Blade that rusteth never, by the Clear Moon, the Light of Neave, the blood I have shed to He Whose semblance I wear—" the murmur flowed over and around me, wove a net to draw me on out of the quiet in which I lay.

"Gillan, short grows the time— By the virtue of the Banebloom, and the Lash of Gorth, the Candles of the Weres—come you back!"

Loud were the words now, an imperative call I could not nay-say. I opened my eyes. Light about me, not that of day, but of green flames. A sweet scent filled my nostrils and the petals of flowers brushed my cheeks as I turned my head to see he who spoke. Herrel stood against a silver pillar, his body to the waist pale silver too, for he had stripped off mail and leather and was bare of skin to his belt—save that across his upper arms and shoulders were welts, angry, red, and on some of them stood beads of blood. Between his hands was a whip of branch broken in the middle.

"Herrel?"

He came quickly, fell to his knees beside me. His face was that of a man who has come from a battle field, gaunted by exhaustion, too worn to care whether he held victory in his hand, or must taste the sour of defeat. Yet when he looked down at me he came alive again. His hand came out as if to touch my cheek, then dropped upon his thigh.

"Gillan, how is it with you?"

I wet my lips. Far within me something was troubled, as if it had reached and been denied. I moved my arm; faint pain, the lingering memory of that agony which had rent me earlier. I sat up slowly. He made no move to aid me. There was a bandage about my arm and I smelled the sharp odor of a salve I knew well; so he had plundered my bag. But as I so moved a covering of flowers cascaded down my body, and with them leaves hastily torn into bits, from which came the scent of herbs. I had lain under a thick blanket of them.

Herrel made a gesture with his hand. The green lights snuffed out. Nor could I see from what they had sprung, for they left no sign of their source behind them.

"How is it with you?" he repeated.

"Well, I believe well—"

"Not wholly so. And the time—the time grows short!"

"What do you mean?" I gathered up a handful of that flowery covering, raised the bruised blossoms, the aromatic leaves to sniff them.

"You are two—"

"That I know," I broke in.

"But perhaps this you do not know. For a space one may be made two—though it is a mad and wicked thing. Then, if the two do not meet once again—one fades—"

"That other Gillan—will go?" The flower petals dropped from my hand, once more I felt that cold within me, that hunger which could not be appeased by any food taken into the mouth, swallowed by the throat.

"Or you!" His words were simple, yet for a moment the understanding of them was not mine. And he must have read that in my face, for now he got once more to his feet, brought down his bare fists against the side of the pillar as if he smashed into the face of an enemy.

"They—wrought this—thinking that you— this you—would die in the waste—or in the mountains. This land has mighty safeguards."

"That I know."

"They did not believe that you would live. And if you died, then would that Gillan they had summoned be whole—though not as you, save in a small part. But when you came into Arvon—they knew. They learned that a stranger troubled the land, and guessed that it was you. So they turned again to the power and—"

"Sent you—" I said softly when he did not continue.

He turned his head so that once more I could

read his face, and what lay there was not good to behold. There were no words in me which I could summon to assuage that wound as my balms and salves could have healed torn flesh for him.

"I told you—at our first meeting—I am not as they are. They can, if they wish, compell me, or blind my eyes, as they did when they brought forth that other Gillan who turned aside from me to welcome Halse—as he wished from the beginning!"

I shivered. Halse! Had that other me lain happily in Halse's arms, welcomed him? I put hands to my face, knowing shame like a devouring fire. No—no—

"But I am me—" I could not set my bewilderment into words clear enough even for my own understanding. "I have a body—am real—"

But was I? For in this land I was a wraith, as its people were wraiths to me. I ran my hand along that bandaged arm, welcoming the pain which followed touch, for it spelled the reality of the flesh which winced from finger pressure.

"You are you, she is also you—in part. As yet a far lighter and less powerful part. But, should you cease to exist, then she is whole, whole enough for Halse's purpose. They fear you, the Pack, because they can not control you as the others. Therefore they would make one by sorcery that they can."

"And if—if—"

Again he picked the thought from my mind. "If I had done as they intended and slain you? Then they would not have cared had I learned the full truth, once I had accomplished their purpose. They do not fear me in the least, and if I had done myself harm on discovery of the murder they set me to, well, that would have merely removed another trouble from their path. To their thinking this was a fine plan."

"But you did not kill."

There was no lighting of his face. Still he was as one who had fallen into Hounds hands and been subjected to their cruel usage.

"Look upon your arm, Gillan. No, I did not kill, but in this much did I serve their purpose. And should this hurt keep us from the road we must take, then I have done as commanded—"

"Why?"

"Time is our enemy, Gillan. The longer the twain of you are apart, so will you fail in strength—so finally you may not reach uniting in time. I speak thus that you may know what truly lies before us, for I do not believe that you are one to be soothed with fair words and kept in ignorance."

Perhaps he paid me a compliment in that judging. I do not know. Only then I wished that he had not thought so highly of my courage, for I was shaken, though I tried not to let him know it.

"I think," I tried to push aside fear for a space and think on other things, "that you are more than you believe—or they give you credit for being. Why did you not carry through this geas they set upon you? I have heard, by legend, that a geas is a thing of great power, not lightly broken."

Herrel came away from the pillar, stooped and took up from the ground a shirt which he drew on over his welted shoulders.

"Do not credit me with any great thing, Gillan. I give thanks to the forces above us, that I

awakened from their spell in time. Or that you
awoke me—since your voice came to me in that
darkness where they had me bound. If you believe you can ride, then we must be gone. To
catch up with the pack is what we need to do—"

He donned leather under-jerkin and then his
mail, belting it about him. But when he picked
up his helm he stood for a long moment, staring
down upon the snarling cat crest and his eyes
were hooded as if he looked upon that which he
would like to thrust from him. However, after
that short pause he put it on his head.

Then he turned to me, aiding me to my feet,
putting about my shoulders not the heavy rug,
but his own cloak. Then he half led, half carried
me from the mound.

The moonlight was waning; it must not be far
from dawn. Herrel whistled and his horse came
to us, snorting a little, glancing from side to side,
as if it perceived more lurking in the forest
shadows than we could see. Yet Herrel displayed no interest in the woodland. He lifted me
to the saddle and then mounted behind me. The
stallion showed no distaste for a double burden
but set off at a steady, ground covering pace.

"I do not understand," I began. Herrel's arms
were about me warm and safe, the mail of his
sleeves not harsh to the touch but rather reassuring in its rigidity. "I do not understand why
Halse wanted me. Was it because his pride suf-
fered when you fared well and he went bride-
less?"

"It may have begun so," he answered me. "But
there was another reason, which came because
you are you, and no maid of the Dales. From the
first, the rest were one with those whose cloaks

they wore in spell. You were not held so. They feared that. There was a chance, a last chance to bind you to us. When that failed, then you were open to what they would do."

"A chance—?"

His voice was low, and I was glad he was behind me, that he did not see my confusion when he made answer.

"That night in the Safekeep, you refused me. Had it been otherwise, then all their spells could not have prevailed."

I broke the silence which followed. "Then you named me witch, Herrel. Was that out of anger—or out of knowledge?"

"Anger? What right had I to anger? I do not take by force that which one chooses to withhold from me—for such must be freely given and in liking, or it has no meaning, not in my sight, nor that of Neave. I named you as what I think you are. Being so—you could do no else than say me nay—"

"Witch," I repeated thoughtfully. "But I am not learned in aught but healing lore, Herrel. That is a craft, yes, but owes nothing to sorcery. Had I been what you named me, then never could I have dwelt at the Abbey-stead. They would have expelled me within an hour of my coming. The Flames and sorcery had naught to do with one another, and the Dames of the Abbey-stead would have thought themselves defiled by my presence."

"Witchery is not the evil the Dalesmen think. There are those of another blood who are born to it. Lessoned in its use they must be, but the power over wind and water, earth and fire, is theirs by natural gift and not just from study. In the old days Arvon was not walled against the rest of the world. For all men then had touch with powers which lay not in their strength of arm, nor their minds, save as their minds could control such forces. We knew of other nations over seas which also used sorcery as a way of life. There was one wherein witches walked. And when we rode the waste, still we heard of that land, or what had come from its dwindling, for as Arvon, it had aged. There are witches still in Estcarp and with them Alizon wars."

"You think then I am of this witchblood?"

"True. You have not the lessoning, but within you lies the force. And there is this. They believe that a witch who gives her body to a man must put aside her witchhood."

"If they never do, then how does their nation survive?"

"It dwindles amain by report. Also, this was not always true. It followed when some blight fell upon them long ago. Not all women of that land are witches, though they may mother daughters with the power. But she who has it is not wont to put it aside."

"But I have had no lessoning. I am not truly witch."

"If the power is in you, then it will strive to make you a proper vessel for its encompassing."

"And the other Gillan?"

"The Gillan they try to fashion is not witch. They would not take such a threat among them."

With each measured word Herrel sent me farther and farther into my own waste of exile. Would there ever be any rate for my return?

"Herrel—when I was with that other Gillan for

a space—in the tent—and called to you—you knew me?"

"I knew—and learned then what had happened."

"They dragged you away—then Halse sent me out of her."

"Yes."

"Would you have come searching for me, even if they had not sent you under geas?"

"I am not greater than the pack." It seemed to me that he wished to evade my question. "I came—to their bidding."

I had never been good at the understanding of people, the weighing of any emotions other than my own. Still, at this moment, was granted me a small flash of insight as profound, perhaps, as that any witch in the glory of full power could gain.

"You came because they could use your wish to lay the geas. Had there been no—no tie between us, then perhaps their bidding would not have sent you—"

I heard a sharp sound, or else a breath drawn in pain.

"Also, it was because of your thought of me that you broke that geas, Herrel! Remember that. For never have I heard of a man breaking a geas set in earnest spell—"

"What have you heard," he demanded harshly, "save what lies in song and legend? The Dalesmen spin tales, and in them the kernel of truth is very small and hid. Do not find in me any virtue that I did not kill you to their bidding. I know well my shame—"

"Too long—" I put out my hands, resting them

on his where he held the reins before my waist, "too long have you accepted a lesser naming, Herrel. Remember, I came to your cloak, when those others laughed to see you leave it. Through their clouds of sorcery, ill meant, have we broken thus far. You have not failed in battle, or you would not have continued to ride with the Pack." I paused, but he said nothing, so I continued:

"An arrow shaft alone can be broken between a man's two hands by small effort. Set two arrows together and the task is less easy. All my life I have walked alone, an onlooker of the lives of others. So perhaps have you. But do not tell me that you are less than Halse, or Harl, or Hyron. That I do not believe!"

"Why did you pick up my cloak?" he asked abruptly.

"Not because it lay the nearest, or because I saw it of great beauty. For, remember, I saw it as it was. But because when my eyes fell upon it, I could not turn aside, or do aught else than gather it up." The mailed arms about me tightened, and relaxed.

"This then—this much I did!"

"And the spell you laid, Herrel, must have been greater than the others, for I saw beneath the illusion. And you as you are—"

"Did you?" The momentary elation was gone from his voice. "Are you sure that you did not rather see the truth this night? Halse showed it you once in your very bed—"

"Truth may be not a sword with only two sides to the blade, so you look upon one and then the other. Rather it is like a faceted jewel with many faces. You may think you know one well, and another; then you discover a third, a fourth. Still they are all truth, or truths. I have seen you as illusion would make you for a bride's beglamoured eyes, as a Were Rider from the waste, as the beast— And I think perhaps there are still more Herrels I have not met. But it was Herrel's cloak which brought me here and I have no regrets of that choice."

Again he made no answer for what seemed a long time. Around us the gray light grew stronger; we were coming into the new day, although in the wood the transition from dark to light might be delayed. The stallion held to his steady trot, now looking forward as if he, too, sensed the need for reaching some goal with as little delay as possible.

"You build too high on a hope—" Herrel might have been speaking to himself rather than to me. "However we only live by hope and mine hitherto has been a poor, weak thing. But, Gillan, listen to me—the worst is not now behind us— rather does it lie ahead. Their geas is broken, but they have that Gillan of their fashioning. And we must get her forth from them. To do that the Riders have to be faced—in one guise or another."

"Will they meet us as beasts?"

"You they can face so. With me, no—to me they must give Pack right—if I have my chance to demand it."

"Pack right?"

"I may demand to meet Halse sword point to sword point in Right and Judgment—since he has taken the other Gillan. And with you at hand I have proof of that."

"And if you win?"

"If I win, then I can demand repartment from Halse—perhaps of the rest. But they will do all they can to keep me from such a challenge. And here in Arvon they can bend much to their will. From this hour on we ride in danger. I know not what they may send against us. Were it otherwise we would ride for the border, but without that other Gillan that would bring you naught but ill."

We came out of the woods at last, but the level meadow lands through which the road had led me before now gave way to rolling country, not too unlike the Dales, though perhaps their rises and valleys were not as steep. A bird flew from nowhere to hang above us.

I heard Herrel laugh shortly. "They are well served—"

"It means us some harm?" I questioned. The bird was small, rusty brown, unlike any hawk or winged instrument of war.

"In this much, it watches our path. But they need not keep such a check upon us. There is only this road for us."

He called aloud in another tongue, that, I believe, of the wraith people. The bird swooped as if to fly at our heads, veered, and shot away into the morning sky.

## XIV THE SHADOWED ROAD

"HAS THIS LAND of yours no water?" I ran tongue over dry lips. "Also, one of humankind can not live on hope and words alone—there needs must be bread and meat—"

"Ahead—" his answer was one curt word where I had attempted to make my complaint light. Broken as the land about us was, yet did it seem empty of all but us and the birds. But the meadows had not been empty yesterday, save to the outer sight. And mayhap Herrel saw more here than I did. That I must know.

"Herrel—is this land empty as I see it under the illusion, or is it inhabited?"

"Under the illusion—how so?" He sounded genuinely perplexed, so I told him of the manor and the village, and how I had run from there because I believe I had been detected, if not really seen.

"This man in the inn room, of what manner was he?" Out of all my story Herrel caught upon that first.

From memory I tried to build a picture of him. When I had done I ended with a question: "Who was—is—he? And how could he have known I was there?"

"He was of the Border Guard by your description. As such he is sensitive, one trained to the ferreting out of any invader. Hard though the way into Arvon may be, still through time men have come into these lands unknowing. For the most part the illusion holds, they see naught but the road, or some ruins. And they are worked upon by threats to the spirit which gives them a dislike of the place, so they pass through. But when you sought the inn, the guard would know an alien presence was there, and that it was aware of more than an empty land. That was why the alarm went forth. You after kept to the road, which was your safety—had you known it—"

"Why can I see only the illusion, save when I call upon my power?"

"You entered not by the gate, but by the mountain." Again his arm tightened about me. "And those are filled with many entrapments. How you came safely by all those snares, that is also magic—yours. Tell me, what of that road, and how did you find it?"

So I went back to my awaking in the deserted camp and when I spoke of the coming of the Hounds, then did I hear his breath quicken with a sound like unto a cat's hiss of anger. I told of the vial and the way I freed it from my bag and there he interrupted:

"True witchery! There is no denying your gift. Had you the proper lessoning in it then—"

"Then what?"

"I do not know, it is not our sorcery. But I think in some ways you might challenge the whole Pack and come off unscathed. So you left those dogs of Alizon asleep in the snow. Let us hope that winter cold made that sleep death! But the Gate was closed—spell laid and bound again—so how found you another way?"

"Up and over the heights—" I told him of that climb, of my blind struggle with the shifting stones.

"Those were the ruins of Car Re Dogan—

reared by wizardy to be a fortress against the evil which once roamed the waste and which is long since gone. You found a very ancient way, one our race has not trode for half a thousand of Dale years."

I spoke of the barrier of light and its overthrow, and then of my coming into the places of the Guardians.

"The Setting Up of the Kings," Herrel identified for me. "They were the rulers of an elder age. When we first came to Arvon those of that blood were very few, but we mingled with them and took from them some customs which had merit. Thus they did use their kings when each died in turn. So was he buried, standing, allowed to look out upon the world. And should his successor need good council he went thither and abode for a night, waiting to hear that wisdom, or to dream it. Also they were ensorcelled to guard this land."

"I felt that I was weighed, yet they passed me through—"

"Because they knew the kinship of your power. But—" Herrel's voice was troubled, "if you came that way, there are other and far worse dangers to be faced—"

I could not repress a shiver. "Yes, one of them I saw—or saw in part." And I told him of that noisome, clouded thing which passed me in the night.

"That which Runs The Ridges—! Gillan, Gillan, you have such fortune cloaking you as I have not heard of before! That you survived even so chance a meeting as that! It can not come into our fields, but it is death such as no living thing should ever meet."

"The rest you know—" Suddenly I was very tired. "Herrel, where is this drink you promised me? It seems an age since I had aught to even wet my lips."

"For once I may give you what you wish as you wish it." He swung the horse off the road and we came to a small shallow stream bubbling along over a pebbled bed. The very sound of that water increased my thirst, so that I wanted nothing more than to plunge head and arms into it, lap at its surface as a dog might lap. But when Herrel aided me down from the saddle I was almost too weak and tired to move.

He brought me to the water's edge and took a small horn cup from his belt pouch, filling it and lifting it to my lips.

"It would seem that I need this and food greatly," I commented when I had drunk my fill. "I am as one emptied—"

"For that also there is an answer." But I thought that he spoke too briskly and avoided my eyes.

"You said that you believed I was one who could listen to the truth, Herrel. It is more than need of food and drink which makes me thus weak, is that not so?"

"I said that time was our enemy. By now they know that I failed them. Now they draw on your life substance to feed their Gillan. They can not slay so, but they can weaken, and so slow your searching, until it is too late."

I looked down at my hands. They were trembling a little, and I could not, by will or muscle, control that tremor. But—

"Fear is also a weapon they may use, my fear."

I do not know whether I meant that as a question or a statement, but he answered me.

"Yes. In any way they may shake your confidence, or your spirit, by that much do they profit."

I returned then to the question I had asked earlier. "Is this an empty land through which we ride, or has it those living here who can be roused against us?"

"It is not as populated as the plains beyond the forest. There are scattered keeps and manors. As to their being set against us—had you been alone they would have mustered against you at the bidding of the Border Guard. Now that you are with me they are willing to let it be a personal thing with the Were Riders."

"But you said we ride a dangerous way—"

"The Riders will rouse what they may to front us."

"I had thought Arvon was a fair and smiling land, without peril."

Herrel smiled a wry smile. "Alas, my lady, one remembers, when one is far apart from one's beloved, only the fairness of her face, the sweetness of her words. Long were we severed from Arvon and our small memories were of her smiling face, which was what we wished most to recall. All lands hold both good and evil. In the Dales of High Hallack such good and evil is born from the deeds of men or nature. In Arvon it may be born from sorcery and learning. I told you once—we rode in exile because we were deemed disturbing factors, like to bring dissension into seeming peace. But that was not altogether so— though we were made to remember it thus. There

have been struggles for power here, too—though
sometimes fought with more fearsome weapons
than sword blade and arrow head or even those
Alizon arms which spit killing fire. We rode in
exile because we had supported lords who went
down to defeat in one of those ancient battles.
And then the memory that exile was of our own
unworthiness was fostered upon us. As there
was a treaty we were allowed our time of
grace to apply at the Gate—and it was opened
to us.

"That war which sent us riding into the waste
is long since done and gone. There are new rulers in Arvon. But also were forces loosed then
which are neither truly good nor ill, but which
can be moulded for the service of either. These
can be commanded by the Riders working
together—"

"Rulers!" I interrupted him. "Herrel, is there
no law which runs in Arvon? Can one appeal to
no overlord for justice?"

He shook his head. "The Riders are without
the law, and you are also an outsider. We have
taken no oath-service. They can not deny us Arvon, for that is our birthright and the terms of the
treaty have been fulfilled. In time the Riders will
take service, with some one of the Seven Lords.
Now no man can move against them as long as
their targets are of their own company—me—
and you, an alien from the Dales. There is
nothing for us save what lies here—" he spread
out his hands, "or here." He tapped his forehead.

Out of his saddle bags Herrel brought food and
we ate. For a little that revived me and I walked
along the stream feeling strength and life rise in
me. So I believed that Herrel could not be sure

they were draining me to build their Gillan the
stronger.

"Have you no kin here, Herrel?" I asked. "You
could not always have been a Rider. Were you
never a child with a home, mother, father,
perhaps brothern?"

He had put aside the cat-crested helm, was
kneeling by the brook laving his face with water
in his cupped hands.

"Kin? Oh, yes, I suppose I have kin—if time
and change have spared them. You have set
finger on my difference, Gillan. Just as you are
not Dale brood, but were fostered so, I am not
wholly Were strain. My mother was of the House
of Car Do Prawn—their hall lies to the north—
or did. She fell under the love spell of a Rider and
came to him across the hills. Her father paid
sword ransome to take her back, and I do not
know whether that was by her will or no. When
she came to child bed her son was accepted as of
her blood. Then, when I was very young—I
shape changed—perhaps I was angered, or
frightened—but it made my inheritance plain to
read—I was Rider rather than Redmantle. So
they sent me to the Gray Towers. But still was I
half blood and so not truly of the Riders either.
Thus my father in time liked me as little as did
those of Car Do Prawn. On this day I can claim no
aid from Redmantle clans."

"But your mother—"

He shrugged and shook the water drops from
his hand. "Her name I know—the Lady Eldris—
and that is all. As for my father," he stood up, his
face averted from me, "he was—is—among
those who have set this ill upon us. It has hum-
bled his pride that he has only a half-son."

"Herrel—" I came to him, put my hand into his. And when he would not tighten the grasp then did I, but still he kept his face turned from me, and I did not try to do more than I had done.

"Well and well," I said at last. "Since we have naught but ourselves, then that must do—" But my words were far lighter than my thoughts and did nothing to dampen my growing fear.

Herrel whistled to the stallion and the horse trotted to him. He put on saddle and bridle and then looked to me, his eyes remote, withdrawn.

"It is time to ride."

We returned to the road. Now it wound through steadily rising dale hills. At last I broke the silence between us to ask:

"You spoke of the Gray Towers. Are they the home of the Riders? Do they return there now?"

"Yes. And it is needful we reach them before they enter the Towers. In the open we have a small chance. To follow them into the Towers is hopeless folly, for there the very stones are steeped in sorcery they can draw upon for aid."

"How far?"

"We are perhaps half a day behind them. They may send on the women, wait for us—"

"Send on the women! If they send Gillan—"

"Yes!" His interruption and the tone of his voice was enough. I had put into words one of his own sharp fears.

"Herrel, can I will myself into the Gillan and so somehow delay them?"

"No! They will be watching her with great care. They would know and when they did— then they would have what they want. This time they would not drive you forth, they would bind you—to become the Gillan they wish."

There was movement behind a bush some paces ahead. I noted the horse's ears a-prick.

"Herrel!" I hardly breathed that.

"I see," his whispered answer was a faint. "This may be their first move. Hold well your seat."

Though Herrel gave no signal I could detect, the horse quickened pace. We came even with the bush. There reared out of it such a creature as might have sprung from some legend. Not furred, but scaled, still also in its body shape like unto a giant wolf-thing, with a kind of mane of stiffened spines across its head and down its shoulders. At the same time it reached for us, horse and riders, Herrel kicked out, striking aside its taloned paw. The thing squalled.

Scales melted into skin. Now I saw not a reptilian monster but a small brown creature a third its size raising a head which was a travesty of human with eyes in it which held no intelligence, only brute anger and ferocity. It was worse in a way than the illusion it—or others— had used to clothe it. I cried out, but I did not move in the saddle.

Herrel flailed down at the thing, using his sword flat bladed to beat, rather then edged to cut. It crouched back, slavering its rage. He shouted words which cowered it more than his blows, and it scuttled back into the bush.

"Wait." Herrel slipped from the horse. Sword in hand, he went towards the brush in which the brown thing had vanished. Just before this bolt hole he drove the sword point down into the earth and rested his two hands upon its hilt, right over-lapping left as he spoke again in that other tongue, this time sing-songing the words until they made the pattern of a chant. Having so done, he pulled free his sword and, using the tip as a writing tool, he drew symbols in the dust of the road behind us and along both sides for a space of several feet.

"What was it?" I asked as he returned to me.

"A wenzal. One alone is no great danger. But where one sniffs, more follow, and in a pack they are no foe to be smiled upon."

"Those marks—" I pointed to those he had traced in the dust.

"To murk our trail. That scout will seek out his kind. They will up the hunt."

"Are they of those whom you spoke—neither good nor ill, but able tool to either?"

I heard him laugh. "You listen well, my lady. No, the wenzal is wholly ill, but it is also cowardly, and it can be routed by knowing the right weapon with which to face it. Usually it comes not down from its high places. Mayhap it was intended for a guardian thing, made to be a lock upon our borders. If so, it was marred in the making, for it turns against all comers."

"Then it might be here only by chance—" I ventured.

Again I heard his laughter, but this time with less amusement in it. "This far from the border? No, the wenzal is not that great a traveler. And, as I said, it is a coward, keeping well away from Arvon's core lands. If a pack runs here now, they have been summoned."

"They must know that you have a defense against them—"

"Against one wenzal, or even five perhaps— against a full pack that is another matter. These creatures gain courage from numbers and their rage feeds in proportion to their company. When that rage reaches a certain point, then they care for nothing—save the overwhelming of the enemy. And stopping them at that moment is far beyond a single sword or any small sorcery I possess."

"There is also this," he added as he took up the reins once again. "Each small delay works to the Riders' favor." Then he fell silent. Perhaps he strove to see with the mind's eyes what new plague they could send upon us. But I had other thoughts.

As I had the day before I began to try to break the illusion, searching the ground before us. And so I was rewarded my marking a mist-walled keep backed against the dale hill side. But try as I would, I could not deepen nor darken its outlines. It would not become solid in my sight. That worried me, for I guessed that my power was lessening. Was it true that the other Gillan grew the stronger on what she drew from me?

"Herrel," I broke the silence. "When we come to that other"—I would not allow myself to say 'if'—"then what happens? How do two become one again?"

He did not answer at once.

"How?" I demanded with more heat. "Can it ever be so? Or is that one truth you have decided to spare me?"

"It can be so, but as to the doing, that I am not sure. It may be that, once face to face, you will be drawn to one another as a magnet reaches for iron. I only am sure of this, apart there is grave danger which increases every moment. And because they have *her*, you are the one under most threat."

"If I only knew more!" Once again I knew that old frustration. "To be half-witch—that is to be already half defeated!"

"Do I not know—" he answered out of his own bitterness. "Hold this in mind—they strive to make you less than half. Had we but time we would ride to the Fane of Neave, but that is half the land away and there is not that much time left us."

"Who is this Neave that he or she has power you may look to?"

"Neave is—no, I can not put name, a single name, to Neave. The wind blows, the rain falls, the earth is fertile and brings forth fruit—and behind that fruitfulness stands that which is Neave. Man seeks maid and she does not deny him, bearing other fruit in turn, and Neave is there also. Neave works not against the natural order of things, but with them. The beginning of life, its natural ending, is Neave's. War sorcery, evil sorcery done for ill purposes—can not exist in the Fane of Neave; only that which nourishes and abides. I could not enter that fane—but you could and perhaps be safe—though of that I am not sure."

"But you are not evil!"

"I am Were—and so against the true course of nature. My kind may not ride in the deep dark, but we go overshadowed through our lives. Our sun has many clouds."

"I hazard you call upon Neave—in the night—"

I could feel the sudden tension of his body through those encircling arms.

"At such times men call upon each and every Power they may know. But I am not Neave's leigeman. I would not be accepted."

So I had been led away from the question he could not answer, whether I might ever be whole again, even if I met face to face that Gillan Halse wooed. It was another fear I must keep at bay by thinking only of the here and now and not of that which lay yet to come.

"You have no plan, except to overtake them?"

"I have a plan, if by nightfall we reach a certain stage on this journey. But only a plan of shadow—not yet of any substance."

I did not press him. Instead I watched for more habitations in the hills and thought that, in the afternoon, I saw a second ghostly collection of walls and roofs. Only this time my second vision was even fainter.

We came to where the road split again about one of those earth mounds. This bore a single pillar at its center and Herrel drew rein beside it.

"Off with you and up." He helped me to dismount. "Swear you will remain at that pillar's foot until I come again. That is a place of safety for you."

I caught at his sleeve. "Where do you go?"

"To find that which I must have to aid us this night. But remember—at the pillar foot you are safe. These are spell encircled and only that which is harmless and of good meaning can so abide."

I obeyed, climbing to the top of that earthen platform. Again that weakness was upon me, and the effort I expended left me spent, willing to drop at the foot of the pillar. Herrel had left the road and rode along the land. Now and then he dismounted to look at what seemed to me to be the protruding roots of long buried trees, where soil had washed away to show the gnarled wood. Perhaps this had once been a forested place, but the trees still growing were small of girth and widely scattered. These, too, he studied, but from the saddle. And at last it was under one that he set to digging with his sword. He hacked at what he had uncovered, and then gathered up a bundle of what he had unearthed and cut up. Bearing this before him, he rode back to me.

At the forefront of the mound he dumped his harvest and I could see they were indeed roots or parts of roots, crumbling with age but with yet a core of hardness. Three times he dug, hacked, and brought that ancient wood, until he had a pile of pieces which, with care, he built into a conical heap. This done, he climbed to join me, bringing the saddle bags with food and the bottle he had filled from brook water.

"What do you with that?" I gestured to the wood pile.

"That will at least reveal the nature of the peril which may creep upon us at moon rise. I think Halse will force the issue. He has never counted patience among any small store of virtues he possesses. But we do not need to watch until dark closes in. Sleep now if you can, Gillan. The night may be long and without rest for us when it comes."

## XV  HERREL'S CHALLENGE

AFTER A LONG space I spoke. "There is no sleep this night for me, Herrel. Tell me what you would do. To be warned by scout horn is to have shield on arm before the foes arrive."

His head turned. Though the upper part of his face was shadowed by his helm, I could see his mouth and chin. He smiled.

"Well do you speak in the terms of war and battle, Gillan. You are a shield mate and sword companion as good as any man could wish. This then is what I would do—I wait not their will, their choice of the hour and field for battle—I summon them to mine! At moonrise I shall set fire to that root heap there—and they will be drawn—"

"More sorcery?"

Now he laughed. "More sorcery. It is laid upon us that our true nature is revealed and we are drawn to flames which dance from wood as old as we. A thousand dale years—even so long a span of time would not suffice to hold a Were from answer if you found a tree of his age. I do not think they will expect me to challenge them even this far. They will believe I shall be content to leave well enough alone—live so on some scrap of hope. For if I summon them thus, then I must be prepared to meet them with full power and array—"

"And you believe this possible?" I could not stifle that question. I must have his reply.

"Fortune will rule the field this night, Gillan. I

do not know what shape they will wear, but if I can name Halse, throw him sword challenge, then they must allow me that right. So can I bargain—"

So many chances and so little assurance that any would be the right ones. But Herrel knew the Pack and this land. He would not choose so reckless a course unless he saw no other way. I could find no protest which was right and proper for me to offer.

"Herrel, it was to me that they did this thing—have I no right of challenge in my turn?"

He had drawn his sword, and it rested across his knee. Now he ran one finger tip down the blade from hilt to point. After a long moment he raised that weapon and held it out, hilt first, to me.

"There is a custom—but it puts a heavy burden on you—"

"Tell me!"

"If you can give a shape changer his name in the firelight, then he must take man's form again. Whereupon you may demand blood right from him and name me your champion. But if you speak the wrong name to him whom you so challenge, then you are his to claim."

"What difference might my success mean?"

"It would give you the right to set the stakes—that other Gillan. If I challenge there is an equal chance they could deem this Pack quarrel only, with no stakes other than life or disgrace."

"Do you think I might not name Halse? He is a bear."

"The beasts you have seen are not the only shapes we may take upon occasion, only those which are the most familiar. And at such a test as this he would not show as bear."

"But you could warn me—"

Herrel was already shaking his head. "That I could not, by word, or gesture, or even by thought! The naming would be only yours and on you the burden of its success or failure. If you stand out before them, holding this sword, then you will be the challenger."

"I have the true sight. Have I not proved that?"

"How well does it serve you now?" he countered.

I remembered the mist-halls I had seen in the afternoon and my feeling that the power ebbed.

"This afternoon—I tried to see—" I was not really aware I had spoken that aloud, but Herrel drew the sword out of my reach.

"It is too great a risk. I shall challenge by Pack right and bargain as I can—"

He sounded decisive but still my mind played with what he had told me, and I leaned back against the pillar, running my hands along its age pitted stone. My sight, if I could but regain that illusion-breaking sight only for the few moments needed for the naming of true names! Up and down the stone my fingers moved, around and around in my mind thoughts spun, seeking some solution. There were herbs in my simple bag which cleared the head, sharpened the senses—as well as those which cured wounds and illnesses. My bandaged arm moved now without pain. Surely there must be some way to strengthen my inner power for as long as was necessary. If I only *knew!*

"Herrel—the healer's bag, please fetch it."

To expend even so much effort as to hunt for it would endanger what I would try.

"What—?"

"Bring it hither! How long have we before they come?"

He moved slowly, gazing at me over his shoulder as if he would have out of my mind what I planned. But he brought the bag and laid it in my lap.

"I do not know. I light the fire at moonrise—then we wait."

But that would not do—I must have a better idea of time. My fingers released the latching of the bag. I searched within for a small bottle cut and hollowed from a prism of quartz.

"What do you plan?"

I opened my fingers. Even in this shadow light the prism seemed to glow.

"Have you ever heard of moly, my lord?"

His breath caught in a half gasp. "Where got you that?"

"From an herb garden. Dame Alousan used it. Not because she would work sorcery, but because it has the power to soothe those who have come under the ill-looking of witchery. Though I do not remember that she used it save twice since witchery is not practiced in the Dales. The last time," I smiled, "was for a man-at-arms who claimed he had been ill-looked by a Were Rider, and so lay with no life in his limbs. Whether it was only an illness born of his fear, or true sorcery, I do not know. But he walked again after he had a few drops of this in his ale for three days. However, it has by legend another property. It can break illusion."

"But you do not know who will come—or which to try it on—"

"That is not needful. It is my illusions which I must break. But I dare not use it too soon. And neither do I know how long it takes these drops to work. If I choose the time wrongly I may be either clear-sighted too soon, or too late. Therefore if you can give me warning—"

"It is a great risk—"

"All we strive to do this night is by chance, good or ill. Herrel, will not this be better?"

"And if you fail?"

"To see ever the cloud and not the sun is to woefully and willingly blind oneself. But can you give me warning—?"

"This much. I can tell you that they come before I sight them. For I, too, will experience the drawing, and will know how strong it grows."

With that I must be content. But as I enfolded the prism in my sweat-dampened palm, I knew how small a warning I must depend upon.

"Herrel, 'til the moon rises, tell me of this Arvon of yours. Not as it threatens us now, but as it might be."

And he told me—unrolling his country before me, with its strange people, its grandeur and might, its dark places. To everyone the hills and plains of their homeland have a beauty and color beyond the rest of the world. More is this the truth when one has been in exile. But still the Arvon which came alive to me in Herrel's words was a country fair beyond the sparsely inhabited, war torn Dales of High Hallack, and like unto a nation—time-set and sunk, that is true— yet mighty.

Though they all, those who dwelt in Arvon, shared in some use of magic and that which can not be weighed or measured and of which only the results may be seen, yet that varied in degree and kind. There were adepts who dwelt apart, wrapt in their studies of other times and worlds which touched ours only momentarily at intervals, and who were now scarsely even of human seeming. On the other hand the people of the manors, the four clans, Redmantle, Goldmantle, Bluemantle, Silvermantle, worked sorcery very little, and, save for their very long lives, they were close akin to humankind. Between those two extremes ranged a number of alien folk—the Were Riders, those who tended the Fanes of personified Powers and Forces, a race which lived in rivers and lakes, one which chose not to be too far parted from woods and forests, and some that were wholly animal in form, yet with an intelligence which set them apart from any animal the outer world knew.

"It would appear," I said, "that there are so many marvels in this Arvon of yours one could ride forever, looking, listening, and still never come to the end of them!"

"As I have come to the end of this telling?" Herrel got to his feet and slid down the mound to the side of the piled tree roots. Then I saw that a silver moon was rising. He touched sword point into the heart of the wood and a small green spark broke from the meeting of steel and wood.

They did not leap, those flames, rather did the wood smolder contrarily, as if it had no wish to be summoned from ancient sleep, to die in ashes. Thrice did Herrel thrust with his sword, each time the point going more deeply into the pile.

Then flames did crawl reluctantly to the air and there arose a smoke which thinned into a gray-white column.

I closed my hand so tightly upon the prism which held the distilled moly that the edges of the crystal cut into my flesh. Already I had loosed the stopper, but I kept my thumb upon it, making sure I would spill none.

Herrel raised his head high. His eyes were glittering green, shadows swept across his face, and vanished, only to return. But the alien shape did not take possession of him as he stood there, naked sword bright in his hand. At last he turned his head and spoke to me. His speech was no longer quite human words, but I understood.

"They are drawn—"

I stood up, away from the pillar. He did not move to aid me down from the mound, it was as if he were held prisoner there. But I came to him and held out my right hand, the left still grasping tight the prism.

"Your sword, champion."

Herrel moved stiffly, as one who fought some force, to hand me that blade. So we waited by the fire. The moon lighted the road, but nothing moved along it that I could see. After a while Herrel spoke again—sounding as if he stood afar from me and not within touching distance.

"They are coming."

How near, how far? When must I put on such armor as a few drops of golden liquid would give me? I thumbed the stopper out, held the prism to my lips.

"They are swift—"

I drank. It was acrid on my tongue, unpleasant. I swallowed quickly. The road was no longer

empty. Beast and bird did not lope or fly as I had
expected, in spite of Herrel's warning, but a multitude of shapes, ever changing— A mounted
warrior who dropped to be a belly crawling
thing out of nightmare. A scaled dragon who
rose to be a man, but one with wings upon his
shoulders and the face of a demon. Ever
changing—I realized I had been over-confident.
How could I find Halse in all this throng mock-
ing me with their disguises? If the moly did not
aid my undersight then, indeed, were we defeated before we ever did battle. I strove to fasten
upon one figure, any figure in that weaving of
disolving and reassembling forms. And then—

From the hand which gripped the hilt of Herrel's sword sprang runnels of blue fire, dripping
down the blade. And I saw—

There was a web of changing forms, behind
which was a company of man-like beings, con-
centrating upon holding the sorcery screen they
had wrought.

"I challenge you!" Though I knew not the
words of custom, I spoke those which came
naturally.

"All or one?"

Did that buzz in my ears, formed by no man-
voice? Or was it only a thought answer which
came so to me?

"One, letting all rest upon that."

"And what is 'all?' "

"My other self, sorcerers!"

Grimly I held to the undersight. Halse, yes, I
had found Halse—to the fore and left of where I
stood.

"Do you name names, witch?"

"I name names."

"Agreed."

"Agreed in all?" I pressed.

"In all."

"Then," I pointed with the sword to Halse, "do I name among you Halse!"

There was a greater weaving of their shadow disguises, a rippling— Then it vanished and we stood facing men.

"You have named a name rightly," Hyron stood forth. "How do you challenge now?"

"Not mine this challenge. It is another's right, all resting upon it." My hand slid from hilt to blade. I passed the sword to Herrel so that his fingers could grasp the hilt and he took it from me eagerly.

"So be it!" Hyron spoke as if he pronounced a doom, and clearly he meant that doom to rest upon us and not those in his company. "Pack custom?" That he asked of Herrel.

"Pack custom."

Men moved swiftly. Hyron took the cloak from his shoulders, laid its glossy horsehide lining down upon the pavement of the road, its dun-gray surface uppermost. Harl and three of the others doffed their helms, set one on each corner of the cloak, their crests facing inward.

Some feet beyond the edge of the cloak men set up four swords, points wedged well to hold them upright, and other cloaks, rolled rope fashion, were laid to connect each, forming a square.

Halse put aside his cloak and the baldric of his sword. He stepped now onto Hyron's cloak and Herrel moved to face him. Halse smiled as I had seen him do and hated him for—as one who has only to stretch out his hand to take what he wants, no one saying him nay.

"So she has more power than we thought, Wrong-hand. But she has made her mistake now—in choosing a sword and you to wield it."

Herrel did not answer, and there was no expression on his face. Rather did he watch Hyron who had moved into the center of the cloak between the two fighters.

"This is the field. You will match swords until blood flows, or one or the other of you be driven over the battle line. By moving so only one foot, it will be deemed he who does so had fled—and full right yielded to the other."

Then he turned his head and looked to me. "Should your champion lose, then you are fully subject to us. And what we wish shall be done."

I knew what he meant—they would give the remainder of my life to their false Gillan. So did he lay the greater burden of more fear on me. But I hoped that he could not read that in my face, and I tried to make my voice steady and cool as I answered:

"When your champion goes down to defeat, my lord, then you shall render freely to me what you have stolen. That is our bargain."

Though I had not made that a question, he replied: "That is our bargain. Now—" in his hand he held a scarf and this he flashed up and down in the air, leaping away from the cloak and its guardian square.

I am no warrior who knows the proper use of the blade, each nicety of thrust and parry, the art of sword mastery. And I had thought, after the brush with the Hounds, that the Riders went to war as beasts who needed no such schooling. But it would seem that though they used claw and fang, they also knew steel.

They circled, ever watching, now and then thrusting as if to try the enemy's skill or strength. And I remembered a bit of war knowledge which I had heard at the Abbey-stead table when kin of the refugee ladies came a-visiting—that it was always best to watch a man's eyes rather than his weapon—

The slow beginning erupted in a flurry of blows aimed and parried, a wild dancing to the clash of steel meeting steel. Then, retreating, they once more circled. Whether Herrel was accounting himself well, I did not know. But no blood flowed and, although he had put one foot off the cloak, he had beat his way back with speed.

For a short time was I so dazzled by that murderous play that I did not sense what else was going on. Perhaps it was the power of the moly which awakened that other acute sense in me. Halse willed his sword hand on the cloak, and so did Herrel. But outside there was a uniting of wills. Perhaps that ill wishing could not reach and weaken Herrel physically and prepare him for the finishing stroke, but it hung as a fog working for his defeat. And, if he were sensitive enough— A man's belief in himself can be delicately poised. All his life Herrel had thought himself less than whole. His anger, our need had worked upon him to refute that. But should seeds of doubt begin to grow—!

I had used my will as a tool—to see—to hold the guard in the hall, to fight the Hounds, to carry me to Arvon. Now I strove to make of it a buckler against the desire of the Pack. And because I had my own fears, this was a thing nearly beyond my doing.

My undersight was failing. Monsters ringed in that fight. I saw not two men with swords in hand, I saw a bear reared upon hind feet, reaching great furry arms to catch and crush a cat which snarled and wove about it.

"You—"

So sharp was that demand for my attention that I jerked my eyes from the fight to look at him who so hailed me. A stallion—a man—a monster stretching forth great crabclaws to my hurt.

"Hyron," I named a name and saw a man.

—You can not win, witch, having chosen a half-one for your service—

The Captain of the Riders was turning his whip of defeat now to my beating, his thoughts thrusting at me as those swords thrust and cut on the cloak field.

—I have chosen the best among you!— Confidence, and I must feel that as well as give lip, or thought, service to it.—This is a man!—

—A man is not a Rider. He fronts those who are more than men—

—Or less—I retorted.

—You fool! Look upon your hand which had held the sword. In the moonlight my fingers were pale, thin, with an odd transparancy about them. And swiftly Hyron gave me what he hoped would be the death blow to my aid for Herrel.

—You waste. Each time you use your power now, witch, you waste. She grows the stronger! You will be shadow soon; she all substance. And what then will any victory here avail you?—

Even as he spoke I felt that draining weakness. Shadow, yes, my hand had a shadow look—

No! They were tricking me, drawing my attention away from the fighters! Herrel was being driven back, he was close, too close, to the cloak rope. If Halse could not wound him, perhaps he wished to give his enemy the greater shame of breaking the square. Herrel's face was set, he was a man still fighting dogged against some inevitable defeat.

—No!—I tried to reach him, build up the wall of strength and confidence. And now there gnawed at me the belief that Hyron had spoke the truth, that my very efforts to support Herrel were death to me. I was trembling; the ground reeled under me. I must let go—keep what I had left.

My hands—they were thinner, whiter. Do not look upon my hands! Watch Herrel, fight the fog of defeat the Pack had raised. Herrel—shadow hands—Herrel—Herrel!

It cost so much to break their united desire—and I was no longer sure I could.

—Fool, you fade—

—Herrel, you can—you can defeat the bear! Herrel!—

There was a mist between me and the men, or did cat and bear still circle on the cloak? I stood, blind, holding to what small strength I still had.

There came a shout—cries—or were those animal growls, screams of bird, neighing of a horse?

I rubbed my hands across my eyes, strove to see— A cat crouched with switching tail, fangs bared. Facing it still a bear, but one of the clawed hind paws was beyond the roping—Halse must be counted fled!

They were men again, all of them, drawing together, ranged against Herrel still. But that wave of defeat they had woven was gone as if torn away by a rising wind. Herrel raised his sword—pointed the tip to Halse.

"He is fled!" His voice rang loudly, a sharp demand in it.

"He is fled," Hyron returned somberly.

"A bargain is a bargain, we claim all—"

When Hyron did not reply, Herrel strode forward a step or two.

"We claim all!" he repeated. "Does Pack law no longer hold? I do not believe you will nay-say our right."

Still the Captain made no answer. Nor did the others. Herrel went the closer. His eyes were green fire in his face, but he was all man, not cat.

"Why do you not keep your bargain, Hyron? We spoke for all, you promised it on our winning—"

"I can not give it to you."

Herrel was silent for a long moment, as if he could not believe he had heard aright.

"Dare you name yourself honor-broke then, Captain of Riders?" His voice was softer, but in it an ice of deadly anger, the more perilous because of the control he held over it.

"I can not render unto you what I do not have."

"You do not have? What has become then of the Gillan you wrought through your powers?"

"Look," Hyron inclined his head in my direction. Herrel turned his flaming eyes upon me. "The tie is broke; that which we summoned is gone."

Tie is broke— I swayed. Where was it, that cold which had led me out of the wilderness into this land? It was gone, I felt it no more— I was adrift. Then I heard laughter, low, evil, gloating—

"She has only herself to blame," Halse said. "She would use her power. Now it has destroyed her. Nourish your bride while you yet can, Herrel. She is a shadow bride, soon to be not even shadow!"

"What have you done?" Herrel sprang then past Hyron to seize upon Halse. His hands closed about the other's throat, he bore him back to the ground. While I watched as one in a dream, far less real a dream then those they had pushed me into, the men struggled.

They dragged Herrel from his enemy, and held him in spite of his efforts to come at Halse, who lay gasping on the ground. Then Hyron spoke:

"We have played as true as we can. But the tie is broke, that other one is gone—"

"Where?"

"Where we can not follow. She was wrought in another world, she returned there when the tie holding her here was broke."

"You brought her to life. Upon you lies the burden of returning her—or go honor-broke." Herrel shook off their hold. He spoke to Hyron but he came to me. "I asked all, Gillan asked all and you gave oath on that. Now, redeem your oath! Gillan!" He reached me, his arms were about me but I could not feel his touch. I strove to raise my hands—they were thin, transparent. No tie— I was tired, so tired, and empty—never to be filled now—never—

# XVI   THE ASHEN WORLD

"ANOTHER WORLD—" Herrel repeated. "So be it!
You have the key to its gate, Hyron. Turn it now
or take the name of oath-breaker on you." He
swung around, giving eye to all of them. "Oath-
breakers—all of you!"

"You do not know what for you ask," the Pack
Captain said.

"I know very well what I ask—that you make
good the bargain. You send us—"

"Us?" repeated Hyron. "She perhaps," he
nodded to me, "since she has been there before,
has survived what lies there. But for you—you
have not the power—"

As a cat might stalk, Herrel moved upon his
leader. I could not see his face, but his whole
body displayed his determination of purpose.

"I am beginning to know that I am more than
you allowed me to be, Hyron. And the need is
now more than life. You shall send us both
and— No, I will not ask of you for myself. That I
have never done. But this I demand for Gillan:
you shall sustain her to the limit of that much
vaunted power of yours. Since yours was this
ill-doing, so must you aid in the undoing."

Hyron stared back at him, almost as if he could
not believe he had heard aright. There was a stir
and murmur among the other Riders, but Herrel
spared them no glance. His attention was only
for their leader.

"We can not do it here and now," Hyron
answered.

"Then where and when?" Herrel demanded.

"At the Towers—"

"The Towers!" Herrel was plainly unbelieving. "You wrought this deed in a wilderness which was far from the Towers, why now must you have them about you to undo it—at least to open the other world to the twain of us?"

"You have asked for our full aid for her after she passes through—I am not even sure we can give that. But we must have our own anchorage—or mayhap we be all swallowed up and lost."

"It is a long ride yet to the Towers. Look upon her. Do you think that time is any friend to her? It is rather her enemy."

To me that argument was a dim, far off thing which had no meaning save words poured into my ears. I was so tired. Why would they not ride away, leave me to sleep? Yes—how good was sleep—to melt into the dark and know nothing—

"Gillan!" I must have gone a little way into that dark, for Herrel was again holding me, and somehow the force of his arms about me was a barrier against my drifting into the waiting dark. Also warning stirred in me.

"Herrel?"

"Gillan, look—think— We must ride, and you must hold to life—this life—hold!"

Hold? To life? A cord—but the cord had snapped, was gone from me. To rest . . . let me rest . . . I was so tired, so very tired.

"Gillan! See—look about you!"

Sunlight? But it had been night and there lay a cloak where two men—or beasts—had fought. A vial was pressed against my lips, a voice urged me to swallow. Feebly I obeyed and then for a short time the mists were gone. We were riding, I held in Herrel's arms, at a pace which was close to a full gallop. Cloaks streamed out from the shoulders of those about us. And it was day.

"Hold—" Herrel gazed on me as if by his eyes, the mind behind them, he could bring me under obedience to that order, "Hold!"

And that will of his coupled with the cordial he had made me drink, did keep me awake. But I saw all about me as if I passed through a dream which concerned me not. Herrel talked, as if by his voice he could hold me. I heard his words but they made no pictures in my mind.

"—Towers and then they shall send us forth and we shall quest for that other. In that world where she was made, perhaps you shall find her soon and your uniting will be the easier—"

Other? What other? But questions only confused one, better not to think of them. I lay passive, watching rising hills about us, green-gold-green. There was a melting, every changing aspect to this land which I dimly remembered—or its like—Once there had been green walls or broken walls which had flowed, trembled, formed and reformed in a like manner. Nothing was stable, though I could feel those arms, steady as mountain rooted stone about me.

The sunlight was gone—gray—all the world was now gray. And that flowing of landscape was performed by shadows melting one into another. Once I thought I heard shouting, and those who rode about us were gone for a space, though Herrel's horse never faltered in that ground-eating stride.

"Gillan!"

It was all a dream—a soft dream.

I was no longer on horseback, I lay on a bed or couch. No, I stood apart and looked down upon one who lay upon a couch, one who was very pale and thin and wasted seeming. And beside her lay another, straight and lithe, well muscled, for his mail and leather had been taken from him. But he was not wasted, nor did he sleep, and the words he spoke reached me as the thin whispers of wind teased leaves.

"Do as you will for our swift passing."

Smoke arose about that bed place, whirling, whirling, whirling, billowing out and the smoke touched me, wreathed about me, caught me into it so I, too, whirled, drifted, and was a part of it.

A wind within the smoke, impelling me ahead of it as if I had no more weight or substance than a leaf or petal—driving me onward through this unseeingness—this place of specters—

Specters? My mind, if I still possessed a mind, clung to that word—specter.

Shadows in the smoke, things which were rooted, for I passed them, they did not float with me. And they became darker, more real —a gnarled trunk, crooked branches up flung against a hidden sky. Uneasiness grew—sometime—sometime, long ago—I had seen their like and they carried a threat of danger—evil. What danger? What evil?

I willed, I reached, I caught at one of those branches, and so stayed my flight within the smoke-mist. Under my fingers that wood, if wood it could be, had a dry, dusty feel, as if dead and falling into rot.

Still the smoke drifted by and I could see only what I held to. There was no sound at all. For a space I held to my anchorage. Then I loosed my grip, was once more pulled forward in the mist, passing other branches, other trees, seeing no purpose in lingering by them.

There was—there was something I must find. It was not a tree, nor anchorage. But I must find it—yes, yes, I must find it! A raging need for that filled me, as if I had drunk it out of a cup—was a fever in me.

What did I seek, and where? Please, I must know—I must find out!

I—I must find Gillan. And who was Gillan? Witch, a whisper in the fog? Maid—bride— Gillan— I tried to open my lips and call that name, but no voice was granted me. Suddenly the fog about me thinned, the charred dead trees stood out of it, to ring me in a forest glade.

Gillan—

There was gray-white ash on the ground and it was trackless. There were no guides to turn me this way or that. Where did one seek Gillan in this alien world?

White-gray skeleton leaves upon the trees, and silence—a brooding silence. Yet still I listened, eagerly—or fearfully—I was not certain which.

—Gillan— My will sent that call questing out, though my lips did not shape the name. —Gillan, where?—

No answer, but I began to walk forward, down that aisle of trees, always the same.

—Gillan!—

On and on. To this always-the-same forest there was no end. On and on and on—no end—no answer. Nor was there any change in the wan light, no rising nor setting sun, or moon, no darkening, no lighting—always the same. So I might not have walked forward but stood in the same place. Still move I did, through those endless rows of trees.

—Gillan?—

Now that hunger which drove me was fed by uneasiness. What lay behind? I turned now and again to look back. All I saw was the silent forest, no movement. But—no longer was I alone among those trees—something had been attracted by the mere stir of my passing, was awake, padding to see what disturbed its world. And with it came fear.

I wanted to run, but I knew that running would bring it the quicker on my trail. So I must walk as always, hunting that to which there was no clue, while behind came something hunting—ME!

—Gillan?—

I had grown so used to the unanswering silence that I was startled when this time there came an answer—or was it but a troubling of the atmosphere, a stirring? But to me it was an answer—and it lay to my right, so I turned aside from the way I had been going. But as I hurried, I knew that same troubling had alerted that which followed me. Now it was more than curious. It was aroused to a hunter's hunger and cunning.

The trees were growing taller, thicker of girth, as if now I headed into the heart of this forest. As they towered so the light was less, I walked in gloom wherein each darker shadow could hold that which was prudent to fear.

—Gillan?—

Again that answer. This time I could not mistake that it was an answer and that she I sought was somewhere ahead of me.

Now I must round trees whose trunks were like small towers of men's building, and among them were other growths, tall plumes of ashy gray, like skeletons of ferns. These fell into thick powder when one brushed against them, leaving on the air a faint trace of the odor of very ancient corruption.

But long dead as this world seemed to me, it had its own life, was home to creatures which were not of my species. I saw a many legged thing of dull yellow flash into a fern bed. And there was something so malignant in even that small glimpse I had, that I detoured well around the spot where it had vanished, and thereafter watched the forest floor with care.

That which hunted—it was no longer alone! Others of its kind had joined it. I tried to control the panic which wished to rush me on at a blundering run through the forest, unheeding of my going. As yet, though, it seemed content to keep its distance.

—Gillan?—

The answer far sharper, clearer! Close—she must be very close. If only I did not have to weave in and out among these monstrous trees—

Among the brittle ferns began to appear great fan shaped growths which gave forth a yellowish glow as if they were carved of phosphorescent putrescence—for they had the look of rottenness frozen before it lapsed into slime. These were so unclean in seeming I tried to keep well away from any contact with them.

Finally there were no more ferns, only the stinking fans, as the odor, faint at first, grew stronger with their numbers. And it was very hard to find a path among them. Some grew horizontally from the trunks of trees, vast ledges of corruption.

—Gillan?—

Surely by the answer she was just ahead! I picked my way along a corridor between noisome, shoulder high barriers of the fans and came out abruptly on the border of a lake. Or was water ever so black and still? Still? A bubble arose, broke on its surface and I swayed as the fetid gas it had released stung my nostrils, choked me.

—Gillan?—

Had I only thought I had had an answer? I stood on the border of the lake, could see around its rim—the fans, the dark trunks of more trees—but there was no one there. And my last call brought only silence. A trick—a trap? I tried to listen with that sense which was not the hearing of the normal world, but here served in its stead—listening for what slunk behind. It was there—no closer—perhaps it had also halted for a space.

Again the water was troubled, but this time twin bubbles arose, an even space between them. Those were no bubbles, but eyes!—eyes regarding me, drawing—drawing—

No!

I trembled, drawn forward by the willing of those eyes, rooted by my own sense of preservation. I must not be swallowed up in that mere, go to meet the death behind those eyes. There was Gillan—I must find Gillan! And the thought of her snapped the spell those eyes had thrown upon me, so I could move, not into the water as they willed, but along the shore.

For a time those eyes paralleled me and I could feel the grasp and pull of the will behind them, tearing at my resolve, trying to force me to turn, look into them—obey—until at last I made each step with the effort of one climbing a mountain cliff, but I made it.

How long did it take me to round the end of the lake, dogged by the eyes? There was no time in this land, only purpose, need and hunger and my own hunger gave me strength to pull away. I turned my back upon the turgid waters and went on into the wood once more. Had that monstrous lake dweller picked up my call and used it to draw me?

—Gillan?—

—Here!—

Another deception, trap baiting? I could not be sure, nor could I not answer. Through the patches of fans, under trees once more—on and on— Those others, the hunters, they came too, still well behind, but coming.

—Gillan?—

—Here—

Fans gave way to ferns, trees grew smaller in girth—was I coming to the other side of the forest? A winged thing planed down, squatting in my way, looking up at me. Bird? How could one equate that name for a warm, feathered, singing thing with this small horror of loose, leathery skin, naked wattled head, a head three-quarters rapacious beak?

It continued to squat there though I walked towards it, turning its huge beaked head from side to side as if to better view me one eye at a time. Then it flapped its wings, ran to meet me in a rapid scuttle. I started back against a tree trunk, and it paused as if startled and perplexed by my action. For a long moment we were so, confronting one another.

—Gillan!—

I stared at that grotesque parody of a bird. That name had come from this monster of the specter forest. Now its clawed feet moved in the dust; it sidled towards me. I flung out a hand to ward the horror off. Trap—this creature, others—they could pick up my call—use it to confuse and entrap me. There was no Gillan—not here—never to be found—never!

Now I ran from the bird, from that place where the truth had faced me. And behind the lurkers at last made up their minds, they fastened to the chase, began to track me in earnest.

The bird did not leave me—if flapped over my head, would alight ahead to wait, each time beaming into my whirling mind its false call:

—Gillan!

Once it strove to get between my feet, as if to trip me, but a last sidewise leap saved me. I waited for it to fly at my head—perhaps strike at my eyes. But at least I was spared that. Only it did not leave me, any more than those padding hunters strayed from my back trail.

There was more space between the trees now, wider areas in which were twisted clumps of grass edged with small saw teeth. And beyond, an open country completely covered because here hung again a smoky mist, and that closed about me as I left the forest, so, glancing back a little later, I could no longer see trees, only a wall of smoke-fog.

Though I was out of the forest, I was not free of the bird. It no longer tried to impede me on the ground, but circled over my head. And once more my control grew stronger, the full force of fear ebbed.

Gillan—who was Gillan? Why—*I* was Gillan! I halted in the sea of grass. I hunted Gillan, yet also was I Gillan. How could that be? Memory, very faint and far away, stirred. Once there had been one Gillan, and then two. Now I must search for the second, that two might be one again. The bird named me Gillan and Gillan I was. Therefore in so much the bird had been true and not false.

I looked up at the circling winged thing. Painfully I shaped a question in my mind.

"Who—are—you?"

It flapped those wings vigorously, circled me more swiftly.

—Come—Come!—

Was it trying to draw me on for its own desires as that thing in the lake had toiled to bring me to its maw? I hesitated—the grass plain was an ocean of unknown ways. I might wander in its mist-curtained hold a long time. Perhaps any guide who would take me through it was to be followed. Another trap—maybe—but I had no stir of uneasiness when I looked again to the bird.

I did not form my acquiescence into any real reply, but the bird now winged away, into the mist. Yet back it came into sight each time I thought it lost. And so we went across that endless plain. Nothing broke the eternal grass, and we saw no other moving things.

—Gillan?—

Once or twice I sent out my silent call to that other who was also me. But now came no answer. Nor did the bird speak again in my mind.

Coming from the forest had not deterred those hunters at my back. I believe that they did hesitate for a space before they ventured out into the open, away from the territory which was their native ground. But that hunger, which was as strong within them as mine was within me, brought them out. And it was when I sensed that that the bird returned to circle my head.

—Hurry—hurry!—

The mist was an envelope which appeared to move as I moved, setting up a barrier against my sight some small distance away, yet never enclosing me. For there was always a clear space about my body and I was ever able to see the path I followed for several good lengths ahead. The bird flew in and out of that fog, always coming back.

It seemed to me that the ground now sloped down, on a slant from the first level of the plain. The grass still grew high, but not as thickly as it had earlier, thinning now and again to patches of open bare ground. And this was not firm, but more like mud underfoot. The bird lit on the edge of one such place, pacing back and forth there as I approached. When I would have passed, it barred my way—standing to its full height, beating its wings as a man might wave off a fellow from some danger.

—Why?—I asked of it.

—Danger!—

It did not take to the air again, but waddled in an ungainly fashion to my left, making passage from one stand of grass to the next in fluttering hops, waiting and watching while I trod in its wake. The patches of ground it so laboriously avoided were smooth surfaced and larger. My foot dislodged a rough clod with grass ends and struck it into one of those patches. It was sucked down as if puckered lips of earth had inhaled it in a breath.

Our pace was now a crawl as the bird was slow and heavy in its earthbound advance. Behind the chase was up, no more loitering along the way for the pleasure of the hunt itself. Those who coursed me were anxious to have the chase finished, to make their kill and return to their specter wood.

—They come!—

I tried to reach what mind or intelligence lay in the flapping creature leading me from one precarious foothold to the next in this treacherous land.

It fluttered faster, made a last leap, springing into the air with beating wings. Before me was a wide stretch of the too smooth ground, and then a grass grown strip promising safety. Still, without wings, I doubted my own ability to cross that trap.

A snuffling—the first real sound I had heard in this nightmare world, from behind me. I must leap that stretch ahead—there was no going back— The bird circled, its urging ringing in my head.

—You must!—

Must? How? How did one perform the impossible? To desire a thing no matter how strongly—to desire a thing! Will—desire—potent, very potent. Potent enough to bring me to safety now? I had no other help or defense except what might lie within myself.

I tensed, drew upon will—any reserve of will which my body might hold. I forgot the other Gillan, narrowed the whole world to that patch of ground and the necessity of reaching its far side. Then I jumped.

A sprawling fall, my hands grabbing at grass. But about one ankle a sharp closing, a grinding pain as if great teeth gnawed at flesh and attempted to reach hidden bone. I pulled against that hold, straining with not only physical strength, but that of will. There was a reluctant loosing. I pulled, fought, lay at last on the grass, free of that which had held me. When I looked at my foot I saw a palid ring, very pale to show against my white flesh, and the foot below that was gray, very cold and clammy to the touch. I could stand, but there was little feeling in it and I went forward at a hobble.

—On!—

My winged guide did not need to urge that. But if my spirit was ready to fly at a speed matching its, my body needs must go slower. Luckily we appeared to have reached a place of solid footing, free of more sucker pools.

—Gillan?—

I clung to a tough strand of the grass, weaving my fingers into it for support. An answer! Not from the bird overhead—not this time. From ahead— To be believed?

Yes! In me a leaping, a straining forward, such as I had not known before—a pull so much a part of me that now I could not turn from that trail, even if I had so wished.

—Gillan!—

I stumbled away from my grasses, wavered on. And it was some time before I realized that I was now alone, that the bird which had brought me out of the forest no longer held its position as my traveling companion. But there was no need—I had now a surer, stronger guide—

The hunters padded behind. Again I caught uncertainty, hesitation from them. Then in my mind and not my hearing—a shriek—a death cry of something which had known life—at least as much as those of this world knew it. And following that a burst of such hate as was like a fire flame licking out to sear and destroy.

I began to run, my numb foot unsteady under me—but still I ran—grass about me, mist beyond. Somewhere Gillan waited and behind me a pack of hunters raged. Once more the ground began to rise from the bottom which held the pools of sucking earth. I stumbled so often that I had, at last, to grasp at the grass, pull myself up and on by those holds.

So intent was I on holding my speed that I must have been running for some time between those blocks before I knew that my path was narrowing and walled. In, in. Higher the walls, more shadowed the way. Behind came death, and before me was what I sought—and now that hungered seeking was greater in me than the fear of what loped behind.

# XVII WHO IS GILLAN?

I CAME TO A place which was walled, yet open to the sky. It was filled with a pale yellowish light which acted to conceal rather than reveal what might walk there. And just within the entrance I halted to peer ahead.

"Gillan?" For the first time my lips moved, my throat produced sound.

And the sound there, in that place, was shattering, breaking some age-old bond. So I needs must set my hands over my ears in protest against the echoes I awakened. For that name came back to me distorted, made into an alien thing which was not mine.

They came in answer, moving through the light, one, two—more of them until they stood in an unending line, stretching back into obscurity. A hundred mirrors, repeating a reflection a hundred times—and each entirely like its companions.

A slender body, white of skin, bearing above her ribs the faint mark of the Hound sword, on her arm the sign of beast fangs, both healing or healed. Dark hair sweeping from an upheld head— I saw myself, but not just once—again and again and again!

And they all made answer, speaking in myriad voices, but still the one and same:

"I am here."

I had been two, now it would seem I was a troop! That which made Gillan had splintered, broken, been cast to the winds, never to be united again. So I stood, watching that company, the hunger in me raging unsatisfied. For I did not know any spell or sorcery which would draw that oft splintered Gillan back to me.

It seemed to me that they watched me at first blankly, as bodies which moved without souls or minds. And then there grew in those eyes a cold hostility to me. I had no guide, the words which came to me were unthought—a protest—

"We are one!"

"We are many," they denied me.

"We are one!" I held to that, as if with that very statement I could make it fact.

The line stirred, their heads turned from me, they were beginning to return into the light— they were going! I moved forward, seized upon the nearest Gillan, held her fast with what strength I had in me. It was as if I had fastened my fingers about polished stone, cold, lifeless, inimical to the flesh which touched it. She looked at me then, that Gillan I held, standing without attempting to throw off my hold, but as if she were a dumb thing obedient to aught which would force its will upon her.

I do not know what I expected then—that she might flow into me, be a small answer to my hunger. Nothing happened, save that she alone of that company stood fast.

"That is not Gillan."

Words, again shattering the air of that enclosure. I loosed my grip in my surprise, looked around to he who spoke.

A shadow? No, that figure had more substance than shadow. However, it was dark, visible only in that darkness and in the two sparks of green which were near its top—eyes? The silhouette it made against the wall flowed and changed as I watched. Sometimes a man stood there, again it was beast or monster.

"There are but two real Gillans," it spoke in a hissing whisper, "you and she whom you seek. And that is the one you must find."

"But—" I looked back to the company. She whom I had held was still to be seen, fading back into the light in wake of those who had gone before.

"She is hidden, one among the many," the shadow told me.

"And how will I know her—the right one?"

"By the power in you, if you use it aright."

"How?"

"That is your own mystery, Gillan. But time grows short. If you linger here, you will be lost, just one more among the many—"

I could not depend upon that tie, that hunger which had led me here. It was as if it fastened me only to this place and not to any of the Gillans. But now—I swung once more to the shadow by the gate and the gate—for the hunters were here! Those which had trailed me from the forest had come.

And the shadow knew that. I saw the turn of his head, the sparks of his eyes vanished. The silhouette changed, was now that of a crouching cat—a cat?

Through the gate scuttled a many-legged thing—part spider, part something out of no world any human knew, larger than a mountain hound. It drew its legs in under it as if crouching to spring. But the cat shadow struck out at it with a large paw and the thing moved with surprising speed to avoid that blow.

"Find—Gillan. I will hold the gate—" came the whisper from the shadow and the echoing sibilance appeared to daunt the spider foe, surprising it.

So I went on into the light, leaving the shadow embattled at the gate, in search of one who was hidden among many, yet not knowing what would be the result of such a finding, if I were able to do so.

I closed my eyes against the dazzle of the light, tried to open instead my mind, to sharpen and hone the desire that was in me to assuage my hunger. My power, the shadow had said. Well enough, this was the only way I had yet learned to use it—as a weapon and a defense. So would I employ it now, a weapon against puzzlement, a defense against my emptiness.

Thus did I stand unmoving, spinning out my power in quest, hunting, searching for a spark of truth among the false. It meant that I must shut out all else, my fear of the hunters, the sounds of battle from behind, my own failing strength—all but the quest for Gillan.

I was no longer a body walking on two legs, swinging two arms, reaching two hands for grasping of what I would take. I was only desire, disembodied, a wraith—I did not see, nor feel, nor think—

Then—I was Gillan! The other Gillan. Curled into her, filling her emptiness! But—my triumph was a quick dying spark—I was no whole. I had found my Gillan true enough among the company wandering in that wilderness of light, now I must return her to the Gillan from which I had fled.

Once more I moved through the confusing

radiance. Muted sounds—the fighting by the gate. The Gillan who had been me had stood near there—I must use sound to guide me. But this body obeyed me clumsily. It needed vast effort to set one foot before the other, as if now I inhabited a semblance of Gillan which could be moved only by concentration on each and every muscle in turn. Thus I stumped back towards the sound.

My awkwardly moved foot touched against something on the ground. I tottered and fell—to lie beside Gillan. She was not cold stone under my fumbling fingers, but flesh, chill flesh. Her eyes were open, but there was no sight in them, no breath filled her lungs. She was—dead!

I think I cried out then as I clumsily gathered the other into my stiffly moving arms so we lay together as might lovers, the dead and that which should never have been wrought at all.

So they had won in the end, had the Were Riders. My mind stirred with memories. There was only one of me, the one who was biddable to their plans, But—that was not true! This was me—the real me! They had not won—yet—

I stared down into that dead face. Now I was in exile. I would never be complete until I returned to my proper dwelling which was this body I held in my arms. But how? Witch they had named me—a witch who knew not her craft.

Gillan! For the first time the two Gillans were together, locked body to body. How had this begun—with one Gillan left behind, struck by an arrow, lying under a tree in this world, and the other taken away by the beasts. Beasts! That promise Herrel had wrung from Hyron—that the Riders must aid me—

If they would fulfill it now!

In my mind I summoned a picture of Hyron—
as a man, not as a raging stallion which was his
shape change. And upon that man I concentrated my pleading.

Was it Hyron's thoughts reaching mind—or
some scrap of witch lore answering my need?
Death and life—they were the opposite in this
world, Gillan had died here afore time, to give
birth to Gillan—this Gillan in whom I now
dwelt. Therefore, this Gillan must die so that that
other could live again. But how? I had no
weapon to hand—did not know whether I would
have the courage to use it if I did—for what I
guessed might not be the truth.

—Hyron—give me death.—

There came no answer. But there was death in
this place. And it did not only lie in my arms. It
was like a creeping, seeping tide, spreading from
the gateway. No longer did I hear the muted
sounds of attack and defense from there. That
shadow which had stood to bar the gate and win
me time—the shadow with green eyes, and a cat
shape for battle—

—Herrel?—

My thought reached out. As it had to find the
other Gillan, so now did I try to touch the
defender.

—Herrel?—

A reply, faint. But—Herrel could grant me that
death which was life. I began to crawl to the gate,
dragging with me that other Gillan. It was a
journey of exhausting trial, for my new body was
so stiff and clumsy, reacted so poorly to my will
that the burden was doubly hard to carry.

—Herrel?—

This time even more faint the answer. I crawled out of the thick of the light into the space before the gate. The spider things lay there, one still kicking convulsively. And the shadow who had fought to buy me time was huddled against the wall, drawn in upon itself as if to nurse a gaping wound, while ringing it were other shadows and these I knew—the masters of the spiker hounds—those twittering things which haunted the ashen forest.

I kneeled by the body which I had brought forth from the light. Herrel had slain the hounds, he still held their masters at bay, but he was hurt. I gazed upon that scene, and remembered, and in me grew an anger such as I had never known before, I who had schooled my emotion through inborn need for control. Had I had the power with which all credited me I would have loosed it in that instant to cleanse the ground of this foul crew.

Anger could strengthen, could rid the mind of shadows and doubts—or so I found it at that instant. I opened myself to anger, held no barriers against it. Then I was out among that pack tormenting what they dared not face in open battle. I do not know whether I struck them with my fists, beat upon them—or whether that great and glorious rage made of me a torch of force, which withered them as they stood. But they reeled from my path, and I drove them before me out of the gate as one might drive timid woodland things by the mere force of one's steps upon a forest path.

Surprise was my ally, but they might return. And Herrel—the other Gillan—time indeed had threaded sand too far through the glass for us. United—did I have a chance to serve us both better?

But when I came back against the wall, green eyes upon me.

"You—are—not—she—" his whisper was very faint.

"I am the other one—" I began.

He winced.

"You are hurt—" I would have gone to him but he waved me off with a sharp gesture.

"Where is she?"

"There—" I pointed to the body I had brought out of the light.

He wavered away from the wall, his form unstable, now a man falling on his knees beside that silent form, now an animal on all fours.

"She is dead!" His whisper was harsher, louder.

"For a space. Listen, Herrel, to make this Gillan I now wear they slew me—in this world. Therefore, should I be now slain, it must follow that I live again—in that body—"

I do not think that he understood or even heard me. So I came to stand above that body and then he raised his head, his eyes blazing—and in them a rage like unto that which had made of me a force only moments earlier. He was not a cat now, but man, still there was a beast's unminding ferocity in his eyes. He struck up and out at me, shadow sword in shadow hand.

Pain through me—such pain as was an agony to tear me apart—

Golden light, and in that light I must find Gillan—that other Gillan—but I had found her! was in her—or was I? I sat up from lying on cold ground. A body—white—but it was fading away like mist! Their Gillan—the false one! Then I was whole again—myself!

I hugged my arms across my breasts, holding in what was me. Then I ran my hands down the length of my body, knowing it to be real. No longer was I empty but filled! Filled with all they had stolen from me.

Herrel! I looked around. The shadow whose sword thrust had set me free— No shadow here, no sign it had ever been, save those dead monsters at the gate.

"Herrel!"

The echoing of my own cry rang deafeningly in my ears. Had he made answer then I would not have heard it. I walked between the dead spider hounds to the gate. If their masters lurked without I did not see them.

—Herrel?— As I had done when I sought the other Gillan, I used the inner calling. But to it came no reply.

Yet I was aware, just as I had been on my first awaking in the ashen forest, that I was, in a manner, still tied to this ghost world. And that which tied me so was Herrel. Must I go seeking him as I had my other self?

I had not closed my eyes, nor sought for any inner vision at that moment. But before me was a shadow horse. He struck out with a fore foot, not at me, but as if to part some curtain for a clearer meeting.

—Come—

The word was an imperative command. But I did not obey it.

—Herrel?—I made that both question and refusal.

The maned head tossed high in impatience. But he gave me no answer and I demanded in turn:

—Where is he?—

—Fled.—

—Fled? That I did not believe. He who had held the gate against the monster, who had bought me time to his own hurt, and who had swordbought my deliverance. Why should he flee?

Hyron must have read my thought for he answered it.

—He flees from that deed he did here.—

—But he freed me! He could have served me no better.—

—Who is Gillan?—The question seemed meaningless.

—I am Gillan!—Of that I had no doubts.

—To him Gillan lies dead, by his hand.—

—No!— So plain was it all to me that I could not readily believe Herrel had not also seen the truth.

—Yes. Come, we can not long hold open the way between the worlds.—

—And Herrel?—

Again the stallion tossed his head.—He chose to tread this road, knowing well the danger. Upon him be his own fate—

"No!" This time I spoke aloud, sending echoes buzzing. "No, and no, and no! Herrel comes forth."

—You also choose your path, witch—

—You are oath-bound to aid us.—

—There comes an end to all oaths. You have now your other self, as Herrel won it for you. Even our united strength can not hold this opening long. Come back to life, or go into nothingness in time and space.—

He had given me the choice. I was not oathbound to any course. Save that I knew this, in this moment I could not take the steps which would win me safety, that there was that in me which refused what I could not share. I eyed the shadowy Hyron as I answered:

—Hold as you can. Mayhap I will also find that which is another part of Gillan, or her life, as I did not know it until now.—

Now the shadow horse stood still, and those golden eyes which were the most alive part of him studied me.

—Your choice, witch. Do not ask for a second one.—

—Knowing you, I do not.—I retorted, and in me again stirred that anger which had sent me at the sulking things.

Hyron's shadow form flickered, was gone. I stood where I was. With that other Gillan I had had a bond, so deep a bond, to guide me. With Herrel—what did link me to Herrel? A sense of gratitude, of shared danger, of dependence (as much as I had ever depended upon another)? None of those were deep enough to form a leading tie.

Hyron had asked me—who is Gillan? And I had answered him out of triumph, pride and knoweldge—I am Gillan. But only because Herrel's sword had made it so could I say that.

Now I must ask myself—who is Herrel—what is he—to me.

I thought of our first meeting in the bridal dell when he had come to me in the mist because I had chosen his cloak out of those lying on the

velvet sward. Taller than I, very slender, a boy's
smooth face, holding eyes as old as the hills of
High Hallack—that was the first Herrel. Then the
feline, lying in relaxed slumber on a moonlit
bed, awaking to the peril of sorcery as a net
spread about us both—the second Herrel. Again
the cat, crouched, eager for battle, sliding down
and away to hunt those of Alizon—and he who
had returned in man-form from that fight to
stand with me against the anger of the Were
Riders.

Another Herrel who had wooed me, to whom I
did not yield, and a Herrel who had sprung at me
in blood-lust. The Herrel I had seen appealing to
forces and powers for my healing while the
Werefires blazed about me and I lay covered
with a blanket of flowers. A Herrel who had
ridden with me through the day, who had waited
for moonrise, telling me of his land and his
loneliness—

A Herrel who was shadow fighting embodied
evil to win me time—and who thought he had
slain a shadow because reality lay dead—

Who is Herrel—all these and more. That was
the truth stripped of all illusion, that of his
people, that of my own pride. Who is Herrel? He
is another part of me, as Gillan was a part. And
without him, do I go bereft and lacking all my
days!

Thus—as I sought Gillan—yes! This was the
right way, the only way! As I sought the Gillan
sorcery had made, so must I seek the Herrel
which had made himself a thing which could
walk this land. Again I put forth my quest call—

I came out from the gate of that place of yellow
light. Must I return to the ghost-wood? Or

plunge farther into this world without sun or moon, change in time?

—Herrel?—

No answer, but a sense of drawing, of that I was sure. Not back to the wood, forward, bending on it all my powers of concentration.

Something scuttled in the rocks before me. A master with more spider hounds baying on Herrel's trail? That trail, so faint for me, might be plain for their sniffing. Still it must be mine also, if I would win to my desire.

If this world did not have a night and day according to the pattern I had always known, it would seem it had changes in weather of a sort. There was a wind rising about me, but, I noted, it blew neither hot nor cold, merely as a wind which brushed my body, tugged at my hair. And I stopped to pull that to the back of my head, fastened it there with a length of grass plucked from a tussock. That mist which had dogged my path across the bog-valley and the plain withdrew, or else the wind tattered it into nothingness.

I was on a hillside, and ahead climbed other hills, up to massive mountains which were a threatening purple against a sky never plain to see. Around the heads of the mountains crackled swords and spears of lightning fire and there was a rumbling—to be felt rather than heard.

The storm, if storm this was, had not yet hit the hills about me. I climbed among the rocks, which were broken and twisted, taking on all manner of evil shapes, suggesting they hid greater horrors, lurking to spring, rend and tear. I reached the top of the rise. Still that thread, thin as any spider's weaving, led me on. I looked down into a dusky dip. There was a trickle of liquid running there and from it arose hazy smoke, while it was as dull red as dying coals.

Along its bank a figure moved. It did not walk straight, but wove a staggering path from side to side, sometimes falling, but ever pulling up again to struggle on.

"Herrel!" Hunters to be roused or no, I cried that aloud, throwing myself at the down slope.

The stumbling one halted, but he did not turn. Then he went on at a hobbling run, reaching out to grab at holds to pull himself along. I lost my footing and fell, rolling down to come up against an earth embedded rock. I put my hand to my spinning head, blinked at stones and earth which were no longer steady.

"Sssssss—"

The thing had scrambled to the top of a boulder facing me, hunkered there, slavering so that the spittle dripped thickly from its almost lipless mouth. Lipless that mouth might be, but it was well equipped with pointed fangs. Above was a slit which must serve it for nose, and then very large eyes, lacking pupils, flat and dull. But that they could well see me I did not doubt.

Its skull was round and hairless, the ears slits like unto its nose. But the worse was its monstrous resemblance to man—though no man could be as this horror. With skeleton fingers to its mouth it produced a kind of whistling, very high and shrill, hurting my ears. And it was answered. I was hemmed in by the hunters I had driven from Herrel. But that they would flee a second time from anger—that was too much to hope. Nor could I summon that super-human rage to serve me.

"Herrel!" The moment that cry left my lips I repented it. What magic could he summon to our salvation? I would merely draw him back into the worst of traps.

The thing on the rock turned its head from side to side. It sat on all fours like an animal, raising one hand now and then to its mouth. Slowly I got to my feet, waiting for it to spring. Another round head came into view, a third, a fourth—How soon would they pull me down? I stopped and caught up a stone. They carried no weapons I could see, and perhaps I could give some account of myself. At the same time all that was sane in me, all the heritage of my own world, shuddered at the thought of any close contact with these nightmare things. The first of the creatures lifted its head high, opened wide its jaws and squalled.

Pride is a great deceiver. We who choose to walk apart from our fellows wear it, not as a cloak, but as an enshelling armor. I who had asked nothing from my fellows—or thought I asked nothing—in that moment I was stripped of a pride which broke and fell from me, leaving me naked and alone. I faced not death as I knew it, as I had felt it in this world, but something infinitely beyond human death, which we have been told is in reality a beginning. From this there would be no issue save a blackness it is not given my kind to face with a mind untouched by madness.

Perhaps madness did possess me now. I think I shrieked, that I called upon gods whose names had no power here, that I cried aloud for any help which might be given me. I do not know this for truth, but I think it is so.

And help came then, stumbling, weaving, but still on his feet, sword ready. Even as I struck with that stone which was my only weapon, so did Herrel come, shadow still, but alive, able to answer my plea.

Of that fighting in the rocky, stream cut valley I remember but little. I do not want to remember parts of it. But the end—that I shall always hold in memory—he who stood between two rocks, pushing me into safety behind him. His sword was a live thing, and from that blade those things flinched and cringed. Though they strove, they could not pull him down. Until at last the survivors fled and left us.

"Who are you?" Herrel held to the rock as if he dared not trust his own strength to stand erect. "Who are you?" He held up his hand, from his wrist dangled his sword by a cord. His fingers moved, slowly, painfully as if this was some effort almost past his making, and in the air he drew a symbol.

Fire, blue, so bright that my eyes were dazzled. But I called out trying to put the truth that was into my voice:

"I am Gillan. Truly, Herrel, I am Gillan!"

# XVIII  THE LAST GATE OF ALL

HE DID NOT come to me, rather he sank to his
knees, one arm thrown across a rock to support
him. But his green eyes were on me, though his
face was still more shadow than true substance.

"I slew—"

"You united!" I threw myself down beside
him. "That other Gillan, she had to die that we
might be whole again—whole! By your sword I
am!"

Herrel bowed his head upon his out-flung arm
and I could no longer see those eyes which were
the most living part of him. I put forth my hand
and touched that which was not firm flesh—
rather a yielding, changing stuff.

"Herrel!" I saw him as a shadow, but I had
expected to touch a man. And this struck new
fear into me.

Now he did raise his head again, look at me.

"I am—far spread—Go—back—Hyron—" The
words came with long pauses between them.

"No! Herrel—!"

But his head had fallen forward again and he
did not answer my call. In me stirred again that
anger, and with it my will. I got to my feet and
this time I did not plead in my summoning, I
demanded:

"Hyron!"

The rolling echoes of that name boomed about
the walls of that unknown valley, appeared to
join with the vibrations set off by the mountain

storm. But could it reach from one world to another?

"Hyron!" For the second time I voiced that demand.

A shimmering—a change in the air—behind it shadows moved—

—Come!— Very faint.

"Herrel!" I stopped, strove to draw up that collapsed shadow. But it was as if I scooped running sand in my two hands, there was nothing substantial in him for my fingers to grip upon. "Herrel!"

I glanced up. That troubling in the air, it was already subsiding—perhaps we had only seconds.

"Herrel!" Once more I tried to arouse him—to no purpose.

And when I looked again—that shimmering which marked the gate between the worlds was gone. I covered my face with my hands, dull despair warring with my will, Hyron had warned me that they could not hold the gate—or was it rather would not—for long. Now they had let it close—we were trapped in this nightmare other existence.

Once more I knelt beside Herrel. Was he dead or dying as this world knew those terms, or sore hurt where I could give him no real tending? Why did he wear this shadow form when my body was real and solid? Or did it merely seem so to me, and he saw me as a shadow? If so—then to himself he was real also— A fleeting scrap of memory touched me—that bed on which we twain had lain when we were sent on this perilous venture—had our bodies continued to lie there while we had put on other forms in this alien country?

—Herrel?— I could not touch him, bandage his hurts, give him any small comfort.

Or could I?

I had found that other Gillan, sent out that which had entered into her. But that had been because she was a part of me. I could not enter so into Herrel. Maybe not myself, my mind worked on, but could a portion of my will, a desire for life, be so shared with another? It was so small a hope, but now my only one.

I leaned my head on the arms I had folded across my knees. In my mind I fastened upon Herrel—as I had seen him—not on our first meeting, or on other occasion, but at what I knew was a moment when some power had touched us both, when he had stood at the moonlit, silvered pillar and called upon forces known to him in my behalf. And that Herrel I held in my mind—intent on seeing him and not the shadow man beside me.

This was like feeling one's way along a dark corridor where a danger one could not see stalked, and there were many sideways in which one could be lost. I tried to make of my will a visible thing, of substance—to reach, touch, be one with the Herrel I held in mind, blotting out all else.

He stood there, his bared shoulders silvered as the pillar was silvered. I could smell the sweet scent of the flowers—I could hear his voice chanting in the tongue I did not know, uttering words that I did—he called upon Neave—

Neave! I made of that name an anchor point for

my will. Neave—-Herrel—and I concentrated the force of my desire on the man who had stood in the moonlight.

—Gillan?—

Perhaps that had been several times repeated before it reached me, locked in concentration as I was.

—Gillan?—

I turned the head still pillowed on my arms, opened my eyes, the shadow beside me had also raised his head, the green eyes were open, watching me.

—Herrel! You are alive?—

—After a fashion, but what do you here? The gate— He sat up straight. —They could not hold the gate so long.—

—So Hyron said— I answered without thinking.

Again those sparks of eyes swung to mine.— Hyron! He told you, but then, why have you not gone?—

I did not answer. A shadow hand balled into a shadow fist, struck down on the surface of a rock.

—Why did you not go. Leave you me no pride at all, Gillan?—

I was startled, and then saw that his way might not be my way after all. That I had delivered hurt where I meant healing. And I made the only answer I had left me:

—Matters being in all ways reversed, would you have done so?—

A shadow face shows no expression for reading, and I could see no feeling in his eyes. There was a period of silence between us until I dared to break it:

—This gate being closed, where is one we may

open?— Not that I expected he could name me any such, but that I might turn his thoughts from within to without himself.

—I know of none. Hyron misled you if he suggested that such might be.—

—Hyron gave me nothing but warnings. But, this is the third time I have walked this land. The other two times I believed that I dreamed. And from dreams there is waking.—

—Dreams?— Again he moved and this time with more vigor. His hand went to his middle as if exploring some hurt with caution. —Gillan—I—my wound, I no longer bleed! I can move— He pulled to his feet, stood away from the rock which had been his support.— I am whole again! What sorcery have you worked, my lady witch?—

—I do not know, truly, I do not. This only— And I told him of my try with will and power.

—Neave! You called upon Neave, and now you speak of dreams. Dreams—

He reached down his hand as if to draw me up beside him. I felt a wisp of mist wreath about me, but with no force. Herrel recoiled.

"What is this?" he whispered aloud.

"To me you are shadow," I told him hastily.

He held his hand up before his eyes as if to reassure himself. "But this is solid! Flesh— bone—"

"To me you are a shadow," I repeated.

"Dreams!" Once more he struck the rock surface with his fist. "If we now share a dream world—"

"Then how do we wake?"

"Yes, the waking—"

His tenuous form swung around, he stared

about him as if to locate in the valley some means for shaking us out of nightmare slumber.

"What do you remember of this world, tell me all of it!"

Why he wished me to retrace in memory I did not know, but I obeyed his order, spoke of the forest, the coming of the bird—

"Bird?" Herrel halted me at that point, demanded a description of the bird. And then said:

"So in that much they kept their oath. That was a guide sent by the Pack. Where did this bird lead you?"

I told him of the passage through the bog, the coming to the place of light where I had found him and the company of Gillans.

"Yes, that was where I awoke, in that place of light, seeing them pass back and forth through it, and knowing that only one was the right one, and only you could find her. But none of this gives us any clue to the gate or our awakening—"

"Do we have a key left us?" The muttering of the storm in those mountains grew louder. There was a kind of menace building up about us which broke through my concentration, as if the alien world was gathering its forces to deal with what we represented, an irritation foreign to it.

"I do not know. But while we can move—and think—then perhaps we still have a chance. I wonder—" I saw his head turn again as he surveyed that narrow valley. "That place of light is undoubtedly a place of power. And so might well be where we could find answers—"

"The times I awoke here were in the woods—" I suggested. Though to cross the bog land without a guide was a journey I did not relish.

"Then you dreamed under their command, awoke by it," Herrel's husky whisper continued. "If we are to go forth from there now it will be by our wills, united. And I believe that power, no matter from what source, can be drawn upon in times of need—"

"But what if the power is evil, a danger to our kind?"

"I do not think that the place of light is either good or evil. We entered therein, the creatures of this world hunting us entered. It took no part in our battle, either for one side or the other. We were apart from it, left to our own concerns. Tell me, how did you drive the hound masters forth—that I did not understand—"

"By my anger—I think," I made answer, but I was considering what he had said. That force of anger, so strong, carrying all before it—never before in my life had I been so possessed. Had that emotion been fired, fuel fed, by some power within the enclosure? Could Herrel be right in his guess that what abode there could be tapped to aid us?

I had said there was no change from day to night in this haunted world. But around us now it grew darker. Either the storm was reaching out from the mountains, or else there was a night coming I had not seen before. We made our way dimly back up the slope to the higher land where stood the enclosure.

Within the light still swirled and around the gate lay small white heaps. Herrel stirred one with the point of his dusky sword, cleaned bones collapsed and rolled, remains of the hounds. But of that which had feasted on the losers, or of its nature, we had no clue.

We had come here, but what must we do now? I turned to Herrel with that question, and it seemed to me that his shadow self was even thinner.

"What do we?"

"It becomes a matter of walking an unknown road, trailing across never charted mountains, my lady witch. In my mind it is that we two still lie in the Gray Towers, that we dream there—so stand within these walls. Unless we can wake, we are lost forever. For the deeper the dream, the less able will our bodies be to escape it. As for how to wake—well, we must try different ways—"

"What ways?" His confidence seemed overly bright to me who had no trace of plan moving within my mind.

"What brought you to that other Gillan, then led you to me?" He counter-questioned. "What led you to summon me from what was death in this world?"

"I thought, I centered my will—on Gillan—on you—"

Herrel looked into the light. "If we do have bodies left in our own world and time, then they anchor us in part there. Perhaps if we strive to be reunited with those bodies, we shall find them. I see no other path for us."

"But—I have no clear picture to fasten upon—" And I did not—that glimpse of Herrel lying in the room which might have been in the Gray Towers—that was too fleeting a thing to serve me.

"I have!" He seemed possessed now by a rising belief in himself, as if, instead of being daunted by our plight, he was stimulated to greater efforts.

"Now listen—" He laid his hand on my arm, and I felt his touch only as I might the passing of a feather across my flesh. "This is as I saw it last—before I came here—"

He told me in detail of that tower room, of the divan on which we had lain side by side, of small things which had been imprinted in his memory in such vivid pictures that he must have rested there with greatly heightened senses before he had gone forth on this strange journey. And such was his telling that he made me see it, too, bit by bit, piece by piece, as if before my very eyes he was setting up figures and furnishings.

"Do you see, Gillan?" For the first time a note of anxiety crept into his whispers.

"You have made me see."

"If I have only done so aright!"

"And now?"

"And now we do what you have done before, we fasten our wills on this—" he paused. "I am counted by half-man among them, since my power does not always serve me as I will. So, mayhap I put now to the test a flawed blade. But that I can not know until I use it. Let us go!"

I closed my eyes upon the light, upon Herrel. For this time him, too, I must shut away. He had his battle and I had mine, to the same end, yet we must fight it singly. I brought to mind that room Herrel had pictured for me—there were the windows—two—one looking north, one south, between them walls covered with tapestries so old their patterns had long since been lost, save for a hint of face here, a trace of a beast's gleaming eyes there. Braziers and from them smoke, aromatic smoke. And in the center of that chamber the divan. On it lay Gillan, Gillan whose face had shown a hundred times, a thousand times from mirrors when I looked therein, Gillan who bore the scars of wounds which had pained me. That was Gillan, the Gillan I must seek and find.

And I centered upon that Gillan, not only the body which slept, but the nature of that which wandered afar from it in dreams. Who is Gillan? No, rather what is Gillan? She is this and this, and she is also that. Some parts of her could I welcome, others I would shun if I could. For this was a measuring and an inner seeing of Gillan such as I had never known and it made me writhe for a nakedness beyond all stripping I have believed could exist. Almost did I wish to forego the awakening of that Gillan who had such small meannesses, such ill within her.

Who is Gillan? I am Gillan, in this way was I fashioned, by nature, by the will of others, by my own desires. And with this Gillan am I united for good or ill, therefore I must pick up the burden of being Gillan and—awake!

But did I wake? I was afraid to open my eyes, lest I see again the light of the alien world. Until at last I had to force myself—

I looked up at gray stone, very old. I turned my head and saw tapestries also faded by the years. I was awake!

Herrel! Swiftly I turned my head in the other direction to see him who must share his couch with me. Empty!

I sat up, reached forth my hand to that emptiness, to prove to myself that my eyes were the

deceivers, not that he was gone. And then I saw
the hand I put forth and I was stricken motionless.

The people of Arvon in that village—they had
been shimmers of light in my eyes, so now was
this hand of mine. Swiftly I pressed it down
upon the fabric covering of the divan—
fingers—palm—my full weight— But there was
no impression!

From my hand I looked to my body. No
body—merely a mist through which I could see
the surface whereon I rested. Then Herrel had
been wrong—we had not had bodies to focus
upon left here—to draw us back to our right
world!

There was a shimmer— No, I had not moved
—it formed beyond me, at the other side of the
divan—Herrel?

I tried to call his name. There was no answer
from my throat and lips. Why should there be—I
no longer possessed throat or lips! I was not
Gillan for all my willing.

That shimmer which lay in Herrel's place
moved. He must be sitting up.

—Herrel?— I tried to reach him by that other
way as we had sometimes spoken together in the
specter world.— What has happened?—

The bar of light stood upright by the divan.

—I think—I think— Slowly, painfully words
came to me (and what *was* me?)—that they believed us dead. Our bodies have been moved
elsewhere.—

Had I had then the power I would have
shrieked aloud. If he spoke the truth what would
now become of us?

—Come—

—Where?—

He had already moved the door, that light which was now Herrel and no man.

—To find what we seek.—

We were back in the familiar world where there was night and day and, suitable to our state as wraiths, it was now night. These Grey Towers must be very old, old and steeped in a life afar from the Dales. It was in all I looked upon—that age and difference.

Along a short hall, and then down a stair which wound and wound about the skin of the Tower, Herrel led and I followed. I heard no sound, saw no one move. Slumber must have claimed those who abode here. And for a fleeting moment I thought of Kildas, of Solfinna, and that company among whom I had once ridden. Did they look upon these ancient walls as now I did, as a shell which held nothing of warmth or welcome? Or would they abide ever under the spells their Were mates wove, seeing only that which would make them happy and content?

We came out at last in a hallway which was paved and walled with stone. At set intervals on the walls were the carved representations of beasts. It seemed that their eyes measured and surveyed us as we passed, even as I had once been measured and studied by those long dead kings set up as Guardians on the frontier of Arvon. But of their findings concerning me I could not guess.

On we went into a space which was shadow hidden as to its width or length. At the far end light burned and towards that Herrel sped, I ever behind. Green was that light and it came from the Were flames I had seen before, those which had burned about me on the mound in the road's parting. Here, too, they burned about two who slept on one bed.

Once more I looked upon Gillan, and this was a Gillan in more splendor than I had ever seen her, or arrayed her with my own hands. She wore a robe of pleasant green overworked with silver, and among the twists of that silver 'broidery were set small milky gems, which a net of the same jewels confined her hair. Her hands were crossed on her breast, and she had, I thought, a beauty which had never been hers in life. For now that I looked down upon this sleeper it no longer seemed true that I was Gillan and this was the envelope of flesh and bone fashioned by birth to hold me.

Beside her was Herrel, his helm by his head so that his face was plainly to be seen. He wore mail and between his clasped hands rested the hilt of a bared sword.

—They do me full honor— He who stood beside me spoke soundlessly.— That honor they never granted me—awake.—

—But these, they are dead!—

—Are we? I say nay to that!—

He was so very sure. Yet when I looked upon her lying so, I thought the truth was as I said. And there was not reason to doubt it.

—Gillan!— Sharp as any warning given when an enemy creeps upon a comrade-in-arms who sees him not. —You are she. Think not otherwise or you are lost. Now!—

The shimmer moved up to those who lay there. By what feat of sorcery he wrought the next I never knew. But those upright flames nearest him bent horizontally and over them he swept me with him.

What is death? Twice in the specter land I had tasted it, perhaps in my world this third time. But still I can not put into words what it is. If I were dead indeed when we so returned to the Towers that night, then death itself was rent asunder by what brought us there.

Gillan was again Gillan, I did not need to open my eyes to know that at long last I was whole. But I did, I raised hands across a firm body finely clad, saw the small, moon radiance of the gems I wore as they glistened with my movements.

"Herrel?"

"Yes—"

He put aside his sword to hold out his hands to me, draw me close. So for a moment we were breast to breast, and I met his eager lips with a need as great as his. Then he held me off a little, his eyes searching, but his lips smiling.

"It would seem, my dearest lady, that we comrade together very well in war; now let us try that state in peace."

I laughed softly. "Right willing shall you find me for such purpose, my valiant lord!"

He slipped from the couch and then raised me to stand beside him. The long folds of the fine robe they had put on me fell heavily about my limbs, hampering my feet. I pulled at the cloth impatiently with my left hand, my right being prisoned in his.

"I go very fine," I commented. "Too fine—"

"Beauty deserves beauty." Herrel did not say that lightly and I think my hand trembled a little for his pressure about it tightened.

"Mayhap, but I would go freer!" For suddenly those weightly robes tied me to the past, and that should be gone. I withdrew my hand from his, my fingers sought clasps and ties, and I shed that dragging magnificence, tossing back upon the empty couch its gemmed skirts, standing in the shorter under-robe.

"Shall we go?" His hand once more sought mine.

"Where, my lord?"

He was smiling again. "Now that I can not answer you, for in truth I do not know. Save we shall ride away from these Towers and this company to seek our own fortune. Do you nay-say that?"

"No. Choose you a road, my dear lord, and it shall be mine. But you do not take your helm, your sword—"

"Nor this—" one-handedly he unbuckled his belt, tossed to lie with my discarded robe. By the empty pillow still rested his cat-crested helm. "Those I shall not use again." And there was such a note in his voice that I did not question him.

As two who would join some formal dance, Herrel led me by the hand down that long chamber until we came forth by another door into a courtyard where we strode under the stars and the moon. Seven great towers were about us. But nothing there moved as Herrel brought me to a stable where in were those dun coated, shadow spotted horses of the Pack. My mare he brought out and saddled, and his own stallion, and leading them we came once more into the open. Before us was a gate.

"When we ride out, my lady, we go into the unknown—"

"Have we not traveled other unknowns, dear lord?"

"Just so!" He laughed. "So be it."

"Who goes?"

From the dusky overhang of the gate came one who wore a rearing stallion on his helm, and the moon was bright on the drawn sword in his hand.

"Yes," answered my husband, "who goes, Hyron? Give us names if you know us."

The Captain of the Were Riders looked upon us. If I had expected a sign of amaze or wonder from him, I was to be disappointed.

"So you found the way to return—" he said.

"We found it. And now we pass through another gate—" Herrel pointed to the portal behind Hyron.

"You are Were blood, these towers are your home."

Herrel shook his head. "I do not know now what I am, for we have been a journey like to change any living thing. But of these towers I am not, nor is Gillan. So we shall go to seek that which we are—for that we must learn."

Hyron was silent for a moment, and then he said in a troubled voice. "You are one of us—"

"No," for the second time Herrel repudiated his half blood.

"You will go to your mother?"

"Do you fear that? You who have chosen not to be my father?" Herrel retorted. "I tell you, I will have none of you, dame or sire. Do you think to hold the gate against us?"

Hyron stepped aside. "The choice is yours."

His tone was now as emotionless as his face. He did not speak again, nor did Herrel as we rode forth. And we did not look back, but Herrel said:

"That, lady wife, was the last gate between the past and the future. And who we are, what we have now, is but Gillan and Herrel—"

"Which is enough," I made him answer, and so it was.